ALSO BY TONI JORDAN

Addition
Fall Girl
Nine Days

Toni Jordan has a BSc. in physiology and qualifications in marketing and professional writing. Her debut novel, *Addition*, was a Richard and Judy Bookclub pick, was longlisted for the Miles Franklin Literary Award and has been published in sixteen countries. *Fall Girl* was published internationally and has been optioned for film, and *Nine Days* was awarded Best Fiction at the Indie Awards, was shortlisted for the ABIA Best General Fiction award and was named in Kirkus' top 10 Historical Novels. Toni lives in Melbourne, where she is a co-director of the Faber Academy's Writing a Novel course.

tonijordan.com
@tonileejordana
facebook.com/authortonijordan

OUR TINY, USELESS HEARTS

TONI JORDAN

ALLEN&UNWIN

First published in Great Britain in 2016 by Allen & Unwin

This paperback edition published in 2017

First published in Australia in 2016 by The Text Publishing Company

Allen & Unwin
c/o Atlantic Books
Ormond House
26–27 Boswell Street
London WC1N 3JZ
Phone: 020 7269 1610
Fax: 020 7430 0916
Email: UK@allenandunwin.com
Web: www.allenandunwin.com/uk

A CIP catalogue record for this book is available from the British Library.

Paperback ISBN 978 1 76029 381 9
E-Book ISBN 978 1 95253 420 1

Page design by Imogen Stubbs
Set in 13/18 pt Granjon by J & M Typesetting, Australia

10 9 8 7 6 5 4 3 2 1

Printed and bound in Great Britain by Clays Ltd, St Ives plc

To Robbie, with apologies for the poor geopolitical analysis
and unacceptably low number of explosions in this book.

The morning after my sister Caroline's wedding to Henry, our mother smashed every dish in the house. Every plate, every glass, every saucer. The bone-china platters etched with roses that she'd piled with sandwiches and little cakes when she was president of our high school mothers club—these she cracked over her knee like kindling. The flutes that were a gift from some great-aunt for her engagement to our father, the set with stems like twigs that lived on the top shelf—these she hurled sideways with her old softball pitching arm and watched spear against the walls to explode in a shower of crystal. She shattered the glass in every framed photograph with her elbow, she overturned vases and fruit bowls. Apples thudded and rolled to all corners of the room, peaches cascaded and liquefied on impact.

I watched her from the doorway of what had been my room and I felt like a small child again, one who would never understand the currents beneath the surface of grown-ups.

She advanced from cupboard to shelf to the divider above the kitchen bench, sometimes pausing to stamp on something particularly offensive and grind it into the carpet, and all the while her face was soft, without any trace of the tight wrinkles that sometimes framed her mouth or the tension stockpiled in her jaw line. Perhaps it was this gentle face, or maybe it was the occasional twist of her hips—it all seemed less Texas porcelain massacre and more avant garde interpretive dance. The early light through the big eastern windows made each individual shard glitter, like a mirror ball dying in a tragic disco explosion. And the noise! I'm amazed the neighbours didn't come running, but that's the whole point of the suburbs, I guess. Nice big yards, lots of space and privacy to start your own hydroponic weed farm or take up nudism or destroy all evidence of whatever it was my mother was trying to erase. When you know people too well, it's difficult to give them a friendly wave as you put the bins out.

When she stopped and everything was quiet again, she wiped her brow with her sleeve. A thread of blood inched down her temple from where some flying chip had grazed her.

'It's all been for nothing,' she said to me. 'All of it. The last fifteen years.'

Caroline and Henry were in Bali by then. When they came home, tanned and massaged and pedicured with their pupils transformed from the usual circles into tiny love hearts, I told Caroline that Mum had been burgled by a well-known criminal bric-a-brac gang. Caroline was living in NewlywedLand, where the air smells of roses and tiny invisible string quartets lurk in every room waiting for your husband to arrive, then

2

launch into 'I've Had the Time of My Life' on their tiny invisible violins.

'Who would want that old rubbish?' Caroline said. 'People are morons.'

Not long after that, Mum sold everything and moved to an ashram in Uttarakhand where she's known as Saraswati, and it was as though our past had been papered over.

Caroline and I haven't seen her since, but every year birthday cards arrive in the mail, randomly. One year it might be August 6th and the next, January 31st. None of these dates coincides with the anniversary of my actual birth, even though my mother knows the date of my birth. She was definitely there at the time. These non-birthday cards all have a colourful Hindu goddess on the front—often wearing gold and red and a great deal of jewellery, sometimes with many arms—and inside Mum writes something like:

> *Dear Janice* (or *Dear Caroline*, when it's my sister's
> non-birthday, or *Dear Mercedes* or *Paris*, when it's
> Caroline's girls'),
>
> *Happy Birthday! I love you! I miss you! This is the
> daughter of Lord Shiva, who was created from the tree,
> Kalpavriksha! Her name is Ashokasundari!
> Remember, don't be too good! Free yourself from
> expectation!*
>
> *GIVE IN TO THE REVOLUTION IN YOUR SOUL!!!*
>
> *Love, Saraswati (Mum) (Grandma)*

*

When Caroline married Henry she was twenty-six and I was twenty-three and Mum was forty-nine. Fifteen years, then, was the amount of time that Mum raised us by herself after Dad left.

I thought Mum was unduly pessimistic. I'd always liked Henry. He was a different breed from the boys in my microbiology lab who strove all year, with some success, to grow colonies of bacteria in the shape of boobs. Henry was not only employed, he owned a suit. He was the most dashing of Caroline's boyfriends and the only one she truly fell for, this big blond rugby player with thighs like legs of ham and sharp blue eyes and a degree in electrical engineering who drove a fourth-hand red BMW with enough dents to make it ironic instead of pretentious. Henry was on the fast track to success at Telstra. They adored each other.

Now it's another fifteen years later. I'm in Caroline's kitchen at ludicrous o'clock on a Saturday morning, leaning against open shelves filled with Caroline's elegantly, eminently smashable dinner service, and I'm beginning to see Mum's point.

Henry waved goodbye to solid some years ago when he swapped rugby for pinot and Foxtel. Now he's soft, with an indoor pallor, and the blond hair is mostly a memory. He's squatting on the floor of the dining room, balancing on the balls of his feet and his leather shoes are squeaking and the seams of his trousers are straining and his bones are creaking. He's looking even paler than usual and his face is damp: a chubby vampire with a fever. He's doing his best to eyeball his girls. My nieces, Mercedes and Paris. Henry, envisaging the

4

world from the perspective of the four feet and under.

'Let me put it this way,' he says to them. 'You like bananas, right? Everyone likes bananas.'

Some conferring is required. Paris stretches on her tippy toes and whispers in Mercedes' ear. 'Bananas are for school but at home we like mangoes better but only when Mummy cuts them up or else we have to sit in the bath,' Mercedes says, after advisement.

'Right. Mangoes. Sure. Well, marriage is like a mango.'

Henry folds his arms as he delivers this gem and from where I stand in the kitchen, it's clear he expects it to make his case. His daughters, though, are a tough audience. None of us got much sleep last night and they are still pyjama-clad with tousled hair and that intoxicating warmth that small children have when they wake, but they're solemn little people, staring steady and blue.

Henry runs his fingers through his strands. 'Imagine if mangoes were all you got to eat, breakfast lunch and dinner. Even if mangoes were your favourite food, you'd be pretty sick of mangoes after fifteen years, wouldn't you?'

'Are biscuits allowed, for little lunch?' says Paris, through Mercedes.

'Mangoes or nothing.'

'Can we have ice-cream on top? Just a tiny bit.'

'Only mangoes. That's it. Forever. You're surrounded by other fruit all right, everywhere you go. Strawberries brushing against you, mandarins slinking around the office in their tight little skirts, bending over the photocopier to fix paper jams. And the lychees. Don't get me started on the lychees.'

'Henry,' I say.

'What's a lychee?' says Mercedes.

'It doesn't matter. What I'm trying to say is: can either of you comprehend the kind of discipline it takes to be married for fifteen years?'

'Not really,' Mercedes says. 'I've never been married. I'm seven.'

'Right, of course. Marriage, girls, is hard time, that's what it is. Monogamy, monotony. Mangoes. They sound the same, right? That's no coincidence.'

'Henry,' I say.

'Seeing the same face every morning, e v e r y s i n g l e morning, day in, day bleeding out. If I took a sawn-off shotgun down to the 7-Eleven and waved it in Raju's face and spent the contents of the cash drawer on crack and hookers I'd get less than fifteen years.'

'Henry,' I say. 'That's a little above their pay grade.'

Paris whispers in Mercedes' ear. 'She wants to know what crack is,' says Mercedes.

'It's an illegal drug, sweetheart. It helps take the peaks and troughs out of the day, like Mummy's sav blanc.'

'Henry.' I walk over and squat on the floor beside him. 'Age-appropriate, remember? I have a great idea. Why don't I take them to the park? I'm desperate to push two little girls on the swings until my arms fall off and if you don't lend me these two, I'll be forced to kidnap a couple off the street.'

Henry holds up his palm. The girls don't move.

'Janice, please,' he says to me. Then, to the girls, 'This is no reflection on any particular mango. Your mango is a wonderful mango. Wonderful. But that's not the headline. The headline is: is it fair to be on an enforced diet of mangoes when the world is an enormous fruit salad?'

Mercedes and Paris squint like talent-show judges. This is an important question, they can sense it. 'Mummy makes us cheese on toast,' Mercedes says finally. 'We like that. And lamb chops. And noodles. And sausages. The skinny ones.'

He slaps his beefy thigh and attempts to pivot out of his squat but unbalances and instead lurches to his knees, which crunch on the floorboards. 'That's my girls. Anyway, Mummy and I still love you very much. That'll never change. Despite the archaic cultural construct that your mother and I find ourselves trapped in.'

All the while he's been talking, I've been aware of a faint clicking and whirring; I wave my hand to deter non-existent mosquitos. Caroline and Henry live in an outer-suburban pocket of dream acre-block farmlets where every home has space for a few chickens and the occasional orchard or kitchen cow. It's the semi-rural 4WD idyll belt and I almost open my mouth to say the crickets are loud this morning, when I feel a sneaking dread. I tell Henry to keep it G-rated until I get back.

When I get to Caroline and Henry's bedroom at the end of the corridor, I'm faced with a scene of devastation. Henry's suits are spread out over the unmade bed like a two-dimensional gay orgy: here a Paul Smith, there a Henry Bucks, everywhere a Zegna. The trouser-half of each and every one of them is missing its crotch and Caroline, chip off the old block, is peering over them with her reading glasses on the end of her nose and the good scissors in her hand.

She's still in her nightie, freshly foiled hair loose and a silk kimono draped over her shoulders. She looks forlornly at her symbolic castration and sighs, just like Mum did all those years ago. 'What a waste,' she says, as she shakes her head.

'Maybe not super-helpful at this point, Caroline darling,' I say.

She shrugs. 'These trousers failed in their primary duty, which is to contain the penis. They have only themselves to blame.'

'Nothing's been decided yet. People make mistakes, Caroline. Marriage is a marathon, not a sprint.'

'Earth to cliché-girl: do you know who took these suits to the drycleaner?' she says, as she smooths and folds the legs of a maimed Henry-surrogate and sits on the bed. 'Who washed all these shirts? Did the ironing? All right, Toula does the ironing, but you get my point. See this tie?' She reaches for a pale blue serpent nestling on the pillow. Crotch-butterflies flutter to the ground at her feet. 'I bought him this tie when he got his last promotion. It was a congratulatory tie. A tie that said your wife loves you. A chastity tie. It was not a tie to preside over the shagging of some schoolteacher young enough to be his much younger sister.'

'You're angry, of course you are.'

'Honestly Janice, do you live on Mars?' she says, as she lops the head off the blue tie. 'Here on this planet, every action has a reaction.'

I take the scissors. 'All the same, let's keep the collateral damage to a minimum. Please, Caroline?'

'Well excuse me. Some of us like being married.' She shoots me a look. 'Are you on Henry's side, is that it?'

I open my mouth, but I'm saved by the doorbell.

'I'll get it!' she yells.

'It's my house too!' yells Henry, from the lounge room. 'That means it's equally my front door and I will be the one who gets it.'

'Neither of you will get it,' I yell back at them. 'You will each stay in your designated corners and I will get it.'

I stalk back down the hall, past where Henry is still squatting and saying god knows what to the girls, who nod back at him. I almost intervene but the bell rings again so I keep going: he's their father, he only wants what's best for them. Besides, they'll need something to tell their analysts when they grow up.

When I open the door, it's Craig and Lesley from next door. What luck.

'Janice,' Craig says. 'It's been ages. You look well.'

'Janice,' Lesley says. 'Aren't you the ministering angel? You must have arrived very early. Or did you stay over?'

In this suburb, everyone knows each other. They pop in for drinks, they pick up each other's kids from drama class, they traipse through neighbours' yards as shortcuts on the way somewhere. Progressive dinners. Weekends at the snow. It's frightening. In the inner city where I live, people have the decency to ignore each other in general, and marital spats in particular. I regularly pass taggers, junkies, half-hearted trannies and any beggar who isn't a bonafide local as though they're invisible. It took six months of nodding in the street before I got to the stage of saying 'morning' to the guy from the flats who dresses like a pirate. Allowing other people room for their private proclivities is the basis of a civilised society.

I step outside and pull the door almost closed behind me. 'Caroline and Henry are just in the middle of something,' I say. 'I'll let them know you dropped by.'

Lesley and Craig exchange meaningful looks. The two of them are always shiny with health, like they've perpetually come from the gym and even their hair—Craig's blond ponytail and close-trimmed beard, Lesley's glossy black bob—is shampoo-commercial-ready. They're both in Lycra shorts and a t-shirt (her) or singlet (him). He has the kind of chest that will happily spend all day in a singlet. She's petite, a good foot shorter than him. Sharper, older.

'It's us, lovely. We heard them last night,' says Lesley.

Craig rubs a hand over his designer stubble in a gesture chosen to simulate thoughtfulness. 'The whole street heard them. Probably the whole valley. Sound really carries out here. It's the shape of the hills. Amazing pitch resonance.'

Craig is a sound engineer by profession and inclination, who works from a besser-block recording studio in their backyard and routinely inserts phrases like 'pitch resonance' into conversation. I've seen him in a t-shirt that says *Sound engineers do it with frequency*. Since Lesley sold out of the IT firm she founded, she makes ceramics: vases and bowls stocked in gift shops and galleries all over the mountains. She has a kiln and wheel in her own studio in the backyard, the mirror image of Craig's. She has a t-shirt that says *Potters do it with a glazed expression*.

'I can't believe he was on with Martha. I literally can't believe it,' says Craig.

'She seemed so sweet on parent-teacher night,' says Lesley.

Craig shakes his head. 'They're the ones you gotta watch.'

'Caroline, the poor love. I can only imagine how she's feeling,' says Lesley. 'Is there anything we can do?'

'He's a sly dog,' says Craig. 'She can't be a day over twenty-five.'

Everyone's fine, I tell them. Every marriage goes through ups and downs. They just need a little space. They're resting now.

'Is that Craig?' Henry is behind me and before I know it, he opens the door. 'Craig, mate. She's gone completely psycho.'

'Henry, mate.' Craig grips Henry's shoulder and flexes his arm and shoulder muscles with little pulses. 'I hear you. I feel for you mate.'

'You'd think after fifteen years I'd have earned a little wriggle-room, wouldn't you, mate? The odd free pass? Wouldn't you think that?'

'I think Caroline has been thoroughly provoked,' says Lesley, detaching Craig's arm from Henry. 'We aren't taking sides.'

'Of course not, of course not,' Craig says. 'Henry, you *dog* you.'

'Is that Lesley?' yells Caroline, and before I know it she's standing on the other side of me, and she's within two feet of

Henry, which is the thing I've been trying to avoid since six o'clock last night. She opens the door even wider.

'All those weekends I was stuck here and he was away on business? Ha bloody ha. His demanding job that kept him so busy and exhausted? Mugsy me, picking the girls up after school and *hello Martha, thanks for giving Mercedes so much extra attention Martha*, and driving them to ballet and swimming and making their dinner and bathing them and putting them to bed and then watching *Law and Order* and eating Lean Cuisine and all the while he's at the motor inn on the highway, shagging.'

'Don't,' says Henry. He sighs it out, a soft *don't*, and in that word I imagine the kind of boy he was: smaller than his size, used to saying *don't* in defence.

'Don't you say *don't* to me. I'm not the one who's been doing anything,' says Caroline. 'I'm the one who's been staying home, minding my own business.'

'Don't say shagging,' he says. 'It's not like that. We have a connection.'

'Your genitals have been having a connection, that's for sure,' says Caroline.

'Now—' begins Lesley.

'Girls,' I yell behind us. 'Back to your rooms please.'

There is a silence, a freezing I can feel from here, and all at once I remember what it's like to be that age in almost exactly these circumstances. Mercedes and Paris will be curled up on the floor in the lounge, splitting themselves in two, trying to decide whether it's best to know or to not-know. You can't win: if you hear, you'll wish you hadn't and if you don't, you'll wish you had. You feel wrong and stupid whichever you choose. Right now, they're trying to make themselves invisible, which can become a habit. It's very hard to stop, even when you grow up.

'Mercedes. Paris. I know you're there. Hop to it.'

A pause. 'We're hungry,' Mercedes yells back.

'You're stalling. I'll make you something really yummy soon but right now, your rooms.'

'All right,' yells Mercedes, after a moment, 'but whatever you make us, we don't like it.'

We all wait until the sound of small feet recede and we hear a door being closed.

'—That's quite enough of that,' continues Lesley.

'Let's everybody chill,' says Craig.

'It's a gross violation of trust, sure,' says Lesley. 'But it's not the end of the world.'

'I know!' Craig clicks his fingers. 'Trust exercises. One spouse leads the other blindfolded through a strange room. Or one spouse folds their hands on their chest and drops backwards and the other saves the first one's head from being smashed in.'

'The girls can change schools. There are male teachers around if you look hard enough, or maybe you can ban Henry from drop-offs and pick-ups,' says Lesley.

'The point is to not let the blind spouse get concussion,' Craig says. 'Concussion doesn't build trust.'

'Two unsettled children dragged away from their friends and two emotional adults at risk of a brain injury,' I say. 'Just the ticket.'

'Some people work at their marriage problems, rather than cutting and running,' Lesley says, and maybe I'm paranoid but she's looking right at me.

'Trust is a muscle,' says Craig.

'I'm pretty sure it's not,' I say.

Lesley threads her fingers through Craig's hand and touches her nose to his shoulder. 'It needs exercise, he means.'

Craig hunches to kiss her forehead. 'It's because we work at it, Pookie.'

'I have a wonderful therapist,' says Lesley. 'She really helped with my OCD. She does couples too. Not that I have direct experience, I don't. It's spray-painted on her door. I'll drop in her card.'

'That's thoughtful,' I say. 'Isn't that thoughtful, Caroline?'

'I guess,' she says.

'Henry? That's a good idea of Lesley's, isn't it? Talking to a professional?' I say.

He doesn't answer. He clasps his hands behind his back and twists from side to side, an Olympic weightlifter before the clean and jerk.

'Henry? Counselling. It's worth a go, isn't it?'

'Really, Janice?' says Caroline. 'You're suggesting counselling? You? I'll tell you one thing: Henry and I will not be taking relationship advice from you, Janice. Will we Henry?'

'Look,' Henry says. 'The truth is. I have a flat.'

'Your car's at the mechanic's, isn't it?' says Caroline 'They'll fix it while it's there, take them two minutes.'

'Not that kind of flat,' says Henry. 'The other kind.'

'What other kind?' says Caroline.

'It's not an affair,' says Henry.

'What is it then?' says Caroline.

'It's love. I haven't known how to say it until now, but I love her. Martha. I want to be with her.' And then he says, 'I'm leaving.'

Perhaps a relationship flashes before your eyes in the moment of its death. *Flash*. I see them, Caroline and Henry, the afternoon they first met outside an Engineering Department mixer, drinking beer and fighting about politics. *Flash*. Here they are again, years later in a crowded pub, each vaguely recognising the other and Caroline drinking too much and Henry driving her home and kissing her on the top step of Mum's house. Here is the first time they made love in the reclined front seat of the Beemer. Here they are, sharing a pizza on a perch of unopened boxes the night they moved in to their first flat, wide-eyed, listening to the strange sounds of the suburbs, planning paint colours and herb gardens. Henry, crying at the altar. The births of the girls. Standing at the sink: him washing, her drying. Sleeping together on hot nights, the tips of their fingers touching. *Flash, flash, flash*.

At the front door, we are all still. None of us dares to breathe. Then Caroline's mouth falls open and her skin yellows and shrinks. She is hollow now. The rage has gone out of her and her shell is upright only from the habit of her bones. She is watching their life together unspool before her eyes and she is thinking of her future, of the years to come without him. She is wondering how she will sleep alone every night in their big bed. Now, after two children, after almost two decades with this man at the centre of her life, she is no longer required.

We all stand on the threshold. No one knows what to say next.

In the long, black nights when I was not much older than Paris, when we were still adjusting to our house without my father in it, I took to imagining where he was sleeping, the particular bed and the pillow and the sheets. Was he warm enough? He liked the kind of orange juice with the leprechaun on the label. The others were too pulpy, he said, and sweet like musk sticks. Who was going to the supermarket and buying it for him? Who was ironing his shirts, now that Mum wasn't?

When he lived with us he would tuck me in and, just before he turned out the lights, bring his face close to mine and shut his eyes. *It's not easy being a grown-up*, he would say. *Take away my day, magic girl.* My hands were pale and soft then, before the bunsen burns and broken beaker scars, and I would raise them to his forehead. I imagined my fingertips as erasers. I started near his hairline, smoothing every furrow, and I then I slid the heel of my hand downwards towards the tufts of his eyebrows then across to his temples. I paid extra attention to the deep wrinkle that curved downwards like a gouge, near the chicken-pox divot above the bridge of his nose. I kneaded and pressed until his frown lines weren't as sharp, it seemed to me, until they blended with the texture of his skin. When I finished, I kissed each of his eyebrows, left and right.

There, I'd say. All fixed.

Now I'm good as new, he'd say. Now I can sleep.

Late some nights after my father left, I would ease my way out of bed as though I was molten, so nothing would creak. Mum and Caroline were sleeping. If I was careful, the house belonged to me in those dark hours. I roamed with bare feet on bare boards, I sat at windows and stared at the moon. It was easy to imagine that this strange house made up of women was temporary and soon everyone would be back where they belonged. My father was only away on a business trip. He would be home in a day or two.

Sometimes on those wandering nights I found myself in Caroline's room where I could look at her big-sister things without her saying *Rack off, Janus*. Or *Vajanus*. Or *Jan-arse Man-arse*. Or some variation of *Can you shut it? Can you possibly give me five minutes of peace?* Asleep, Caroline looked like herself again, despite her black sheets, dyed by Mum after a long negotiation involving compulsory minutes of sunlight exposure. I touched the white foundation on her dresser, the lipsticks with names like Nosferatu and Daughter of Darkness, and ran my hands across CDs of bands that sounded like a Harley-Davidson being tortured. She was a heavy sleeper, a snorer and a snuffler. Even without the makeup, her naked face was pale against the black pillow. She often seemed on the verge of waking, but she never did.

Mostly, though, I would sit on the floor beside my mother's bed to watch the rise and fall of her chest beneath her covers and the rhythmic wave of her sheets. Occasionally she stirred and reached one arm towards my father's empty space. On her bedside table beside the scattered blister packs was a picture of the four of us, smiling, taken at Torquay months before any of us knew of the storms ahead. Mum is wearing a swimsuit with spaghetti straps and a white ruffle that curves around her waist. Me and Caroline have our mouths inched open, as though a photo is the last thing we're expecting. Dad's face is tilted down but he's looking up and to the side. Maybe there is someone standing behind the photographer who's caught his eye. He has a lock of dark hair curled across his forehead like James Dean.

I didn't realise how young they both were, when we were a family. They were younger than I am now.

It took years for Mum to replace the photo with another one of just us three, taken at a school fete where she was running the plant stall. It took even longer for her to sleep in the middle of the bed.

Now, after Craig and Lesley make their excuses as though fleeing an outbreak of ebola, the girls and I are watching Caroline sleep on top of Paris's princess doona, surrounded by stuffed toys. Caroline's chest moves up and down in a ragged rhythm and her mouth is tight and her hands are tucked between her knees. I know that sleep, I've seen it before. The brain has withdrawn in the hope that when she wakes, everything will be better. Henry is packing. When Caroline wakes, things will only be worse. She is right to sleep now, while she can. The insomnia will come later.

'Mummy's like Sleeping Beauty.' Mercedes is squatting on her haunches on the floor beside me.

'She's just very tired,' I say. 'Mums get tired sometimes.'

'We know. If her door is closed, it means we have to stay downstairs in the playroom and not make one peep until she comes to get us. Then, do you know what? Ice-cream.' All at once Mercedes jumps to her feet. 'I know!' she says. 'Maybe if Daddy kisses her she'll wake up.'

I reach for her and hold her tight limbs in my arms. She comes to me reluctantly, a folded origami child all elbows and knees and sharp edges. She smells of soap and fresh milk and I have a precious moment to feel her weight heavy on me before she wriggles clear.

'Well? I'll go get Daddy, yes?' She bounces on the spot with her legs straight.

'I think Mum'll wake up when she's ready, and then you and Paris can be the ones to kiss her. What do you think, Paris?'

Instead of answering, Paris opens her eyes wider still and reaches for a sad-faced octopus at the foot of the bed. It has pearly fur, shiny black eyes and stretched stitches along the joins where legs meet torso from too many years of demonstrative love. I'm surprised Caroline hasn't had it renovated. Paris creeps forward and prises one of Caroline's hands from where it's tucked, and then she slips the octopus in the crook of her elbow.

Paris hasn't spoken to anyone except Mercedes since last night. I wonder if I'm the only one who's noticed.

'Grown-ups are hard to understand,' Mercedes says.

'Sing it, sister,' I say.

'You'd be a good mummy, Auntie Janice,' she says. 'How come you don't have any kids?'

Just then, Henry sticks his head around the corner. 'I'm almost done,' he says. 'I've got as much as I can here, clothes and stuff. One trip, clean as possible. Surgical. No point dragging it out. The CDs and booze can wait.'

'How very efficient of you,' I say. 'You're a regular hero.'

He opens his mouth, then closes it again. We follow him back to the bedroom: all the de-crotched pants and the bisected tie are in a pile in the corner and the bed is hidden beneath suitcases and sports bags and shopping bags filled with clothes. The wardrobe doors are open and his side is mostly empty except for a blotchy raincoat, a plaid jacket with a blue ink stain over the top pocket and a couple of Essendon scarves hanging over the rail. Metal coat hangers litter the floor. The dresser drawers are ajar and there's a trail of potpourri from a broken sachet leading to one of the suitcases. Novels and boxes of tissues and odd socks are spilling from the bedside table. He's stormed through the room and taken the things he wants. The person leaving always takes what they want and the one staying behind has to deal with everything else.

Henry's four-wheel drive is having the transmission recalibrated so I offer to drive him. He doesn't want to put me to any trouble, he says, as he checks the zips of the cases and carries them down the hall, and I refrain from telling him he

21

might have thought of that last night. Anyway, he'd feel better if I stay with Caroline and the girls for a while. What would make him feel better is what matters now, apparently. He's made a call. Someone is coming to pick him up and I have a sick feeling about who that someone will be.

He carries one load out to the front door.

'He's not coming back, is he?' Mercedes whispers to me.

'Let's go and sit with Mum,' I say. 'She'd love to see you both there when she wakes up.'

But Caroline sleeps on. After another ten minutes of watching her and listening to Henry open and close drawers in the ensuite, I hear a car pull into the driveway. It gives a jolly toot.

Henry appears in the doorway. 'That's Martha,' he says.

Mercedes reaches for my hand. Paris yawns, ostentatiously, with the back of her hand against her open mouth like a child actor. For the first time I sense the fury in her.

'Caroline,' Henry says. 'Take care of yourself.'

Caroline opens one fish eye from where she lies and deliberately closes it again.

He squats down beside the girls. He brushes the hair out of Mercedes' face and he straightens the elastic on Paris's sleeve. 'Daddy is going to stay at a friend's place for a while,' he says. 'Miss Roland. From school. Martha. Martha's place. Martha is Daddy's friend. You be good girls for Mummy and Auntie Janice.'

The girls say nothing and their presence helps me say nothing. I walk him out to the front door and they follow us.

Halfway down the slope of the circular driveway, a jaunty

orange Beetle is parked, seemingly reluctant to approach the house. The woman behind the wheel opens the door and steps one leg out. She taps her sandalled foot, she looks at her watch. She's as young and pretty as I feared—although perhaps it would be worse if she were older and plainer— and there's a businesslike tilt to her head that doesn't quite match the tiered peasant skirt and khaki singlet. Her hair is a cascade of shaggy dark blonde ringlets: the kind of haircut that takes three different products to texturise it, the type that has its own name—the Rachel or the Gwyneth. She keeps one hand on the wheel and one foot on the pedals as though she's a fighter pilot about to dismount and take her helmet off.

'Henry,' she calls. 'Tick, tock, babe.'

Henry sets off up the drive, then stops halfway to the car. He looks at her, he looks back at me and the girls, then he introduces us.

'Hi.' Martha waves with the flat of her hand. Wax on, wax off. 'You're the sister-in-law, right? The divorced one? Something to do with science? The one with the ex-husband everyone liked so much. Adam? Aaron?'

'Alec. His name was Alec. Is. Alec.'

'Alec,' she says. 'That's right. And you're Janice. I'm trying to get everyone straight in my head. It's still a blur, really. Relatives, in-laws, exes, friends. Henry knows a lot more people than me.' She sweeps her sunglasses up on top of her head and her eyes are clear and bright.

'That's probably because he's a fair bit older than you,' I say.

'I could have waited out on the street,' says Henry. 'You didn't have to drive down.'

'Henry, relax.' She sighs and shakes her head in a gesture that reminds me of Caroline. It's disturbing. 'He's worried this might be awkward,' she says to me. 'We're not eight-year-olds, fighting over a boy. We're grown women. It's not awkward at all, is it?'

'Maybe a bit,' I say. Paris edges closer to me and Mercedes grips my t-shirt.

'Good morning girls.' She does her flat wave again.

There is no answering *Good morning Miss Roland*.

'You're shy today girls, aren't you? To be expected. I can't wait to get to know them better, away from school. I know, Henry—we could get a kitten, for when they visit.'

'Should we wave at Miss Roland?' Mercedes whispers to me.

'If you want to.'

'Would it make Mummy sad?'

I kneel beside her. 'If you decide not to wave to Miss Roland today, you can still wave to her another day. You can wave to her whenever you like. You can talk to her too, if you want to, at school, or at home, any time you want. You don't have to make up your mind right now.'

Mercedes looks at Paris, then back at me. 'We'll wait, then,' she says.

'Is Caroline up for a quick chat?' says Martha.

'I'm sorry?'

'I mean, we're not cavemen. Cavewomen. I mean, hello? What year is it? We can behave like civilised people. Set a great example for the girls, be adults about this.' Her smile is, frankly, adorable. She could be a tooth model.

Henry goes on loading suitcases into the car.

'Maybe not the best time to disturb her,' I say. 'Under the circumstances.'

'Sure, sure, of course.' She drops her hand down to her side and a nest of bangles tinkle down her arm. 'Maybe next week. We could have lunch, talk it over. We've got so much in common. Believe me, we'll be ringing each other to complain about Henry before you know it.'

I cough, then, and Mercedes slaps me on the back.

'It's super-common to start over these days,' Martha goes on. 'It's a trope, practically. You can't move in Chapel Street for women Caroline's age, sometimes even older, learning to live again after years of marriage. Free at last, free at last. Please tell her from me: no hard feelings.'

'No hard feelings. I'll let her know.'

'Excellent. And maybe you could pass this on: as someone who's devoted their career to early childhood development and pedagogical theory, I know about co-parenting. Support and consistency. Keeping a unified front. There'll be no video games at our place, she won't have to worry. No reality television. Strict bedtimes. No junk food. The psychological health of the girls, that's what matters.'

'Isn't she amazing?' says Henry.

'Amazing,' I say.

'Oh, stop,' she says.

Henry turns and looks back at the house, at the timber he sanded and painted last year, at the stairs, the windows, the row of red rhododendrons in pots along the patio, the bedroom balcony with its cane chairs just a few metres above the garden bed, the guttering he's emptied of leaves. He looks at the lawn he's spent years mowing, at the lavenders and the roses and the tree full of lemons waiting for his famous G&Ts.

'Henry,' says Martha. 'We don't have all day, babe.'

'Who'd like avocado on toast for breakfast?' I say. 'How about you, Miss Paris?'

'Mummy makes us pancakes on weekends,' says Mercedes.

'Does she? That's because avocado on toast is normally just for grown-ups, so don't tell anyone. How many pieces would you like?'

'Two for me,' said Mercedes. 'But only one for Paris because she's little.'

'Bye girls,' says Henry. 'I'll see you soon, OK?'

'OK, Daddy,' Mercedes says.

'Be good at school, won't you.'

They nod.

'And pay attention at swimming classes. Water is dangerous, always remember that. Never go near the water without an adult.'

'OK.'

'Also, never pat a stray dog. If you see a dog, always ask the owner's permission before you pat it and even then give it the back of your hand to smell first. Even nice-looking dogs can rip your face off. And then where will you be? Faceless, that's where.'

'Henry,' I say.

'Avoid Punt Road if you possibly can. Not just during

football season, everyone knows that. All year round. You can waste half your life on Punt Road if you're not careful.'

'Henry,' I say. 'You'll see them again. Well before they get their drivers licence.'

'Right, sure,' he says.

He doesn't come closer or hug them. He doesn't even touch their hands. He's containing this, acting tight and fierce, keeping a lid on it for everyone's sake. They'll all have to get used to goodbyes like these. There are years of them ahead.

He walks up the hill around to the far side of the car. The back is filled with luggage and when he folds his bulk in the passenger seat, his knees are up near his chest because of the bag at his feet. It takes him two tries to close the door properly, then he leans his head back and shuts his eyes.

Martha zips the window down. 'Bye Janice, nice to meet you! Bye girls! See you at school!' she calls, and the jolly car toots and scurries around the circular driveway. It strains a little as it climbs the hill, then at the top it turns left toward the city. We watch for a while after it's gone.

I make breakfast for the girls, and for Caroline when she wakes. She doesn't touch it. I do the dishes and put a load in the washing machine and take the rubbish out while she paces beside me.

'You haven't been telling people about me and Alec, have you?' I say to her.

'Is that what you think of me?' she says. 'I'm your sister. You think I'm blabbing your private business to everyone I know? Thanks for the vote of confidence.'

I tell her I'm sorry. I'm a little oversensitive, I guess.

'She's pretty, isn't she. Martha. Did you think she was pretty?' Caroline says.

'Not very. Fancy a tea?'

'Of course,' she says. 'Of course she is.'

'Something green, something herbal, or something single malt?'

'She hasn't given birth, of course. She's pert. Did you think she was pert? Her breasts probably stand up by themselves. You could put a pencil under them and it'd fall straight to the floor. You could fit an entire stationery drawer under my breasts. You could wedge a laptop up there.'

'Mum,' says Mercedes. 'Can we have pizza for dinner?'

'Of course,' Caroline says. 'She probably hangs on his every word. She adores him, doesn't she? She doesn't wash his Y-fronts and put him to bed when he's had too much to drink. He forgets my birthday, did you know that? I have to write it in his diary myself.'

'Mum.' Mercedes pulls on her sleeve. 'I need a present for Avery because her party's on Tuesday after school and everyone is going. And you're supposed to buy my raffle tickets and if you win you get a hamper and the money goes to the library. You promised.'

'Of course,' says Caroline, and then she sits up, straight and stiff. 'What?'

'Pizza. Present for Avery. Raffle tickets,' I say.

'Do I have any money?' she says.

'I can manage it,' I say, 'provided Avery has simple tastes.'

'I don't mean that. I mean, in the bank. We have a joint

account. Henry could have cleaned it out for all I know. The man is coming to trim the trees this week. We need groceries. There are bills. Also, I may need more wine.'

She asks Mercedes to get her laptop, and she opens the screen and types furiously. After a few minutes, she looks up and closes the screen halfway.

'Girls,' she says. 'Go downstairs to the playroom.'

'Again?' says Mercedes. 'There's no one here for you to fight with except Auntie Janice.'

'Go on. Toot sweet.'

After they leave, stomping their little feet, she calls me over. 'Look,' she says. Her finger points to the bank account screen, to the transactions on their joint credit card. Qantas, it reads.

'For work, maybe?'

'Different card. Let's just have a teeny peek at his frequent flyer transactions, shall we?'

She types, pecking the keys like each one is Henry's face, and before I can say gross invasion of privacy, another screen pops up. I have a sneaking certainty this isn't going to end well.

After a few moments of waiting, she squeals. 'That bastard. That pert-bimbo–shagging bastard. He's gone to Noosa. Noosa. Right now, today. He booked two tickets last week. Oh my god, he's flying business class. He's been planning this for ages, the ferret-faced weasel.'

'Caroline, calm down,' I say. 'Ferrets and weasels are completely different species.'

'Do you know where he took us at Christmas? Dromana.

29

For a weekend. He took his wife and kids to Dromana and he's taking Martha, that skinny ferret-ess, to Noosa. Business!'

'I think you'll find a female ferret is called a jill. Honestly Caroline, let it go. What doesn't kill you makes you stronger.'

'That's garbage,' she says. 'What doesn't kill you joins forces with all the other things that don't kill you. Then they all gang up together to kill you.'

She jumps to her feet and runs to the bedroom. I run after her. She leaps on the bed and bounces on it, on top of the piles of discarded clothes, like it's a trampoline. She's trying to see the top of the wardrobe.

'Bastard. He's taken all the suitcases. Never mind.'

She dismounts and takes a largish handbag from a hook behind the door, stuffs it with undies and a bra, then grabs a shirt from her half of the cupboard.

'You'll be right with the kids for the weekend, won't you Janice? You haven't got plans for tonight? Of course not. What am I thinking. You don't have to feed your Petri dishes or whatever? Look, it's midday Saturday now. I'll be back by Sunday night at the very latest. Where are my car keys?'

'Caroline.' I grab her by the shoulders and she stops moving at last. 'Don't do this.'

'You don't understand,' she says. 'It's my fault.'

'Darling, don't say that. Don't even think it.' I try to reach my arm around her back, but she pulls away.

She squeezes the bag to her chest. 'It's true,' she says. 'I haven't been the perfect wife. I've done things I regret, I know that now. Stupid things. But I never thought it'd come to this.' She grabs me by the arm. There's a mad kind of look in her eye, the kind of look that could lead to anything. 'I blame myself, at least for part of it. I have to go after him. I'm not going to rot away, the way Mum did. I need him to see me. This is my last chance.'

So of course I find her keys, and her phone, and I think about what to tell the girls while she books her flight to Noosa. The bedroom is even worse by the time she finishes: clothes strewn everywhere, every door and drawer open, bags and shoes across the floor. She gives me a list of garbled instructions: pizza delivery menu is on the hall table, don't give Paris liquids within two hours of bedtime, don't move any of the pot plants on pain of death because she has them perfectly positioned for the exact amount of sunlight and if I move them, they'll spontaneously combust.

I don't remind her that my entire job is keeping things growing. I'm barely listening. I not only let her go, I help her pack.

The girls and I don't spend the afternoon wrapping dampened slices of bread in plastic to see how long it takes furry blue mould to spread, and we don't gasp at slides of insect monsters under the microscope I bought them a few Christmases ago. There are no experiments today. Me and science: our relationship is complicated.

Instead we build Lego towers on the playroom floor, where maidens wait to be rescued by knights and mummies are surprised by daddies coming home from work, and I don't say a thing. The way we press the blocks together is deliberate, as though they might slip and skitter away beneath the pressure of our hands. We are all pleases and thankyous and excuseme, except for Paris, who still isn't talking. They sit too close to me and pat my hand and twirl my hair around their fingers. They take it in turns to curl up in my lap and they walk me to the toilet and wait for me outside the door. I'd like to tidy Caroline's bedroom but they'd follow and I don't want them to see the desolate wardrobe, the void Henry's made abandoning ship. Their faces hold no clues to what is going on beneath the surface. This is what worries me.

When I was their age, no one knew about my obsession with the workings of bodies, how I would shut my eyes and imagine each red blood cell bumping along like a tiny balloon inside its capillary until it reached the airy sponge of my lung. I caught insects with a child's casual cruelty so I could examine them with my magnifying glass. When I grew up, I thought I'd understand the way the world works. Science was like constructing a very high wall with tiny pebbles, I thought: no single one meant much on its own but added to all the other pebbles, all the other discoveries and bits of knowledge gained by scientists from every country stretching back centuries, the wall grew high enough to climb and see forever. Science was glorious. I thought it would always keep me safe.

Now that I'm a grown-up, I'm resigned to never understanding the first thing about the world or the workings of the body. When people ask about my job, I no longer say I'm a scientist. I don't even say I'm a microbiologist. I'm a technician, I tell them, who once held aspirations of discovery. Every day I gown up and sit in front of my fume hood and streak my plates of bacteria. It's my job to make very small things grow in the same way for generations without the kind of stress that causes mutations, and it's the job of these small things to make the same enzymes, daughter after daughter. A lot is resting on them and they are in my charge, these tiny, teeming forests. Their lives depend on me. I am a gardener in my coat and mask and booties, with a loop instead of a hoe.

33

Surely I can manage two children for a weekend.

'Isn't this fun?' I say, after two-thirds of a castle.

'Fun slash boring,' Mercedes says. She rests her head on my shoulder and her hair is silk on my cheek.

After I moved out of our flat, mine and Alec's, I stayed in the spare room at the back of their garage. The girls were easy to amuse. In my state, I spent days lying on Caroline's couch and they pressed damp washers to my forehead and poured tiny cups of invisible tea and all I had to do was lean up on one elbow and take a pretend sip from time to time. One rainy Saturday, Paris appeared with her junior doctor kit, ready to diagnose what ailed me.

There, there, she said. She slipped a plastic thermometer under my tongue and hit me on the knee with a tiny reflex hammer. *You catched a germ but this will make it better.*

Then Mercedes held the disc of their stethoscope on my chest under my shirt while they listened. Their golden hair mingled as their heads touched, one ear tip each. Teeth pressed against lower lips.

You've definitely got one, Mercedes said. *I can hear it thumping.*

Phew, I said, as I took out the thermometer. It was a relief to know something was still beating in there.

She moved the disc to my forehead where it sat, hard and cool, then she called out to Caroline who was unpacking the dishwasher. *Mummy*, she yelled. *Auntie Janice definitely has a heart, I checked. Do you want me to see if she has a brain too?*

Of course she does, Caroline said. *Where on earth do you get such silly ideas? Come and get a yogurt and leave Janice alone.*

34

Then she stuck her head in the fridge.

Mummy would love a painting, I tell them now, and I set up the easels on the concrete near the laundry. The paints are lined up in rainbow order in a cupboard, with brushes and paper and bulldog clips to keep the paper in place on the easel. Paris brings ironed aprons for them both.

'Mummy needs a hobby,' I say.

At first, Mercedes focuses on squelching globs of red and yellow and blue in egg cartons and mixing shades of green and orange and turquoise but eventually she paints a mauve cat sitting in a basket. It's a representational cat with a spherical body and a smaller round head and a twisting tail, Cheshire grin and triangular ears. Mercedes loves animals. *We could get a kitten, for when they visit*, said clever Martha, who's been Mercedes' teacher for the whole year. That's quite a tactical advantage.

Paris, on the other hand, dives right in, half conviction and half carelessness, glooping paint straight from the bottles to her brush and getting some on her apron the instant she moves her arm. She's uncoordinated but sweeps the brush with flair, an attempt at scale and interpretation. She paints six people with their arms spread wide and their feet turned backwards. Two are smaller and wear aprons smeared with colour, so I can confidently say they are the girls. Caroline is identifiable by the blonde ponytail and pink dress, and Henry is thinner on top with a sad face. He's the only one in profile, looking somewhere else. Caroline and Henry are holding hands. The last two are a mystery. They're also holding hands: a brown-haired woman in a white dress with buttons and a taller man with open hands. Perhaps it's a wedding.

'That's you,' says Mercedes, and now I see that the white dress is a lab coat. 'And that's Uncle Alec. We don't have to paint Miss Roland, do we? She's not in our family, not really. She belongs at school.'

'You remember Uncle Alec?'

Mercedes rolls her eyes. 'Of course. He's our only uncle.'

I step back and knock over a bottle of red paint that I've left near the landing. We watch it run on to the concrete and then the grass, as though someone's killed a pig.

'That wasn't us,' says Mercedes. 'That was you.'

It's almost enough to bring on the waterworks. The girls aren't too happy either.

'I have a great idea. How about we clean this up later and have a nap now?'

'No,' Mercedes says. 'Don't go.'

'I'm not going anywhere, except to snoozyland. I think we're all pretty tired.'

They both fold their arms and drop their chins.

I pull Paris to my lap; there is a tiny pause before she yields. 'I hate resorting to extortion, but there's a good chance Santa will ring this afternoon. I'd like to be able to tell him how good you are.'

Mercedes twists her fingers through mine. 'Will you still be here when we wake up?'

'That's a definite yes.'

Mercedes' hands are small against mine but stronger than they look. Her nails are chips of mother of pearl with sharp edges, her fingers are thin and spiky. They are skinny, lithe children who climb trees with their monkey fingers and monkey toes. They love lifting things, provided you tell them the thing is too heavy for girls their age, and they adore running as fast as they can manage, lap after lap around the house, to beat their best time from yesterday. They are young enough to be proud of their girl-strength and girl-speed. I suppose all children have skin this pure and tanned, without a blemish. Golden shiny hair is probably as common as grass, and pleases and thankyous, most of the time at least, are not even slightly remarkable—yet some days I can hardly look at them for amazement. How lucky Caroline is. The impossibility of it. The miracle of them, the one-in-a-million sperm-meets-egg.

They both stretch their arms high. 'Carry us?'

'Are you joking? Look at the size of you two. You should be carrying me.'

After the junior literalists put me down, they're convinced about our nap. My overnight bag is in the spare room but I bring it upstairs: I don't want them to wake confused and disorientated, unable to find anyone. For a few strange weekends when we were little, Caroline and I stayed at Dad's flat, before he moved away. He made up the couch with old flannelette sheets from home, with a pillow at each end and our legs entwined in the middle, and we lay awake all night watching strange shadows creep up the walls and listening to growling sounds from the flat next door. I decide to sleep in Caroline and Henry's room.

I tuck the girls in and stagger to the bed. The late night, the early morning, the high drama. Everything will be all right, though. Caroline will go to Noosa and find Henry and they will reconcile and everything will be all right.

I leave the door ajar so that I can hear the girls if they wake, then I shut the blinds and open the balcony doors a little. They won't stay put, they keep blowing closed, so I take a potted rhododendron from where it sits on Caroline's dresser and use it to wedge them open, just a crack. It's dark in the bedroom now, with the doors almost closed and the blinds drawn. I crawl across Caroline's bed, feeling my way amid the mess. My clothes feel heavy and tight so I strip off down to my undies.

The bed is firmer than mine but it'll have to do. The walls are bare, plain and white and soothing, rather like my lab. There are precautions required when you're handling bacteria and my stock culture collection is serious, so we work in demountable buildings in the middle of a great shed and every building has its own filtered air and water and there are alarms and emergency showers in case one of us—what? Makes a mistake and contaminates herself? Has some kind of breakdown and throws plates in the air and kicks over hundred-litre vats and rubs some strange pathogen over her skin, something that would wipe out the world's cotton crop or cause every cow in the country to cough its lungs out?

When I first started working there, environmental monitoring was part of my job. Every week I tested the air and water inside the lab for bacterial contamination and compared it with control samples I'd take from the air outside and water from the tap. Most people have no idea what bacteria they ingest. I'd culture my control samples into beautiful and strange miniature gardens: round globules of fuzzy burnt orange, a glossy slick of sunset yellow. For weeks I was conscious of every breath and every mouthful, once I knew what was lurking in the open, hiding in plain sight.

The world we see is not the only one on this blue planet. Sometimes it's better not to know these things.

It's too quiet: how can anyone sleep out here without the city hum? I pull the covers up and put my head under the pillow, and an instant later I feel myself falling.

I dream of Alec.

I dream that he has come to me. I haven't had this dream for over a week but in the months after I left, I would wake gasping every night and for a few seconds would have sworn he was beside me. I could feel his musky warmth in the space where his body used to lie, the sleek muscle of his thigh, the soft white flesh under his arm. I was not really alone in my bed. That was an illusion. Even when I woke properly, if I kept very still with my eyes shut I could convince myself he had nipped out to the kitchen; any moment he'd be on his way back to me with a tray of tea and toast.

Sometimes, when we were married, he would rest one finger on my hip as we lay in bed. Just one finger. Every cell of my skin, every breath of mine would reach toward him as though the whole of the universe had contracted to that one point where our skin was touching. Then I would nestle my bottom backwards, into the hollow of his hips. Then I would feel his hand, flat on the curve of my bottom, sliding under the side of my pyjama pants.

In my dream, I never left Alec and we were never divorced

and we do not sleep apart even now. In my dream I can feel his hand sliding under my waistband and running over my stomach and cupping the underside of my breasts. I can feel his feet against mine, his legs against mine, his arm diagonally across my chest like a seatbelt holding me safe in a speeding car. It's been so long since I felt a man's skin down the length of my body. This feels so real. So real. I can feel his breath hot on my ears, I can feel his beard nuzzle the back of my neck. I want his hand lower. Lower. I run my fingers over his hairy forearm and push his arm down.

Wait.

I can feel his beard nuzzle the back of my neck; I run my fingers over his hairy forearm.

Wait, what?

Alec's arms aren't noticeably hairy.

I bolt upright and fumble for the bedside lamp. In the sudden flare of light I turn and, lying beside me under the covers, with his hand tucked in the side of my undies, grinning up at me, is Craig.

Craig, from next door. Ostentatiously married Craig. Tall, bronzed, muscles-on-top-of-muscles Craig. Unrobed, de-clothed, utterly buck-naked. He's the one who's been kissing my neck and fondling my bottom.

He sees me and I see him. His mouth opens and his eyes widen and he barrels backwards, propelled from the bed as if by jet pack. He tries to grip the sheet as he lurches, but I grab the other end and we tussle for a moment before he loses, then he trips over a nest of hangers and smacks against the wall in the corner of the room, cupping his genitals.

'What, what, what,' he gasps.

'Who, how, what the fuck,' I pant.

'Oh man, oh man, Janice, you just about gave me a cardiac arrest.' He tilts his head back to lean his crown against the wall, panting. His pecs are hard and waxed smooth. Shiny, like a Ken doll's.

'Are you out of your mind? Are you deranged?' I manage.

'Give me a minute. Phew. Let me recover.' He bends at the waist and puffs like a sprinter, then he removes one hand from his crown jewels to lay it on his chest. 'Whoa. Feel this. Seriously, my heart rate must be hitting 150 or 180 right now. My monitor would be maxing out.'

'You should be locked up,' I hiss at him. 'How dare you creep into my sister's bed and fondle me, you big creepy creep.'

'Jeez, calm down. You make it sound so sordid.'

'That's because it is. It is sordid. No, keep your hands where they are. And keep your voice down,' I say. 'The girls are at the end of the hall.'

'Well I'm sorry,' he stage-whispers, 'but they're usually downstairs in the playroom.'

Oh no. My stomach flips, my skin feels chilled and clammy.

'Usually?'

'They didn't see me, if that's what you're worried about. I'm like a ninja.'

'A ninja.'

He jerks his head toward the balcony door. 'See that trellis? There, behind the roses. That side of the house is only five feet off the ground. It's a poor design, actually. Terrible

41

security. I had to reinforce it to take my weight. Lucky I'm handy like that. I could spend the whole day wandering around Bunnings.'

'I couldn't give a flying fuck if you built a replica Taj Mahal in the middle of your lounge room out of Doritos and dental floss,' I say. 'What. Are. You. Doing. In. This. Bed?'

'Steady on. Way to blow everything out of proportion, Janice. The rhododendron. In the pot? That one, right there, on the balcony.'

He gestures with both hands this time. I squeeze my eyes closed.

'I can see it from the kitchen window at my place,' he says. 'Not with the naked eye, obviously. I keep binoculars under the sink. The coast is clear, it means. Come on, be reasonable. It was dark and you were under the covers and there is a family resemblance. So, hey. Will you open your eyes? I can't talk to you like that.'

I flutter one lid. 'Please tell me you're here because you're moonlighting as a surprise volunteer naked door-to-door mattress inspector.'

He crosses his eyes, then uncrosses them. 'I literally don't even know what that is. Jeez, I thought you were the smart one. I'm sleeping with Caroline, obviously.'

She hasn't been the perfect wife, she told me. I think of the secret life we all have, the one that no one else knows about. I think of her wedding, her children, our parents, my divorce.

'I cannot comprehend this,' I say. 'I cannot mentally grasp what you're saying.'

'Lighten up,' he says. 'It's not the fifties. It's a little

extracurricular activity, that's all. If I was meeting your sister a couple of times a week to play squash no one would give a rats. We're both adults, Judge Janice. Face it: life is short. Let's make the most of it while we're breathing.'

He raises one eyebrow. All at once, I long for a shower. And a loofah. And some hospital-grade disinfectant.

'Don't just stand there cupping yourself,' I say. 'Get dressed.'

'I can do that, sure,' he says. 'If that's what you really want. Because what I'm thinking, Janice, is maybe you moved those rhododendrons on purpose.'

'What? I had no idea it was the bat-signal. And I certainly didn't know you were the bat.'

'Maybe that's true, maybe you didn't know. Or maybe you did. Maybe, just maybe, your conscious mind is not in the driver's seat, Janice. Maybe your inner Freud called out to me.'

'You are a complete muppet. I find you utterly repellent.'

'You're very defensive, you know that Janice? You're allowed to experience lust. It's natural. I hate to see female passion being suppressed by the societal conventions of the male-dominant paradigm of the phallocentric patriarchy.'

'I moved a plant, Craig. That's all.'

'But *why* did you move it?' He wiggles his eyebrows up and down. 'Because you put the plant's needs first. You're a kind woman, Janice, I can tell. Also, you have very soft skin. The twins are at a pony club camp and Lesley's spending the afternoon looking at some new clay. She loves clay. She loves poking it and squishing it and oozing it through her fingers. She won't be home for hours.'

I pin the sheets under my armpits and grab the lamp from the bedside table. 'Take one step. Go ahead.'

All at once, we freeze. We both hear it: the unmistakable sound of a car pulling up in the drive.

'Who's that?' whispers Craig.

'How should I know?' I whisper back, still clutching the lamp, and then I look at him properly. There's something glinting on his chest. 'Oh my god. You have pierced nipples.'

'It's probably someone turning around. It's very handy, a circular drive on these hilly roads. Lesley's been at me to put one in. For her friends, most of them can't reverse up that hill. Not for me. I'm excellent at reversing. And yes, they heighten sensation. You don't know what you're missing, vanilla Camilla. Let me give you a little tweak.'

'Try. You'll never use that hand again.'

I hear the car engine stop.

'The car has not turned around,' I say. 'I thought you said it was turning around?'

'It's probably a delivery,' he says. 'They'll leave it at the front door and get back in the car, I bet. Maybe Henry is sending flowers to apologise, or a box of cheese. Lesley is forever ordering boxes of cheese. I'm not a mouse, Janice. I'm a man. I have needs.'

Then the doorbell rings.

'Maybe it's a once-in-a-lifetime opportunity to change electricity suppliers,' whispers Craig. 'Or a Jehovah's Witness. Someone taking a survey. Girl guides. Just don't answer it. If nobody answers it, whoever it is will go away.'

Just then, I hear Mercedes' door open down the hall. 'I'll

get it!' she yells. She's running to the front door. I hear Paris running behind her.

'No! Don't get it!' I yell.

Small children should not be opening doors by themselves. Some wandering axe-murderer is probably ringing doorbells all over the neighbourhood to find small children in the care of naked negligent aunts in bed with nipple-ringed neighbours. So he can murder them. The small children. With an axe.

'Girls! Stop! Stranger danger!' I yell.

I rifle through the bed and there are clothes everywhere but none of them are mine so instead, as I get out of the bed, I tighten the sheet around me. Craig saunters over to look out the window and as he turns around, I get an inadvertent eyeful of him, standing to attention in all his throbbing glory.

'Cover up!' I throw a pillow at him. 'I do not want to see that.'

He catches the pillow but holds it against his chest. 'I hear you've been living like a nun since you dumped your husband. Must be tough. It's a waste, Janice. What are you, thirty-seven, thirty-eight? You're overwhelmed right now, I bet.' He glances down at himself. 'All your hormones are going crazy. You're probably feeling somewhat intimidated.'

'I'm feeling somewhat nauseated.' I open the bedroom door, wrapped in my sheet, trying to peer down the hall. I hear the front door open. I hear a man's voice. The axe-murderer's voice. He's inside the house now. The girls have let him inside.

I hear Mercedes say, 'Daddy's gone away with Miss Roland because he loves her more now and Mummy's gone too because she's been naughty. Auntie Janice is in charge. She's in Mummy's room.'

Then she sings out: 'Auntie Janice! It's Uncle Alec.'

The last time I saw Alec was outside the bookstore in Bourke Street, almost two years ago. I can't remember why I was in the city. Maybe a dentist appointment or maybe something to do with finalising the divorce. Papers that needed signing, something like that. At first I thought he was another of the faux-Alecs, the men whose resemblance faded on close inspection and left me sad for them, those watery imitations. After my heart started up again, I saw it was actually him, the real him, standing on the footpath, looking in the window at the new releases not far from the beautiful people lunching outside the Italian restaurant. He was eating a green apple and his left hand was in the pocket of his jeans.

He was wearing glasses I hadn't seen before, rounder ones with a tortoiseshell frame, and they slipped down his nose as he bent his head. He pushed them up again with the back of his hand, the one that held the apple. He didn't notice me as he ate his apple: first, big bites through the sharp skin, then little nibbles as he ate the whole core. He always ate cores. He ate the prickly green hulls of strawberries; he swallowed mandarin seeds. He didn't eat citrus peel, of course. I was forever finding long orange streamers coiled on the bedside table or in his pockets in the laundry basket. That kind of thing drives people crazy when they're living together. It leaves a different recollection when you're not.

Alec never rushed. Even when playing tennis or riding his bike, his was a leisurely action: the centre of him seemed undisturbed, balanced there on top of his strong legs, a passenger along for the ride. This inner stillness I supposed to be the result of his job. Historians see their lives in the context of millennia, although the past was more than a job to Alec. He knew the names and occupations of his ancestors back five generations, and anecdotes about their lives, and it mattered that his great-grandfather had been a butcher on the Darling Downs, that his mother's family came from Poland. He knew that time stretches forever in both directions, that we are all but specks in eternity and so our hectic, self-important busyness doesn't matter a jot. On that day in the city, he was looking through the window of the bookstore as though it was a very important thing that needed doing, the only thing he had scheduled for the whole day.

He was alone, and all at once I realised that one day soon I'd run into him in the street and he wouldn't be alone. He'd have someone else with him, a woman and maybe children who looked like him, a baby in his arms or strapped to his chest in a carrier, or a little boy or girl also eating an apple. I could see this girl. I could see her blue dress and her red Mary

Janes with appliqué flowers, the way she handed him the core of her apple to finish, all the while holding his hand and tilting her head right back to look up at him, and I couldn't breathe for a moment. I stopped in the middle of the footpath and a young woman with headphones clamped on her ears walked right into the back of me. I'm sorry, she mouthed, even though I was the one at fault.

Perhaps I could move to Antarctica on some kind of research mission. There must be bacteria down there. Or perhaps I could develop an allergy to the twenty-first century so I'd never have to leave the house again.

We had already decided who would get the fridge and the washing machine and how we would split our mingled books and the DVDs. We did this while perched on stools in a wine bar not far from what used to be our flat. We worked our way through half a bottle of Tasmanian whisky while making two lists: one of things we wanted and the other, of things we deeply, seriously didn't, like the toaster with two settings, cold and black, and the his-and-hers reindeer mugs his aunt gave us for Christmas. We did this in a spirit of determined cordiality, of a gritty kind of gaiety. He had his pride. He had no desire to be with me if I was too stupid to love him.

After that, everything was fresh and vivid, like the world after a heavy storm. There was nothing outstanding that needed to be resolved. And now, outside the bookshop, there was no reason to speak to him at all. I could have backed away and nipped down the lane and chances are he wouldn't have seen me. There was only one thing I still owned that caused me grief.

That thing was the weight on my third finger, left hand. When we were separating, I hadn't given it a thought but now I couldn't forget it. I couldn't leave it at home out of my sight—it throbbed in my dresser drawer like kryptonite— yet as the months passed, it had grown so heavy I could barely move my arm. It dragged me lopsided to the ground, Quasimodo-style. It caused a creeping paralysis as though my finger had been bitten by a redback while I slept. That day in the street, I knew it was my chance to be rid of it. It was the last thing left of us. Perhaps if I gave it back, things would start to get better for me.

I inched it down my finger from this side to that, bit by bit until it was off, and held it tight in my right hand. Then I stood beside him, also looking in the window as if those books were the most fascinating thing ever and they alone could make some kind of difference to the way my life had turned out.

'Of all the footpaths in all the towns in all the world,' he said, after a while. He didn't turn his head. He kept his focus on my reflection in the glass next to his, staring into the image of my eyes.

'Some day you're going to eat one core too many,' I said, 'and pow. You'll find an apple tree growing right out of your belly button.'

The likeness of his eyes was distorted through the lenses of his glasses, as though he was a rare tropical fish in a tank. 'My former wife. This is a surprise. Unless you're stalking me. If you're stalking me, it wouldn't be a surprise.'

'Not stalking, no.'

'So, luck then.'

'I guess you could call it that.'

'Luck. Wow. I thought I'd never see that baby again,' he said. 'If it's luck, it'd be a crime to waste it. It's a rare thing these days, luck.'

I envied him then, for his clear-cut, dead-wrong understanding.

'A drink?' he went on. 'A quick, insignificant drink between two ex-spouses. A Campari and soda? It's not too early.'

It was too early, but that wasn't the reason I said no.

'A wine?'

I shook my head.

'Bloody mary? Cointreau? Château Lafitte-Rothschild 2008? If you've started drinking again, of course. It's fine if you are. Off alcohol. A lemonade? Or a juice?'

'I'm drinking extra, actually, to make up for my sabbatical, but no. Thank you. No drink.'

'Of course not. A drink is a bit intimate, now that we're no longer married. We're strangers, practically. How about a coffee? Coffee is what you have when you don't know someone at all. When it turns out you never really did.'

I extended my arm. He thought I was offering to shake his hand, I could tell. He honestly thought I was that cruel and maybe he was right, maybe I was, but not today. Instead I handed him the ring, the solitaire he'd spent so long choosing that the man in the antiques store snibbed the lock and swept the floors around him, statue-still in the middle of the shop, ring glinting in his palm, imagining it on my finger.

Imagining me at forty, wearing that ring. At fifty. At eighty.

'What's this?' He held his hand flat, as though the stone would cut him if he softened.

I never wore it in the shower, I took it off to do the dishes. Soap scum builds up on diamonds, it cuts down the brilliance. I couldn't bring myself to leave it at home but the talc inside my work gloves left it dusty, so every week I washed it in warm water with a few drops of ammonia and polished it with a soft toothbrush I bought specially. I made it shine. I took it back to the antique shop every year to have the claws checked; I wrote the date in my diary in case I forgot. I never forgot. The jeweller remembered Alec. Of course he did. *How's that husband of yours*, he'd say, as he tested the claws, loupe in his eye. *The chatty one.*

'I gave this to you,' Alec said, palm still flat. 'It's yours.'

That was only partly true. He gave it to me, yes, but even as he placed it on my finger I knew he had chosen it for the decades to come, for the hands of women and the pledges of men who hadn't been born yet. It was meant as an heirloom. I was holding it in trust.

I put my hands in my pockets.

'Give it to charity,' he said. 'Sell it. Throw it off St Kilda pier if you want to. It's a bloody stone.'

'It's too much responsibility. Please.'

'Why should I?' he said. 'You accepted it, as I recall. You were the one who said yes. What is it about the word "forever" that you don't understand?'

'I don't want it.'

'What makes you think I do?'

'Please,' I said. 'Please take it.'

He plucked it up and held it to the light, in the street, in front of the bookstore, in front of dozens of witnesses who didn't notice a thing. He held it close to his face as though it was some strange foreign thing he needed a microscope to identify.

'We didn't have to keep going,' he said. 'We could have stopped. Called the whole thing off.'

'It had nothing to do with that. I told you,' I said. 'I made a mistake. I don't love you anymore.'

'I keep turning it over in my head, every little thing I can remember. Trying to find clues. When did everything change? Why didn't I see it? Or maybe nothing changed and I was an idiot from the beginning. A deluded, naive idiot.'

'We've been over this,' I said. 'I'm not having this conversation again.'

A police car passed us, heading up Bourke with its siren on. It was on its way to an emergency. This was a good sign, for somebody. The siren meant it wasn't too late.

'Amazing things, diamonds,' Alec said. 'One hundred, two hundred kays underground, billions of years of unbelievable pressure. Surely that means there's hope for us all.' He smiled without showing his teeth, and he buried the ring deep in the pocket of his jeans. 'I'll mind it for a while, that's all. It still belongs to you.'

I thanked him, and then I let my legs walk me down the hill to Swanston, and I hopped on a tram and went straight home. Not *home* home. Not back to our old place: there were strangers living there by then. Home to the flat I was renting, where I sat on unfamiliar furniture and breathed the strange air, where I took off my shoes and climbed straight under the covers, still in my jeans, and when the phone rang later that afternoon, I didn't answer it.

The white circle around my finger has faded now. I haven't seen him since.

'Who's Uncle Alec?' says Craig, and, 'Oh,' when he sees my face. 'That Uncle Alec. Awkward. What's he doing here?'

I drop to the floor and begin manically sorting through clothes, pitching the rejects across the room. Patterns and fabrics swirl before my eyes. What was I wearing? It seems like hours, days since I lay down. Nothing looks familiar, like it could be mine or even Craig's. Alec is here. I am no longer safe anywhere.

'Wow,' Craig says. 'Look at the state of this place. Caroline's really let things slide.'

I stop searching and lift my head. 'Get out on the balcony.'

'I'm getting a very hostile vibe from you Janice,' Craig says. 'Normally we have a sherry afterwards. Caroline keeps it under the bed.'

I lift the back of my sheet-train and crawl one-handed to where he's standing. 'I'm sorry if I sounded hostile. I'm terribly sorry. This has all been a misunderstanding. Let me rephrase. Get out on the balcony, please, Craig, and climb down the trellis and go home, before I throw you off.'

'Nope.'

'What?'

'I'm not going to let you do this to yourself. You're

repressed, Janice. You've got to stand up to your past. This is not the 1950s. You're single, you're entitled. There's no need to be sneaking around just because Alec's here. Think Beyoncé. You're a single lady. You've got to roar, Janice. Let me hear a roar.'

'A what?'

'Roar. I am woman, Janice. Katy Perry. Let's hear it. R. O. A. R.'

'Please, Craig. No, no roaring. Go out on to the balcony. Go home.'

'Let me ask you one question Janice, and tell me if you think this is too personal.' He sits on the bed with the pillow balanced on his crotch and takes his weight on his arms, behind him. 'Do you experience genuine multiple orgasms? Or are they more like "indifferently sequential"? Are your orgasms like the V-line service to Ballarat—great if they show up but more often than not you find yourself waiting on a cold platform with a book and a large mochaccino?'

'Get out.'

'I'm trying to help you, Janice. You can't spend your whole life afraid of what other people are thinking. I'm not leaving.'

'You don't understand. Alec is out there. My Alec. I mean, my former Alec.'

He scoots back further, to lean against the bedhead, and folds his arms. 'Not my circus, not my monkeys.'

There's a knock on the bedroom door.

'Hello? Janice? Are you in there?'

It's his voice. Alec's.

'I can go, if you'd rather,' says Alec's voice. 'I had no idea you'd be here. I can come back next weekend.'

'That's not fair,' says Mercedes from the hall. 'We're supposed to fly kites today, you said.'

I wrap the sheet tighter, still clutching it with one hand, then I open the door half a body width. And there he is, in front of me. Alec. He's in black jeans I haven't seen before. A long-sleeved shirt with a collar, god help me, open at the neck and sleeves rolled up to his elbows. Those new tortoiseshell glasses that are no longer new. My pulse is crashing in my ears. I'm still not gay, apparently.

Clearly he's a regular visitor, one more thing that Caroline neglected to mention. Alec was like a brother to Caroline for years, and to Henry, who is an only child. Of course he would still come by to see the girls: of course he would. We were family. Alec is not the kind of man to have been an uncle to Mercedes and Paris for all that time and then vanish from their lives as soon as we divorced. That would go against the fibre of him. Anyway, he loves children. That was the reason for our demise, after all.

'Janice,' Alec says. 'Hello. I hope I didn't wake you.'

'You didn't. You didn't wake me.'

'You look well.'

'I am well, thanks. I'm very well.'

'Me and the girls.' He jerks his chin toward Mercedes and Paris, standing just behind him. 'We had a date. To fly kites. In the backyard. You could come downstairs. Fly kites with us. It'll be fun.'

'You should see how high Uncle Alec's kite goes,' says Mercedes. 'As high as a plane. You can have the red one.'

'Caroline and Henry are OK, I hope?' he says.

From behind me, Caroline's bed squeaks. I can see Craig out of the corner of my eye, lumbering about like a naked Bigfoot with the pillow dangling from one hand, looking for his clothes. The pillow is aggressively floral and has a frill around the edge. He's a big fan of manscaping. His lunchbox sways against his thighs as he walks.

'Is there someone in there with you?' says Alec, at the door.

'Don't be silly. Mercedes, would you and Paris like to go to the lounge room and watch television? Loud television?'

'Not really,' says Mercedes.

'If you take Paris and go to the lounge room and turn on the television, loudly, right now, you can watch anything you want.'

'Even the kissy shows?'

'If you don't tell Mummy, I won't. Go on, sweetie. Now please.'

'You used to be my favourite,' says Mercedes. 'But you've turned very bossy.'

Still, she takes Paris by the hand and heads up the hall. I wait, and soon I hear the television blaring.

Behind me, though, Craig is still muttering.

'You've got the television on as well,' Alec says. 'Sounds like an odd kind of program.'

'It's a renovation spectacular,' I say. 'Some handyman is fixing something. If he isn't careful, though, he'll get whacked in the face with a piece of four by two.'

'Threats of violence, Janice?' calls Craig, from behind me.

'Is that really the kind of person you aspire to be?'

In my fantasies of seeing Alec again, I am always in a strapless evening gown and my limousine has crashed over the railings of a bridge and is teetering over the side above a vast, raging river. I am going to die. I am going to die with secrets and longings and regrets when Alec, who is no longer a historian and is, for some reason, a firefighter, arrives. He's wearing tall black Darcy-esque boots and has a three-day growth and his hair is longer and wilder than it was the last time I saw him. It must be hot in this fantasy, or maybe he's come from a raging fire, because he's sweating and he's taken his helmet off. And his shirt. It's an emergency, there's no time for recriminations. He inches forward on his ladder and holds out his arms. Come to me, he says. I've got you. I won't let you go.

In none of my fantasies was I ever wrapped in a sheet with a sleep-squashed face and mussed-up hair in the company of a naked idiot. There is nothing for it: I'm cornered. I open the door wide, step back and hang my head.

'Alec. This is Craig.'

Craig swiftly presses the pillow low in front of him, with both hands. 'G'day,' he says.

'G'day,' says Alec.

'I'd shake hands, but I'm a little indisposed,' says Craig.

'I can see that,' says Alec. 'It's fine. Keep that pillow right where it is.' He looks to me in my sheet, then back to naked Craig. 'So you and Janice are—?'

'Yep,' says Craig. 'We are, we *so* are. You could power a city the size of Newcastle off the energy we generate.'

'OK,' I say. 'This is not what it seems.'

'You wanted to be single,' says Alec. 'You made that very clear. And now you are. You don't owe me any explanations.'

'That's just what I've been telling her,' says Craig.

'Look. This has been such fun and I for one will treasure the memory forever, but the girls are probably watching Latvian porn on SBS so let's get those kites in the air, shall we?'

Alec folds his arms and leans against the door jam. 'I'm delighted that you're seeing someone, Janice. Delighted. So. Craig, is it? Where did you kids meet?'

'Meet? Where did we meet? We met at, what's the name of that place again, Janice baby? The club?'

'Really. I thought Janice hated nightclubs. Just goes to show, you never really know somebody as well as you think you do.'

'You must be thinking of someone else. Janice loves clubbing. Loves it. She's an awesome dancer,' says Craig, wiggling his eyebrows.

'I thought you might have met at work.'

'I work from home, dude. I don't work at the same place as Janice.'

'And where is that?' says Alec. He's facing Craig now, as though I'm not even here.

'Where is what?' says Craig.

'Janice's work,' says Alec.

'I have no idea,' says Craig. 'We don't do much talking, if you get my drift.'

'I do. I do get your drift. Actually, what is her job again? It escapes me.'

'You oughta know,' says Craig, gaze darting at me. 'You were married to her. You should know the kind of work that she does. Her career.'

'Which is?'

'Her gig, man. Her nine-to-five, the way she makes her moolah. You know. Jeez.'

Alec would sometimes interview elderly people for their recollections of events of long ago. He used an old-fashioned tape recorder for this, a fat, squat one, with archaic reel-to-reel tapes. At night he'd sit at our dining-room table and play back his tapes and if he heard something that didn't sound right, he replayed it over and over. He'd bite the thumb nail on his right hand as he tried to reconcile the memories of the person on the tape with historical accuracies he knew to be true.

'Nothing could please me more than knowing Janice is happy with you and you two are lighting up Newcastle,' says Alec, with his hands behind his back like a soldier on parade. 'And good on you, for taking pressure off the grid with your carbon-neutral sex. To be honest, though, you don't seem like her type.'

Craig stands taller. 'Thanks, mate, thanks. When we hooked up, she wasn't exactly thinking with her brain if you know what I mean. Me, I love older women. Know what they want, know how to get it.'

'I'm three or four years older than you. Five at the very outside. Never mind. Craig can't stay and chat, unfortunately,' I say. 'He's got to be somewhere. Urgently. In fact, he's late already.'

'And here? In her sister's bed, with the girls in the house

and Caroline and Henry away? That's a bit odd, to me. When we stayed over, back when we were married you understand, many moons ago, we slept in the spare room. It's very comfy, the spare room.'

'He's due to donate blood, aren't you Craig? It's a regular thing. The life you save may be your own,' I say.

'We couldn't wait,' says Craig. 'We couldn't even hold off long enough to get down the stairs. We're at it day and night. She goes off like a cracker. Isn't that right Janice.'

My mouth has dried and shrivelled and I've lost the power of speech.

'Janice,' says Craig. 'Come on, roar. You've come a long way, baby.'

Back when I was married to Alec, the four of us, me and Alec and Caroline and Henry, would sit around the fire and drink Henry's shiraz and talk about one day taking holidays together when we had kids. Our future babies would be cousins, part of each other's lives for ever. Henry and Alec would sometimes go to the movies together to see car-chase films, and Alec would sit on the edge of the bed when he came home and tell me all about it, every ridiculous fight scene and explosion, while I struggled to keep my eyes open. How lucky Caroline and I were back then, that our husbands were so close. How lucky. Alec still visits, still sees the girls, is probably still friends with Henry. I think of my sister, her marriage, the position Alec would be in if he knew Caroline was having an affair, what it would do to Caroline and Henry's chances of reconciling if Henry found out about this.

'Tell him, Janice,' says Craig.

'Night and day,' I say. 'Craig's powers of recovery are unbelievable. A feat of hydraulics rivalled only by the Snowy River scheme.'

'I'd like to take credit, but some things are a gift from the gods.' He flexes his biceps.

'I see,' says Alec.

'OK,' I say. 'Craig really needs to go now, and there are two little girls waiting to fly kites with you. You don't want to break their hearts, do you.'

'That's the last thing I'd do,' says Alec. 'Little girls' hearts are absolutely sacred.'

Just then, there's a scrabbling kind of noise from the garden below the balcony, just a few metres from the bed. It sounds like a dog digging up a bone or a possum stripping flowers.

'Yoo hoo,' a voice calls. 'I knocked at the front door but no one answered. Caroline! Are you there?'

Craig freezes. His face droops and stretches like he was painted by Munch and, to complete the picture of the picture, he claps both hands to his cheeks. The strategically placed pillow falls to the floor and I can't help but notice his nether regions shrink before my eyes, as though he's waist-deep in an ice bath.

'What?' says Alec. 'What is it?'

'Oh my sainted aunt,' I say. 'It's Lesley.'

Henry and Caroline moved here to the semi-country when Mercedes was a baby. It's a hyper-Anglo, relentlessly middle-class nuclear-family monoculture with a killer commute, stratospheric mortgages and no footpaths. It smells of nothing. Out here, political parties are genetic and European cars are acquired and the quality of your lawn defines your character. Women preserve organic fruit in Vacola jars while wearing floral pinnies, their irony only moisturiser-deep. Cafes served lattes in Irish coffee glasses with wee handles and a long spoon within living memory.

Henry and Caroline wanted a yard. They wanted French cricket and tree houses and pets of numerous species and tadpoles caught in a creek, a childhood idealised from television and nostalgic for one of the founding myths of our nation: suburbia. Caroline and Henry laughed at their own impending dagginess. They were unafraid of what they might become.

To me, it seemed a blanket acceptance of their parents' choices instead of their own. Everyone Caroline and Henry knew lived in the city. How would they meet people, make friends? Who would visit them?

Ha. In fact, Caroline's bedroom needs a control tower and ground staff wearing earmuffs and high-vis and waving paddles, because it has more arrivals than Tullamarine. I'm single, I live in the city and my entire flat hasn't seen this much action in two years. To be truthful, though, being naked with two men in a bedroom is proving much less fun than the internet has (occasionally) led me to expect.

Craig's mouth opens and closes but no sounds come out. He looks from me to Alec and back again and his eyeballs bulge as though he's contracted some kind of instant hormonal disease. He looks like a desperate, naked, waxed goldfish with prepubescent genitals made from moulded plastic.

'Speak, Craig,' I say. 'Spit it out.'

He can't. He's making underwater noises, melding his eyebrows together. His stomach distends and flexes and his cheeks bulge and then empty themselves flaccid in a huge whoosh of air.

'Do you need a glass of water?' Alec says. 'Janice? Is your friend all right?'

'It's Lesley,' Craig finally squeaks. 'Oh my god she's here. I'm going to faint. Everything's literally fading.'

'Who's Lesley?' says Alec.

'"Who's Lesley?"' Craig's breathing is shallow and he's noticeably paler and as I watch he scratches his throat and leaves four long jagged white tracks down to his collarbones.

I tell Alec she's Craig's wife.

'Oh,' he says. 'Right. Awkward.'

'Hello, Caroline?' sings out Lesley, from the foot of the balcony. 'Are you there? Darling Caroline, I'm concerned for you sweetheart. Let me in. We'll have a nice chat.'

Lesley's voice is melodious, all lightness and femininity with a gentle lilt. She's an artist who makes beautiful things with her hands, an earth mother, a nurturer, the kind of woman with two children despite only one pregnancy; an ovular over-achiever who is not just fertile but aggressively so. Live and let live, judge not yet ye be etc., what goes on in other people's bedrooms is no concern of mine, but she's one of those people who flaunts their lifestyle choices in your face with their stick-figure families on the back windows of their SUVs.

In the context of her naked husband in my sister's bed, though, all at once I'm seeing her anew.

'His wife.' Alec shakes his head. 'Janice, Janice. You've changed.'

Historians. They think the truth is a simple thing that can be understood and written down instead of the messy fuck-up it truly is. Facts twist and flop like beached fish. It does not matter what he thinks of me.

'Caroline? Let's have a cup of tea, lovely, and talk about how you're travelling,' calls Lesley.

'Nobody move,' Craig whispers. He jumps behind Alec and presses up against the bedroom door with his bottom cheeks, closing it with a click. 'Don't answer her Janice. Be very very quiet and she might go away.'

Alec turns to face him. 'Maybe don't stand behind me, bouncing that thing. Urinal etiquette 101, mate.'

'Craig! Cover up,' I hiss, hand over my eyes.

'Let me give you some friendly advice about wooing Janice, Craig, man to man,' says Alec. 'You need to keep an air of mystery, not wave it all over the place. It's not becoming, mate. I'd put that pillow back where it belongs if I were you.'

'You don't understand.' Craig considerately cups his privates in his hands. 'I'm on my last chance. Don't speak. Don't even breathe. If she climbs the trellis, it's all over. She catches me one more time, that's it. Curtains. I wouldn't want to be in your shoes either, Janice.'

'Me?'

'Her ancestors were gold miners around here in the 1800s. Stringing up claim-jumpers is in her blood. If she thinks we've been shagging, we're done for. Both of us.'

'Please don't say shagging,' I say. 'I'm begging you. It's making me feel sick.'

'Where are my clothes? Please, please, where are my clothes?' Craig is panting like a golden retriever. His face is pink and blotchy and the scratch marks on his neck have turned red. His looks down to the floor, to the patchwork of clothes on the carpet. It's intimate, this detritus of a marriage, this ocean floor of wreckage. He seems incapable of searching through it and I can understand. It would be a violation.

'Are you going to be sick? Don't be sick, Craig,' I say.

'Calm down, mate.' Alec raises his palms to Craig, as though he's cornering a wild animal. 'Slow and steady, in and out. Take it easy. Do you need a puffer?'

'I'm OK, I'm OK. I just need to breathe into a paper bag or something. Do you have a paper bag Janice?'

I pat the nonexistent pockets of my sheet. 'Not on me,' I say.

'How about some valium?'

I shake my head. If I had any valium, I'd have popped them five minutes ago.

'Sit down and put your head between your knees,' says Alec. He takes him by the arm to lead him to the bed, but Craig pulls away.

'The backyard. I can jump down.' He darts across to the other end of the room and pushes open the rear windows, the high ones that look over the backyard with the Hills Hoist and the tyre swing on a branch of the poinsettia and beyond, to dots of houses and green rolls of fields and forests. 'It's, what, only ten feet down? Maybe twenty. That grass looks soft as. I can make that, easy. The ground will break my fall.'

'If you're going to jump, let me call the ambulance first,' says Alec.

Craig sticks his head out the back window and twists his neck as far as it will go. 'On the other hand, I could go up. That gutter looks sturdy. Reasonably. Chin-ups are my thing.' He squeezes his pecs with one hand. 'I can stand on the sill and jump up and grab hold of the gutter, then swing my legs up onto the roof.'

'Of course you can,' I say. 'Because in your spare time, you're Jason Bourne.'

Craig pulls his head inside again, and he cricks his neck from side to side so that his ears almost touch his shoulders.

'I'm hearing a lot of negativity and not much in the way of constructive suggestions from you two. The good news is: I'm an ideas person. My brain's like…' he clicks his fingers, 'pow pow pow. I know. I can go through the house. I can hide under the dining table.'

'Don't you dare. The girls are out there. If you take one step outside this room, I'll deliver you to Lesley myself.'

'After all we've meant to each other?' He darts his eyes to Alec.

'If you expose yourself to my nieces, I'll confess everything.' Then I turn to Alec. 'You, on the other hand, can go whenever you like. Go on, toddle off. My life is not a spectator sport.'

'And miss this? Not a chance. If I'd known today was going to be this entertaining, I'd have brought popcorn.' Alec sits on the unmade bed and leans on his outstretched arms. Those arms. The arms that extend beyond his rolled up sleeves. I feel my ovaries spasm and whimper.

There's another noise, from outside.

'Ssssh,' says Craig, flapping his elbows.

We're all quiet for a while, listening, trying not to breathe. She'll quit any second. It's impossible to imagine even someone as unselfconscious as Lesley would force her way into a bedroom. A bedroom is a private space. It would take an unprecedented amount of chutzpah, a lack of subtlety rare in people who aren't backpackers moonlighting as shopping-strip charity muggers. Lesley is a gentle soul. She's probably on her way home right now. Perhaps she'll phone later. Perhaps she'll calmly wait for Caroline to phone her.

'I think she's gone,' I say.

'I envy you, Janice,' says Craig. 'Oh, she's not gone. Of course she's not gone.'

'Caroline?' calls Lesley again, from outside. 'I know you're there. I can hear voices. Are you alone? I'm beginning to feel concerned, darling. Is there someone in there with you?'

'My life is over,' says Craig. 'She's going to find us, I know she is. I'm doomed.'

'You're not doomed,' I hiss at him.

'You're right,' he says. 'I'm going to envy the doomed. After she's through with me, I'm going to nip down to the newsagents and buy Hallmark envy cards and mail them to the doomed and those cards will say: you lucky, lucky doomed bastards.'

'Caroline?' calls Lesley. 'I'm beginning to think you've got something to hide.'

The lilt is gone. Now she sounds like a traffic cop telling me to keep my hands on the wheel.

'Caroline's not here,' I call back. 'It's me. Janice.'

'Great, just great.' Craig glares at me. 'Go ahead and pick out my plot. Start carving my headstone. Call every woman in a twenty-mile radius so they can drop in to Spotlight to pick up black sackcloth for their sexy funeral minidresses. To think I was trying to help you awaken, Janice.'

'Janice?' calls out Lesley. 'I heard a man's voice a minute ago. And I definitely saw a man, through the gap in the door. A naked man-shaped person. I know Henry left this morning, with Martha. So who's in there with you, Janice?'

The voice is closer. I peek through the crack in the door. I can see a dark head, bobbing, through the railings. Lesley is coming. She is climbing the specially reinforced trellis, hand over hand with the determined movements of a weekend warrior scaling K2. She's halfway up the balcony. I can see her head peek over the top. She's lifting herself, she's swinging one leg over the balustrade.

'Please god please god please god,' mutters Craig. He sinks to his knees in the corner near the door.

'Janice,' says Lesley, even closer now. 'I'm coming in.'

'I'd let her, if I were you,' says Alec.

'Are you crazy?'

'You can't live in a world of half-truths forever, Janice. You'll never be happy that way.'

I can try.

'No. Lesley. Don't. Don't come in.' I leap for the balcony door and the sheet twists around my legs and I try to close the door but I can't, the pot of rhododendrons is in the way so instead I pull the handle toward me with all my strength with both hands and the sheet tucked under my armpits. 'Don't come in. I'm naked, Lesley. And I'm shy. I'm shy and naked.'

'Don't be ridiculous,' she says. 'You've got nothing I haven't seen before. You can't be uptight about your body at your age, Janice. You sound very stressed. Maybe you need a massage.'

She's on the balcony now. She's holding the door handle, she's pulling it a little. Now she's pulling it with more strength. And more. She must have muscles on top of muscles from making pots, or else she's turned into superwoman in the intensity of the moment, like those mothers who can lift a Torana if their baby is trapped underneath. The handle is almost flying out of my grip. I'm going to lose control of the door. I'm going to be pulled out on the balcony head first, in my sheet, so instead I ease off a little so that the door opens, just a smidge, and I wedge myself in the space with my foot on the rhododendron.

'Lesley. Hi. Hi Lesley,' I say. 'Sorry. I was having a nap.'

She's out of her gym gear. Tweed skirt, tailored linen blouse and black boots. 'A nap? At this time of the afternoon?' She blinks. 'Where's Caroline?'

'I'm in a sheet because I was sleeping. Naked. I always sleep naked. Clothes are restrictive, don't you think? Caroline's not here. She's out. Away. What can I do for you?'

'I just got home. I've been out looking at clay. What a waste of time. I've never seen such shitty clay. What do they think I do, make coil ashtrays in my conversation pit and sell them at school fetes? If I was offering clay like that to a professional ceramicist, I'd be embarrassed.'

'I'm so sorry to hear about your clay. Perhaps we could get together later to chat about it.'

'It's not the first time.' She leans closer and rattles the door handle. 'But anyone who thinks they can pull the wool over my eyes is making a big mistake.' Her voice is low and clipped, like a Mafia don. Her lips are tight and curled.

I swallow. 'I'm sure you set them straight.'

'I set them straight all right. Certain people think I'm a pushover. They think because I'm an artist and a mother, I'll put up with anything.'

She stamps her black boot on top of the rhododendron opposite my bare foot. Her boot looks bad-tempered; a boot that used to work for the Stasi before it retired and Lesley bought it on eBay.

'If I ever sell you clay, I'll be careful. Bye now.'

I attempt to move the rhododendron out of the way with my foot so I can close the door, but Lesley's totalitarian boot is on the other side, holding it in place, forcing the door to remain open.

'Then, I arrived home,' she says. 'And do you know what I found?'

I shake my head.

'Not Craig.'

'Not Craig?'

'His car is in the garage. His phone's on the kitchen bench, but my husband was not there. I looked everywhere. I can't help but think: where could the father of my children be, without his car or his phone?'

'He's probably getting some exercise. Out for a walk, or something.'

'A walk?' She snorts. 'Where do you think you are? I know for a fact that Craig hasn't walked since 2007. He has a personal trainer, like a normal person. If he needs to get to the top of the driveway to collect the mail, he hops on Henry's ride-on mower. I don't like it Janice, not one little bit.'

I feel a tic in my left eye. I wipe my sweaty palms on the sheet, one at a time, without letting go of the door. I feel like the Person You Would Least Suspect in a British crime drama. I'm in Midsomer and any second Inspector Barnaby will jump out from behind a quirky spinster and yell, *You're nicked, sunshine*. Lesley doesn't seem to notice.

'Oh well. He's a grown man. I'm sure he'll be home soon. Bye now.'

'I'm at the end of my tether, Janice,' she says. 'I'm coming apart at the seams. Don't let this bucolic village setting fool you. There's a seething, writhing underbelly out here. There are a lot of untrustworthy women in the world. Women who think with their vaginas. And Craig, well. You've seen him— he's catnip to them. Drives women out of their minds. Do you hear what I'm saying?'

'You're being excruciatingly clear.'

She peers through the gap in the door, her eyes boring like lasers into mine, and pulls the handle again so I hold it tighter and tighter again, until my knuckles are white. 'Open the door, Janice. I won't ask again.'

'It's not convenient right now.'

'There's a man in there with you. A naked man. I know there is.'

I attempt to laugh. 'Of course there isn't.'

'Is it my naked man? Is it Craig, Janice? Maybe that's how you people behave in the city, with your celebrity baristas and Mexican street-food vans. Grown men getting around on skateboards, for heaven's sake. Are you some kind of cougar?'

'Me?'

'Look, I have two children, innocent kids who love their father. Let me in, Janice. If you've got nothing to hide, you've got nothing to fear.'

'You might as well open the door,' says Alec, from behind me, 'and stop sneaking around. I think it's time you were honest.'

My Alec—at least, my former Alec—is taking Lesley's side.

'I don't think it's that time,' I say. 'In fact, I'm certain it's some other time.'

'Who is that? Who's that speaking? Out of the way, Janice,' says Lesley. 'I don't want to hurt you if I don't have to.'

When I was small, I thought, like most people, that dogs were boys and cats were girls. It wasn't the most sophisticated understanding of either species or gender, but it explained the shaggy boisterousness of dogs, their energy, the revelling in mud and water and the way they ran for sheer pleasure, versus cats: cooler and neater and sleeker, desires hidden and furtive, appetites more refined, movements measured and fluid. Males were bigger and stronger and did the chasing, at primary school, anyway. Females were smarter and softer. We did the running away.

It was so clear to me back then, and so wrong. Both sexes can be strong and soft and all those other things. The chasing, the running away—we do both of them, all the time.

Opening the balcony door might prove the end of Craig and Lesley's marriage, with everything that will cascade from that, for them and their children. Will Lesley believe that today is the first time Craig has climbed the specially reinforced trellis to my sister's balcony? I doubt it; the trellis will bear the evidence of her husband's handyman skills, and the brave Sir Craig, currently in the middle of a nude anxiety attack, will crack under the smallest amount of pressure. Then everyone will know about him and Caroline, and any chance Caroline had of reconciling with Henry will be over.

Mercedes and Paris will face the same childhood as Caroline and I did; Caroline will face the same years alone as our mother did.

The same. Perhaps we recreate patterns in our lives, attempting to give ourselves another chance to solve problems that defeated us in the past. Problems we didn't have the capacity to fix the first time around. Perhaps this is why we fail, time after time.

'Open the door, Janice,' says Lesley.

'Open the door, Janice,' says Alec.

There is nothing for it. I let go of the handle. I stand back and the door opens toward her. She steps over the rhododendron and comes inside.

'In Caroline's bed? That's icky,' Lesley says. And then she says. 'And who's this?'

I turn. The messy bedroom is just as it was a moment ago—clothes everywhere, unmade bed, doona on the floor—but Craig has vanished as though there were never three of us here to begin with. There is, however, a naked man standing behind me as I expected there would be, and he is holding a pillow in front of his crotch with his very fine arms.

'It's wrong, I know,' says Alec. 'But we just can't keep our hands off each other.'

I've forgotten nothing about Alec. The former me, when it was part of the former us, knew every inch of him and I don't need to look now and I shouldn't but I do anyway. His skin is right there, radiating in front of me. I can feel the heat of his blood as it throbs in the veins of his legs and those arms and that stomach and those hidden places that were so him, so Alec, that I could pick them out of a line-up: the stretched skin on the back of his knees, the blue veins in his oddly delicate wrists, the wrinkle behind his ear. He's thickened a little. His forearms holding the pillow are taut, defined, but his face bears the marks of life. His face has always moved with every thought and every emotion. That face is rubbish at poker: one memorable winter our heating broke, and when spring came I was up a year's worth of fridge clean-ing, pancakes in bed for a month of Sundays and a dozen movie choices. I've sat toasty on our couch, cards in my hand, wearing jeans and a t-shirt plus gloves, a scarf, two pairs of socks and my Ugg boots while he shivered in socks and jocks.

There are no socks and jocks now. There's no clothing of any description. It's ridiculous, how beautiful he is. There's a glint of gold on his chest reflecting the light coming through the open door—a thin chain with a pendant on the end—but that's all he's wearing. I've never seen him in jewellery. Someone would have chosen that necklace for some special occasion, someone would have given it to him. He has a new life now, separate from mine. You cannot go backwards. I don't know him anymore. I check my sheet is securely wrapped.

Alec introduces himself and Lesley gasps. 'Not *Alec* Alec? The ex-husband Alec? Didn't she dump you?'

'I'm not the kind of man to hold a grudge,' says Alec.

'Oh, now I feel terrible.' She plonks herself on the bed. 'I've interrupted some kind of reunion. Janice. Janice?'

'Sorry. Yes. I mean no. Not at all, not at all. Though we could use some privacy.' I take Lesley's hand and try to pull her to her feet. She isn't budging but the effort makes my head spin. Maybe I need to sit. Yes. Yes, I definitely should. I fold down, cross-legged on the floor near the foot of the bed. My pulse is throbbing around my body, the sound of distant warning drums. My face feels ladybird red and might explode at any second. I've caught something. A fever. All at once, I'm clammy. I'm eye level with those arms and the pillow. The pillow and its strategically hidden equipment is right there. I can hear myself swallow.

'I must say I'm surprised to see you two back together.' Lesley says, as though strange men wearing pillows and women in sheets are her usual conversation partners. 'After everything Caroline told me.'

'Is that right?' Alec sits on the bed next to Lesley. 'What did Caroline say, exactly?'

'My feet have gone numb,' I say. 'My hands are tingly and my feet have gone numb.'

'That's diabetes. My mother has that,' says Lesley.

'Janice doesn't have diabetes,' says Alec. 'Do you?'

'Your face looks like a big tomato,' Lesley says. 'Maybe it's an allergy. Have you had any peanuts today?'

'It's not an allergy.'

'Maybe it's a seizure.'

'A what?' says Alec.

'An assistant I had, in my former life—she had a seizure. Come to think about it, you don't look like that. You need more convulsions.'

'Should we get you to a doctor? What is it you're feeling, exactly? Describe it.'

Lesley leans down to peer at my face. 'Nope, not a seizure. Maybe you're having a turn. A turn can lead to a seizure,' she says. 'My assistant started with turns before she moved on to seizures. She can see auras now. She has a stand at the Vic Market telling people the colour of their soul. I'm buttercup yellow.'

Alec takes one hand off the pillow and places his palm on my forehead, which doesn't help one bit. 'You do feel warm,' he says. 'Maybe a little flushed?'

'You're wrapped too tight,' Lesley says. 'You look like a tomato in a burrito.'

'Let me loosen this,' says Alec, reaching for my sheet.

'No, no,' I manage, as I wriggle out of reach of his hands. 'I'm OK now. I don't need to feel my extremities. They're optional, really. I hardly use them.'

'Maybe it's premature menopause,' Lesley says. 'Maybe your ovaries have just shrivelled up and are sitting there taking up space in your abdomen like two useless dried prunes. Does it feel like a nuclear reactor is igniting your whole body from the inside? Because I've heard that's what it feels like.'

'Nothing like that.' My laugh comes out like the cackle of a homeless woman hunched over a shopping trolley full of soft drink cans and pictures of Princess Diana torn from magazines.

'Maybe Alec should help you into the shower,' Lesley says.

'Sure. I could carry you. Just put your arms around my neck, here.'

'No. No no no no no.'

'Peri-menopause can go on for years,' she says. 'It must be a relief to have all those sexual urges behind you. Free from the tyranny of your hormones. Eat what you want, no more heels, no more makeup. Hello track pants. The crone years. I'm almost looking forward to it.'

'I feel better already,' I tell her. 'It was one of those two-minute seizures. Let's talk about something else. You and Craig, tell us all about it.'

'Well,' says Lesley. 'It all started on our honeymoon.'

'Actually Lesley, let me stop you right there,' I say. 'I hope you don't mind. Alec and I were right in the middle of something.'

'Darling,' says Alec. 'Don't be rude. Lesley's clearly upset. Take your time, Lesley. Tell us anything.'

'Obviously we're here for you, of course. But we're naked. I'm naked, and Alec is extremely naked. I think we'd both feel so much better in clothes.'

'It occurs to me that you're exactly the woman I should be talking with, Janice,' says Lesley. 'You're perfect. I should have thought of it sooner.'

It's probably true. At uni, I was always the one listening to everybody's problems. I almost swapped from microbiology to psychology in my second year. It can be a burden. I feel the responsibility of lost people asking me for advice, of my ability to guide and suggest and transform lives.

'I mean, you're not intimidating,' Lesley goes on. 'You've completely failed at marriage and still you manage to crawl out of bed every day and face the world, like you haven't broken the most important vow you'll ever make. You reach deep inside yourself and somehow you find the courage to look in the mirror every morning. What are you now, nearly forty?'

'No, no. No. Not even close. I'm thirty-eight.'

'Thirty-eight. Wow. I'm not even thirty-seven yet.'

'It's just a number, right?'

'A seriously big one. Half your life is over, yet still you carry on. You get out of bed every morning and dress and continue to battle your way through life as though someone will one day… as though you won't be alone for eternity. Do you have any cats yet? Because let's face it, what are the odds of marrying again at your age? I can tell you what they are.

Like giving birth to quintuplets right after hitting a hole in one.' Lesley unzips her boots and kicks them off, then she wriggles her way up the bed and rests against the wall.

'Is that the time?' I say. 'Craig's probably home by now. You don't want him to come looking for you and find you here, in bed with a naked man.'

Said naked man is sitting on the bed and has propped himself on his elbows on top of his pillow. He's batting his lashes and listening like a girlfriend.

'You're wrong, Janice,' she says. 'I'd love that. I couldn't think of anything better. You don't know what it's like, being married to a man like Craig. I've spent our entire relationship waiting at home for him, worrying about him, imagining other women seducing him. What's he supposed to do when they throw themselves at him? He's naive, that's the problem. He's oblivious to his own sexual power.'

'Maybe you could go home and make him a lovely dinner and start fresh.' I crawl up on the bed and reach for her arm. In a caring gesture, I rub my thumb across the bones on the back of her hand, then I take hold of her wrist and try to pull her off the bed toward the balcony. It's like trying to haul a dead body. She doesn't move.

'I'm sorry I suspected you, Janice. I don't know what I was thinking. It's a ludicrous idea, now that I think about it. You and Craig.' She chuckles in a way that isn't complimentary.

'It's not that ludicrous,' I say.

'Yeah, it is,' she says.

Not a dozen feet away from where she sits, I see the wardrobe door only slightly ajar now and through the gap, a hairy, brown, naked leg folded at the knee, and beside it, a scrotum. Then I see a t-shirt on the floor, half way to the wardrobe. I can make out the writing: *do it with frequency*.

'Oh,' I say.

'Oh what?' Lesley says.

'Ohhhh,' I yawn and stretch, ostentatiously. Then I look toward the balcony door and flatten my hand above my eyes, also ostentatiously. 'Wait. I see something, in your front yard. Is that him coming home now?'

'Where?' says Lesley. She gets up from the bed and, as she moves over to the window, I dash, as fast and as nonchalantly as possible for a woman wrapped in a sheet, to stand on the t-shirt and simultaneously block Lesley's line of sight to the wardrobe.

'I can't see anything,' she says.

'My bad,' I say, stretching and fanning the bottom of the sheet over the incriminatory t-shirt. I'm standing firm now. I'm only missing a torch to look like the Statue of Liberty.

'Talk about irony.' Lesley raises her arms to us, sheet-woman and pillow-man. 'You two, reconciling, whilst my perfect marriage to my perfect man is in tatters.'

'Tell you what,' says Alec. 'Why don't you give us a couple of minutes to get dressed, and then we'll make you a nice cup of tea. You can tell us all about it.'

'Or maybe you'd rather go home and wait for Craig,' I say. 'I find that being alone is very helpful in these situations. I feel quite restored after some time to myself.'

'Oh that's so sweet of you both,' Lesley says. 'But I couldn't. That would be too self-indulgent. I'd be taking

82

advantage of your kindness. I should really let you get back to your reunification shagging.'

'Completely up to you,' I say. 'I'll tell Caroline you dropped by.'

'It would be no trouble at all,' says Alec. 'You could tell us whatever was on your mind.'

'Maybe just one quick macchiato,' says Lesley. 'Caroline has a nice single origin Brazilian. With just a stain of frothed milk. If it's no trouble.'

In twenty minutes, Alec and I are dressed. The girls have been consoled with the promise of pizza for dinner, and bribed with ice-cream topped with sprinkles and a new Barbie outfit each into playing quietly downstairs, but they've driven a hard bargain: Alec is eating with us. It's not unusual, Mercedes tells me. Sometimes he babysits when Mummy and Daddy go out and he makes macaroni cheese. Even Mummy and Daddy love Uncle Alec's macaroni cheese.

Caroline is full of surprises. I can't wait to discuss it with her.

But that's a conversation for another day. For now, I am sitting with Alec and Lesley in Caroline's dream kitchen, drinking coffee that I summoned by pressing random buttons on a machine. Caroline's kitchen looks as though it was hand-carved by Quakers from timber that died of natural causes, not designed on a computer by an architect, supervised by a project manager and built by a crack team of kitchen specialists out of high-tech materials and reconstituted stone. It has a deep farmhouse sink and white ceramic taps and, hidden behind the olde-worldeness, enough technology to launch a space shuttle. Alec and I dance around each other, fetching cups and saucers, finding the spoons and the milk.

'Just like old times,' he says. 'You and me, in a kitchen.'

We reach for the sugar bowl at the same time. I almost touch him but jerk my hand away with seconds to spare.

'I don't bite,' he says.

'Are you sure this is a macchiato?' Lesley sniffs it.

'I swear it on my life,' I say.

'Does Caroline have any biscuits? I think my blood sugar is low. The homemade ones, from the cake stall, with jam in the middle? Or anything really. I'm not fussy. But without dairy.'

'I put milk in your coffee.'

'Milk is OK,' she says. 'I just try to stay away from dairy.'

I find some Scotch Fingers in a plastic tub in the pantry and tip them on a plate. Alec has pulled out Lesley's chair so she's positioned with her back to the windows. Outside is impossibly green and impossibly blue and it stretches for ever, and it's safe and idyllic and a good many perfect childhoods must be taking place in the immediate vicinity. A great many parental sacrifices, spiritual and financial and sexual and psychic, must be taking place to ensure those perfect child-hoods and a great many children must live totally unaware of them.

Lesley helps herself to sugar, and as she leans forward I see the back of Craig, dressed now, darting back toward their house, bolting from tree to tree like a spy.

'I should have known it was too good to be true,' Lesley

says. 'Craig played lead guitar when I met him. Why didn't I go for the drummer? I want to sleep with a married drummer, said no woman ever. Isn't Craig the prettiest man you've ever seen? That's his natural hair colour you know, and his original eyelashes. He's prettier than me. Brilliant with the kids, does all the housework. So what if he doesn't make much money? It's the twenty-first century, that's completely irrelevant. Besides, I've got enough for the two of us.' She's scoffing the biscuits with grim determination. Hoovering them.

'He's lucky to have you,' says Alec.

Over her shoulder in the middle-distance, Craig hurdles the low hedge that divides the two yards, clearing it by a good hand span. He's got a fair technique, although he lifts his knees too high. There's an exuberance in the way he moves. Run, Forrest, run.

'It's rare to find someone who's not threatened by their partner's success,' she says. 'Imagine your marriage in reverse, Janice. After all, Alec's a doctor.'

'I'm not a doctor doctor,' says Alec. 'I'm a historian. Very limited emergency skill set. Sudden labour pains? Fractures and sprains? Useless. Urgent contextualisation of the Boxer Rebellion? Stand back ladies, I got this.'

'I'll tell you a secret, Dr Alec.' She lays her hand on his forearm. 'Marrying a doctor is every little girl's dream. My parents would have been beside themselves.'

'I have a PhD too,' I say.

'That's nice,' says Lesley. 'Good for you, holding your own.'

'Let's get back to Craig,' says Alec.

'If only he'd left me a note,' she says. 'Is that too much to ask? A note? Something might have happened to him. He might have seen an injured animal from the kitchen window, someone's lost cow or something, and he might have gone to help it. He might be trying to lift the cow and the cow could have fallen on him. Cows are heavier than they look. We could be sitting here drinking coffee while he's trapped, having the life squeezed out of him.'

'I'm sure he's not underneath a cow,' I say. 'Not right at the moment.'

'Or maybe he's collapsed. He might be a physically perfect specimen of masculinity but he works too hard, looking after the kids. That big beautiful heart of his might be failing. He could be turning blue.'

'I don't think Craig's the type to turn blue,' says Alec.

'He's probably down at Bunnings,' I say. 'He's wandering around in Craig heaven looking at routers and he's forgotten the time.'

'Without his four-wheel drive? Do you think he transported himself to the router aisle telepathically?' She starts to take a sip of her cooling coffee, then she stops and her eyes narrow. 'How did you know he loves Bunnings?'

'All men love Bunnings,' Alec says. 'You should see me down there. Screwdrivers. Nails. I'm gone for hours.'

To the best of my knowledge, Alec has never even been inside a Bunnings. He wouldn't be able to find one with a map, a compass and a starving sniffer dog trained on Rotary Club sausages.

'Oh Janice, I'm sorry. There's no excuse for that kind of

behaviour,' Lesley says. 'I'm suspicious of everyone. You're right, though. Craig's not just handy. He's some kind of genius. He's like Michelangelo with a spirit level. The things he can do with his hands, it's incredible. And not just around the house.'

'I honestly don't want to know.'

'I was completely unaware of the things my clitoris could do before I met him. It was like living in black and white, like the beginning of *The Wizard of Oz*. Like the whole world was AM radio instead of stereo. He can play me like a violin, when he makes the effort.'

'Lesley. I have the best part of fourteen dollars in my purse,' I say. 'If you stop talking right now, it's all yours.'

'You're right,' she says. She's hardly sipped her 'macchiato' and now the froth has dispersed into the brown. 'I'm being selfish. Enough about me. How did you two get back together? You and Alec? I mean, what triggered it?'

I look down at my ringless hands, holding the coffee cup. I need to say something flippant here, and fast, but my tongue's stuck to the roof of my mouth.

'I did,' says Alec.

For many, many mornings, his face was the first thing I saw when I opened my eyes. I know his face better than my own. I have no need to stare at it now.

'It was an easy decision, in the end,' says Alec. 'I've gone out with other people, of course. I've met some terrific women over these past months. But I could never imagine spending the rest of my life with any of them. I couldn't stop comparing them to Janice. All the important days in my life, the days that really mattered, were the ones we spent together. I realised I'd never be happy unless I tried to win her back,' he says.

Lesley reaches across and rubs his arm again. 'Aren't you the romantic? And what about you, Janice? How did you know that you two should get back together?'

On a normal Saturday, I usually nip in to the lab. Not for any pressing reason. Just to check on my little guys. To potter. I stand in front of the mirror and poke my hair lock by lock under the blue paper cap until I look like a patient ready for open-heart surgery before I go in to see them, hunkered down in their Petri dishes, stacked in whichever temperature incubator was best for them, getting on with things. If I do my job right, if I'm very careful, they don't give me any surprises. On weekends I have the prep room all to myself so while I'm in there it makes sense to start on a few weeks' worth of media and solutions. This takes some concentration, a precision in the weighing and measuring. I make the media, then I pour it, and then I might run some loads through the autoclave and maybe I'll wash test tubes by hand with the wire brush because the machine is hopeless, we get the repair guy time after time for nothing, and the next thing I know, it's past midnight. The whole night has gone. When I get home, I eat some fruit because who can be bothered cooking for one and then I water my plants in case their brown, desiccated appearance is just a stage they're going through, in case any of them spontaneously resurrects. I love my dead plants. There are some things I can't bring myself to give up on.

Then I turn the TV on and fall straight asleep on the couch without any tossing or turning. It's easy. No insomnia.

No lying awake, longing for something I can't have. This is a sign of a life well-lived. Though sometimes I think it'd be more efficient if I slept in the lab. Perhaps I could get Megan the research director to put in a bed for me. Something simple. A fold-out, maybe, that doubles as a couch in the daytime.

I wish I was anywhere else but Caroline's kitchen, right now. It's a Saturday night. I have a life to get back to. I'm free. I have no one to answer to. I can do anything I want. My wonderful, wonderful life.

'Janice?' says Lesley.

All at once, I hear footsteps, loud and stagey, at the front door. Then the bell rings.

'Hello? Anybody home?' a voice calls out. 'I seem to have misplaced my missus.'

It's Craig.

'It's wifeless, back at mine,' Craig says, as he sticks his head in the doorway. 'It's like a morgue over there. Ah. There's my little Stradivarius.'

He is dressed again in his t-shirt and jeans, which look fresh and ironed. His shoes are on the appropriate feet and his hair is untousled. It's a skill, composing yourself: buttoning, smoothing and removing evidence. The world would seem manageable if you could remake yourself anew for each fresh encounter with a different person. If you could wake up every morning with your shed skin in a papery pile beside your bed, life would rest lightly upon you.

'Ooh,' says Craig. 'Biscuit.'

There is one lonely shortbread left on the plate. Lesley shoves it in her mouth as though she's trekked the post-apocalyptic wastelands eating nothing but the raw flesh of her companions when she stumbled across the last baked good in existence, a sad dodo of a biscuit.

'You're right babe. Thanks for saving me,' Craig says, with his hands up. 'Confession: extra gluten I don't need. Oh, hello Janice. Long time no see. And who's this stranger?'

I introduce Craig, the winner of the daytime Emmy for best performance by a guilty rat in a soap opera, to Alec as best I can. Alec's performance is adequate but there's something stretched in his delivery; he's not in the same league as Craig, who sounds for all the world like he's never laid eyes on Alec yet is exhilarated beyond reason to meet him. They shake hands like captains before a match, arms pumping with forced bonhomie and the suppressed aggression that, I now realise, is how it goes between men who've seen each other naked without any practical means to gauge superiority.

'So what do you do for a crust?' Craig says, and when Alec answers, he says, 'A historian? Seriously? Mate, I would have faked my own death to get out of history at school. Who needs to know that stuff in the real world? No one. Prime ministers and kings and explorers and whatever. Seriously, it's pointless, history. There are so many dead people, you can't keep up. You're outnumbered. And you know what else? Back then, you could actually be the first person to climb some mountain or sail somewhere or discover something. Now everything's already been done. It's depressing. Dead people, they're just like live hipsters.'

'Alec thinks there's nothing more important than history,' I say. 'Go on. Tell him.'

I've heard Alec explain this, full flight on the idea that the only way we can interpret our nerve-racking present is by understanding the past. He talks of the responsibility, the joy of being a historian, whose job it is to help all of us stand on solid ground. He's evangelical about it, as though he's waiting for strangers to take the love of history into their hearts on the spot so he can dunk their heads in really old water.

'Actually Craig has a point. These days, I'm more a fan of the present,' says Alec.

'You? Since when?' I say.

'Since a few years ago. Something I was so certain about turned out to be rubbish. I guess I'm discovering the joys of subjectivity.'

'My history teacher, man, he was a fossil. We had to learn all these dates, and for what?' says Craig. 'Everything you need to know about history has already been made into movies. *Gladiator, 300, Indy and the Last Crusade.*'

'Right. Well. Were you two looking for each other?' I say.

Craig nods. 'Where have you been hiding, baby? I was worried. You could have left a note.'

'I could have left a note?' says Lesley, biscuit crumbs flying. 'Me?'

'It's a tiny bit inconsiderate, just taking off like that. I've been looking for you for ages.'

'Wrong turn, Craig,' says Alec. 'Dead end. Reverse it on outta there.'

'Anyway, we should leave these good people to it,' says Craig. 'What would you like for dinner?'

But Lesley is lost, staring into space.

'Lesley? Sweetheart?' Craig says.

'No more, Craig. Not one more day,' she says. 'I know exactly where you were. Not precisely, not geographically. But

I know the anatomical vicinity. Pan-fried you-can-get-stuffed, that's what I'd like for dinner.'

'What?'

'I'm sick of spending my life waiting for you, worrying about you. I'm not coming.'

'Of course she is,' I say. 'She doesn't mean it. She's coming. Where are your keys, Lesley? You don't want to leave anything behind.'

Her bag is on the table. I slide it toward her.

'Oh, I mean it all right.' She slides the bag back in my direction, then folds her arms. 'My mother told me this day would come. On my wedding day, she told me. You take a man like that into your life, you're asking for trouble. She had Uncle Eddie park around the back of the church in case I changed my mind.'

'I thought she liked me,' said Craig.

'She's my mother. She likes me more,' said Lesley. 'I'm not budging from this spot.'

'You can't stay here all night,' says Craig.

'The girls will be thrilled,' says Alec. 'It'll be like a slumber party.'

'Mate, I'm sure you mean well,' says Craig.

'I've turned the other cheek time after time, but this is the straw. The *straw*,' says Lesley.

'If Caroline or Henry were here, it'd be different,' I say. 'It's putting me in an awkward position. This isn't my house. It's not my place.'

'If you're sure it's no trouble,' says Lesley. 'I'll be perfectly comfortable in the spare room downstairs. You two will be up in Caroline's room. You won't even know I'm here.'

'No no. We won't be in Caroline's room. We won't be anywhere. I mean, I'll be in Caroline's room but Alec's not staying. Alec's going home tonight, after dinner, aren't you Alec,' I say.

'I thought I'd stay over too, actually,' he says. 'I am deep in debt to the tune of one mammoth kite-flying session. I'd like to get it off the books tomorrow.'

'You can't. You've got that thing on, first thing in the morning. Remember?'

'What thing?' says Alec.

'The thing. You need an early night so you can get up bright and early for the thing you've got on.'

'No I don't,' says Alec. 'I hate things, especially early-morning things. The fate of the early worm should be a warning to us all.'

'But it's an important thing, your early-morning thing.'

'Oh, that thing? The early-morning thing, the thing I need a good night's sleep for? They cancelled,' he says. 'I can stay over too. Isn't that good news?'

'Come on home, Lesley baby,' says Craig. He purrs at her, then he growls and swipes pretend claws. 'The kids are away and you know what that means. We've got the whole house to ourselves. That means the kitchen bench tops, that nice hard granite. Ice from the fridge dispenser. It means the bean bags in the rumpus room. The stairs. Anywhere you want. Let's not waste it.'

'And they say chivalry is dead,' I say.

'You think you can sweet talk me with your romantic

promises,' says Lesley. 'Enough is enough.'

'You can't stay mad at me forever.' He winks at her.

'I can give it a red hot go.'

'At least tell me what I did.'

'You figure it out, Einstein.' She grips the seat of her chair like it's about to fly. 'I have an MBA. I was a regional finalist for Businesswoman of the Year. How did I get here? What the hell happened?'

'But what am I supposed to do at home without you?' Craig says.

'Eat two-minute noodles and watch internet porn, for all I care.'

'If you're not leaving, I'm not leaving either,' he says. 'It's not a home without you.'

'So, Craig's staying for dinner? I'm glad that's settled,' says Alec.

'I'm sure Craig doesn't want to stay,' I say. 'We're having pizza, Craig. With extra gluten.'

'I'm good with pizza gluten,' says Craig. 'It's the other kind I can't manage.'

'There's no sleeping with him afterwards,' says Lesley. 'Dutch oven. You have no idea.'

'Lucky for me, I'm not sleeping with him,' says Alec. 'Who votes for margherita with furry fish?'

The girls don't mind anchovies but they've ordered pineapple on everything. I ask Paris direct questions while we set the table: where does Mummy keep the napkins? Which pizza is your favourite? I get nothing but big eyes. One half of me is screaming that this is some kind of emergency, that I need to call a team of speech pathologists or child psychologists to put the sirens on, stat. The other half admires her fortitude. If all the grown-ups around her insist on acting like children, why shouldn't she behave however she likes? Why should she dignify any of this nonsense with a response? She should have as much time as she needs, without anyone dictating correct behaviour for a five-year-old.

'Wine?' says Lesley.

'Undoubtedly. Girls, where does Daddy keep the wine?'

They take me downstairs to the garage. I hadn't noticed, but there's a whole wall of wire racks filled with bottles behind the laundry.

'It's only for grown-ups,' says Mercedes. 'It's sour, but when you get old, that's what you like.'

The three of us walk along the wall of wine. Mercedes and Paris start pulling bottles out and looking at the labels and then pushing them back in, like little connoisseurs. Paris draws hearts in the dust around the necks with her finger.

'Wow. Daddy's spent ages collecting all these. I bet he's organised it by vintages. I bet he knows the location of every vineyard.' I kneel down to their eye level. 'Which one is the most expensive, do you think?'

'This one has lots of gold medals.' Mercedes lifts a bottle by the neck and hands it to me.

'Ah, a cheeky little Beaujolais. Madam has made an excellent choice. Which one do you like, Paris?'

She stands in front of the rack with her hands behind her back, and rises up and down on her toes, then she dives for a bottle tucked away in the far corner of the bottom row. It's some kind of sparkling, with a foil cap and dust on its shoulders and cursive French on its label. She passes it to me without a word.

'This looks frightfully expensive,' I say to her, wiping it with my sleeve. 'Daddy must have been saving this for a very special occasion. Good work.'

'You've got to write it in the little book,' says Mercedes.

I pick another bottle at random, because faced with a little book, two doesn't seem nearly enough. Until our parents saved the deposit for their own home, Caroline and I grew up in the sleep-out of our grandparents' house under the flight path, and we would lie on our backs on the buffalo lawn between the incinerator and the Hills Hoist and wait for the fat white bellies of the jets to appear. Every afternoon when the wind changed, the rendering from the pet-food factory was all we could smell until we couldn't smell it anymore. Granny said things like *What do you call this, bush week?* and *What's that when it's at home?* Our pop had his trannie on day and night, listening to the races, dogs and trots in strict, hushed rotation while he filled up his prized stainless steel tankard from lukewarm longnecks. Now, Caroline has a wine book and a pen attached with string to her wall of wine. I fill in 'wine', 'grape', 'producer', 'vintage' and 'region' as accurately as I can then, under 'occasion', I write: *Celebrating! Dinner with gorgeous nieces! Thanks so much for your generosity! xxx Janice.* Then I carry the wine upstairs with the girls trailing behind me, in time to see Alec paying the pizza delivery guy at the front door.

'Hello, Brayden,' says Mercedes.

'Mercedes. Paris,' says Brayden the delivery guy. 'It's been a while.'

'Pizza is still our favourite,' Mercedes says. 'But we're not the boss around here.'

'Listen mate, I never want you to worry about that,' says Brayden. 'Sure, I could sook about it. I could carry on like a pork chop. But the way I see it is, there's seven teas a week. That's 364 teas a year. There's plenty of room for everyone. I don't mind the odd palak paneer myself, within reason.'

'There's 365 dinners a year,' says Craig.

'Call me old-fashioned,' says Brayden, 'but I think pizza for Christmas is a bit much.'

'Can Brayden stay for dinner?' says Mercedes.

'Brayden's working, darling,' I say.

'Actually this is the end of my shift,' he says. 'I've been going since lunchtime. Didn't you have the telly on? Dees vee Swannies, in Sydney this arvo. I've been run off my feet. I've got an extra porcini in the car. Gonna eat it at home. Alone. All by meself. Leaning over the sink.'

'Please?' says Mercedes.

I shrug. 'Sure,' I say. 'What could possibly go wrong?'

After the introductions, Brayden retrieves his porcini from the car and I open the wine and Alec sets the table and we pile the pizza boxes in the middle and the seven of us sit. Lesley and Craig pick off each piece of pineapple and leave it on their plates. Brayden, Alec and I endure.

'Are we having a salad?' says Mercedes. 'Because us kids are supposed to have two serves of vegetables a day.'

'I coulda brought one but to be honest, they're not much chop,' says Brayden.

'Extenuating circumstances,' I say.

'What does that mean?' says Mercedes.

'It means that today, pineapple counts as a vegetable. So does tomato paste.'

'It's OK,' she says to Paris. 'Mum will be back soon.'

'What are you? Twenty-two? Twenty-four?' says Lesley to Brayden.

'I'm twenty,' he says. 'And a half.'

'Twenty,' she says. 'That's young. You must have a lot of stamina.'

'You have no idea. I'm on my feet for the whole shift. Stairs, no-shows, people with the munchies too stoned to find their wallets. The pizzas only stay in peak condition for so long in the cardboard and if you take one corner too fast, bam, that's it. Topping all over the inside of the box. That's why I put in all that time at the gym. Upper body, mostly. Quads look after themselves.'

'The gym?' says Lesley. 'I can tell, now that I look closely. More wine? How tall are you, six-one? Six-two?'

'One-seventy-two,' says Brayden, raising his glass. 'And a half.'

'So,' says Craig to Mercedes. 'How's school?'

'Good,' she says.

'What are you going to be when you grow up?' says Lesley. 'A scientist, like your auntie? Or a businessman, like your dad?'

'You'd make a fantastic Wonder Woman,' says Alec, to

Mercedes. 'Maybe Super Girl for your chatty friend there.'

'We don't have them anymore,' says Mercedes. 'They're really old and they've retired. Now we have Black Widow and Scarlet Witch.'

'Old? Wonder Woman?' says Alec. 'You must be joking. She's perfection.'

'Captain Marvel, for mine,' says Brayden. 'She is made of awesome.'

'I'd rather be a villain,' says Lesley. 'Then you get henchmen and a lair of one's own.'

'Perhaps you could be a scientist and a superhero,' Alec says to Mercedes. 'Lots of potential in that kind of work. Close proximity to radioactive spiders. Gamma rays careening all over the lab willy-nilly. Ability to make your own arc reactor. It's a wonder the CSIRO doesn't make better recruitment ads.'

'I'm not a scientist,' I say. 'Not really. Besides, Mercedes' parents are alive. They frown on that at superhero school.' The pineapple is glow-in-the-dark yellow and is making my teeth ache.

'Let me put in a good word for the transport industry,' says Brayden. 'Less chance of a useful genetic mutation, sure, but you can work your own hours, make tips, listen to your own tunes. Plus as much food as you can eat. You've got to go the extra mile, of course.' He laughs. One laugh, a single *ha* exhaled like a baritone's warm-up. 'No pun intended. Lots of billionaires, that's where they started.'

'You seem like a young man with a bright future,' Lesley says.

'You look after the present, the future looks after itself. I feed people. Look after them, you get me? I'm like a bee going from flower to flower.'

'You're a bee?' says Craig.

'It's a lot of responsibility, sure. What if I forget an order and some family are waiting for hours, starving, kids getting cranky, everyone on edge? *OMG, no pizza, no pizza.* Bingo, massive domestic aggro scenario. Or what if some lads are, you know, relaxing with a bit of herbal assistance? *No pizza, no pizza,* one guy who's under the weather gets in the car to hit the drive-through at the chicken place, bam! Multi-car pile-up when he runs the red.'

'If you work nights, does that mean you have all day free?' says Lesley. 'To buzz around and visit flowers?'

'I guess,' he says. 'Provided Mum doesn't need me to take her shopping.'

'Do you want my pineapple?' Craig passes his plate to Mercedes.

'Daddy doesn't live here anymore,' she says. 'He's going to have another house, with Miss Roland. That's where he'll sleep.' She tips Craig's plate so that half the pineapple pieces fall onto hers, then she sweeps the rest onto Paris's. She holds her fork like a dagger and spears and eats it, piece by piece.

'That's a piss-off,' says Brayden.

'Harsh,' says Craig, and I don't know if he means Henry, or maybe Martha, or Brayden or Mercedes.

'Me and Paris'll have to share a room there,' Mercedes says. 'We're going to get bunk beds, and mine's on top.'

'If this new place is on my turf, you give me a hoy. Extra

pineapple no charge, no worries.' Brayden reaches to the middle of the table and drums his fingers on the closed pizza boxes with surprising rhythm.

'You have great digital agility,' says Lesley.

'Ta,' he says.

'We don't know where it'll be yet. We'll have new pyjamas and some toys there, but most things will stay here because this is our first house. If we spill things, Miss Roland will get really mad. If we leave things behind at the wrong house, oh boy. Everybody will get really mad.'

'None of that has happened,' I say. 'We don't know it will happen. Where did you get that from?'

'Olivia. She's in my class. She has two Barbie bikes. The one with the broken wheel is at her old house and the new one is at her new house. When her daddy got married, she got to be flower girl which is a very important job because if you mess up, the whole marriage is ruined for ever and ever and it's your fault,' says Mercedes. She turns to Lesley. 'Plus, we're going to get a kitten for the new house. And a pony called Aurora.'

'Oh,' says Lesley. 'That's nice.'

'Kittens cost a lot but not as much as kids,' Mercedes says. 'Kids cost hundreds and hundreds. More than a car, even. Plus, I'm going to need braces, probably. Daddy'll have to pay for that. I've got his mother's teeth so don't think he can get out of that, because he can't.'

'Sweetheart, it's got nothing to do with money,' says Lesley. 'Sometimes mummies and daddies just can't live together anymore.'

'And sometimes mummies blow one tiny thing way out of proportion,' says Craig.

'Another slice?' says Alec. 'How about you, Paris?'

'Daddy's golf clubs are downstairs,' says Mercedes. 'He left them behind so we can use them as swords to fight any bad men who come.'

'He left them behind because nothing more could fit in that little car,' says Lesley.

Mercedes turns to me. 'If Miss Roland had a bigger car, would Daddy have taken more stuff?' says Mercedes. 'The furniture? The TV? This is still our house, right?'

'Bad men?' I say. 'What bad men?'

She turns up her mouth at me like I'm a moron, like I've never stepped outside my front door or watched the news. 'They'll come,' she says. 'We're only girls here now.'

We are all quiet for a moment. We look down at our plates, littered now with congealed cheese and dobs of sauce and chunks of crust. We look into our wine glasses, as though the perfect words to say in reply are floating there in the Beaujolais. Finally Alec speaks.

'Everyone feels scared sometimes,' he says. 'Even grown-ups. Especially grown-ups.'

'I'm not scared,' she says. 'You know what I'd do? I'd punch them like this.' She lets fly with her tight pink fists, straightening and bending her arms one by one. Then she pulls up each sleeve and flexes her muscles with her forehead to her fist.

'Whoa,' says Brayden. 'Have you got a licence for those guns?'

'As soon as I figure out who the bad guys are,' she says, 'they're going to get it.'

After dinner, after ice-cream, after Mercedes leans back in her chair with her hands on her stomach and says *where are my stretchy pants?*, after Brayden entertains the girls by pulling dollar coins from behind Paris's ear, Brayden and the girls exchange complicated handshake-fist bumps and Lesley gives Brayden an affectionate hug before he heads off to his car. *Youse are the best*, he says. *Next time, garlic bread, on me.*

Lesley holds firm and Craig hikes alone across the yard, slowly this time, glancing back over his shoulder with puppy-dog eyes. Lesley stares at his back and fiddles with her rings and clanks the plates against each other as she stacks the dishwasher, but she doesn't yield. I fetch her an extra blanket and a towel for the morning and a glass of water for beside her bed.

'I'll walk you downstairs,' I say.

'I know the way.' She stands in the hall, and then she turns back to face me. Her hands are tight around the glass and her nails are broken and short and stained and there are remnants of clay trapped in her cuticles. Hardworking hands. She doesn't deserve this, that I know something important that she doesn't.

'Look, Lesley,' I say.

'You think I'm stupid, don't you,' she says.

'I don't think you're stupid.'

She laughs like someone who's not slept for many days. 'Well you're wrong,' she says. 'I am stupid. I'm an idiot. I just can't figure out if I'm stupid for staying with him or stupid now, for not going home with him.'

'Lesley,' I say.

'Mercedes and Paris, they're lovely girls,' she says. 'They know how to sit at a table for dinner, which is more than I can say for my two.'

'Lesley,' I say.

'Don't worry about Henry and Caroline. They'll sort it out. He can't seriously be leaving her. Caroline will forgive him. Henry is a great father. He'd be bereft without them. Children are the most important part of a man's life. Nothing else can possibly make up for losing them.'

'You're absolutely right,' I say.

'Is there something you wanted, Janice?'

The light from the stairwell gives a golden glow to her hair. It's like she's wearing a crown.

'Just to wish you goodnight,' I say.

'And to you,' she says, as she starts down the stairs.

Caroline's decreed bedtime has come and gone, just one more promise broken. The girls are nodding at the dining table. Alec lifts one in the crook of each arm and their small bodies fold against his chest and at the sight of them, all my assurances about teeth-brushing fly out the window.

'How old are you two?' says Alec, as he balances them. 'Twenty-five and twenty-seven? You were just little kids the last time I carried you. I'm going to get a hernia. Two hernias. I'll name them after you. What will I name your hernia?'

'Princess Starlight,' says Mercedes, with her eyes closed. 'And Paris's can be Princess Moonglow.'

'Good names for hernias,' he says.

Mercedes lifts her head an inch. 'You love us, right?'

'Take it to the bank.' He kisses the tops of their heads, one by one.

Then he straightens and leans back to balance their weight as he takes soft steps down the hall to their rooms. He sways and the girls make drowsy, closed-eye smiles as he turns sideways to pass through the doorway. They nestle their faces in his neck and make quiet noises in their almost-sleep. I wish I were as lucky as they.

And now. Everyone is in the correct beds, everything is washed and dried and put away. The house is quiet and I would offer up everything I own to be somewhere else. Uhura to transporter room: my lovely flat with my friendly brown plants for company, please, and step on it.

'They wanted a story but they were both out cold before the dingos smiled and the emus shrank,' Alec says, when he comes back. 'Looks like it's just you and me.'

'Don't think I'm not grateful,' I say, 'I am. I am grateful. But I've wasted enough of your time.'

'So I'm dismissed.'

I move Caroline's oil and salt containers and wipe the bench, then I move them back again.

'It's Saturday night. I'm sure you have plans.'

'We lied straight to Lesley's face and now I'm superfluous to your needs.'

He's leaning on the back of a dining chair, rocking it

backwards and forwards on its legs. His eyes look vaguely hollow, bruised, as though he's witnessed the sinking of a crowded liner far out to sea and been unable to save a soul. Perhaps, despite everything we've been through, he's only seeing me clearly now.

'Grow up,' I say. I wipe the bench again.

'You're a horrible person now, is that it? That's your story.'

'Maybe I've always been horrible. Maybe I've always been a terrible, selfish person who only thinks about herself, and I fooled you for all those years.' All at once it seems too dark in here so I find the panel of light switches and flick them all on. Now the kitchen looks suitable for night cricket.

'Janice,' Alec says. 'I have no idea what you're doing. But if I leave it'll look suspicious. You've just told Lesley we're back together.'

'I'll tell her it's early days and we're taking it slowly. Or we had a fight. Or I felt embarrassed, being sprung by her. Whatever.'

'Wow. You're a really good liar, you know that? I, on the other hand, am a rubbish liar. I promised the girls I'd be here in the morning, and I will be.'

'Go home. Go back to your life.'

He shakes his head. 'Once more, with feeling.'

Prayer might be my only option. I drop to the floor but instead of divine intervention, now that I'm eye-level, I open the oven door.

'Look at the state of this.' I lean inside the oven up to my shoulders, the full Sylvia Plath. 'It's a disgrace. Can you hand me a sponge?'

'Now?'

'There are bits of lasagne in here that pre-date the fall of Saigon. I'm amazed this oven is not already populated with tiny, miniature archaeologists with tiny, miniature shovels. If Children's Services were to drop by, the girls'd be in foster care before you could blink.'

'I've got a better idea.' He takes my arm and guides me to my feet, then he shuts the oven door with his knee. 'It's Caroline's oven. She can clean it. Let's go to bed. Together.'

'Or we could watch TV.' I remove my arm and head back to the lounge. 'The remote must be here somewhere. If we're lucky, there'll be a rerun of *CSI: Wagga Wagga* on Fox. Or *NCIS: Bermagui*. I think there's a whole channel that plays nothing else. The acronym channel.'

'Tempting, but no.'

'I might binge watch one of these box sets. Maybe *The Tudors*. Something to put our humble infidelity dramas in perspective. Who thinks things were better in the good old days? Not me. At least our cheating heads remain attached to our necks.'

'Janice.'

'How about a few hands of canasta? Monopoly? You're chicken, aren't you? I always kicked your arse at Monopoly. You're no good at strategy, that's your problem. Monopoly is like chess for greedy people. You need to have objectives, you've got to have discipline, focus, and an obsession with property. They should give Monopoly sets to new migrants for citizenship training. You're un-Australian if you're not obsessed with property.'

He says nothing. The tips of his teeth: I can remember how they nipped the skin of my inner thigh. Those hands, how they moved and stilled and moved again. He's standing too close.

'Pictionary? Scrabble?'

Ours was not a long courtship. We were in bed together within four hours, before I knew his last name, as if there was no time to waste. Which, as it turned out, there wasn't. We dated afterwards. Surely that will offer me some kind of protection? Edward Jenner figured out the smallpox vaccine in 1796. My blood should be chock-full of anti-ex-husband white blood cells, ready to pounce.

He blinks at me. 'Don't you think we're a bit too old for games?'

'"Too old for games"? That is so corny. That's corn salsa on top of corn filling on top of corn-flavoured corn chips. It's four levels of corn. Plus cheese. It's corn with extra cheese. It's chorn. Come *on*. Monopoly. One game, for nostalgia's sake. Not nostalgia because we used to play it. I didn't mean that. I never think about being married to you. It never crosses my mind. Nostalgia for capitalism, I meant, now that it's in its global death throes. I'll let you be the shoe.' I gulp the remains of my wine.

'Can you stop talking?' He yawns with his arms and his neck and his open mouth. 'I'm exhausted. All that stripping off to bail you out of trouble has made me very very sleepy.'

'You have no respect for the sanctity of divorce. This is a terrible idea. Terrible. Really.'

'I've had worse.'

'It's on a par with that time you bought that barbecue and tried to put it together yourself, despite my telling you to phone someone to do it, and got your hand caught between the spanner and the gas bottle and broke your finger and I had to drive you to the emergency room. What a big baby.'

'Are you going to tell me you're in love with Craig?'

'Yes, Alec. That's it. You've met Craig so you can totally understand why I'm head over heels in love with him. He's my soulmate.'

He comes close to me. Closer.

'Are you in love with anyone? Just tell me and I'll disappear.'

'I've been busy. I do Zumba now.'

'Forget about love. Is there anyone you like? Anyone you fancy? I would never want to get in the middle of anything.'

'Don't think I haven't had offers. I've had offers, believe me. I can hardly move for offers.'

'Dating? Surely you're dating. It's been two years.'

'You make it sound easy. It's not easy. I take school nights very seriously. Imagine if I didn't get enough sleep. Imagine a sleep-deprived bacteria culture error. Like the Exxon Valdez but with *Haemophilus aegypticus*. Chernobyl, that was sleep deprivation. Five Mile Island. I have responsibilities.'

'That leaves the whole weekend.'

'Friday night is for football.'

'The off-season?'

'It's always football season somewhere.'

'Saturday?'

'Surely you understand the pressure of a Saturday night?

If you spend Saturday night with someone, it's a statement. It's like a save-the-date. I just got divorced five minutes ago. I'm not ready for that kind of commitment.'

He buries his face in his hands for a moment. 'Janice. I'll make this as simple as I can. Is there anyone, of either or any sex, that you could tolerate, however briefly, on a one-off, naked, recreational basis?'

'Why is this all about me? Surely there's some woman out there waiting for you as we speak.'

'I'm single. That's all that needs to be said. Are you single, Janice?'

'No,' I say. 'I am totally not-single. I'm in a very serious relationship.'

'With who?'

'Whom. You don't know him. He's working up north on a contract. A long contract.'

He leans against the fridge.

'Really. Tell me something about him. I'm dead curious.'

'Well, sure. Easy. He has a complicated relationship with his family. He used to live with his father and stepmother but she absolutely hates him and that's why he took the contract. He has three half-brothers and two half-sisters. And a dog. He loves his dog. It's a big, hairy thing.'

'What kind of work does he do?'

'Walls. He works on walls, if you must know. Wall work. Maintenance, repairs. And security systems. Wall maintenance and security. Et cetera. He's much cuter than you, that's for sure. He's got long dark curly hair and these adorable lips and a kind of permanent ten-day growth. You think you're scowly? He could scowl you under the table. He's insanely scowly.'

'What's his dog's name?'

'Pardon?'

'This insanely scowly wall guy who works up north? His dog.'

'Ghost. His dog's name is Ghost.'

'So,' says the man who might still know me better than anyone else alive. 'You're in a serious relationship with Jon Snow.'

It might be time to confess, at least part of it. Why am I even embarrassed? It's nothing to be embarrassed about. I should have a t-shirt made with it right there, printed on the front.

I swallow. 'OK. If you must know. I haven't had sex for two years.'

'You can't be serious.'

'I think I've forgotten how.'

'What?'

'It's not like riding a bicycle. It's more like studying for an exam. Like French, say, at high school. The minute you hand in that paper and walk out of the room, your brain empties like pulling the plug from a bathtub. *Bonjour?* What the hell is *bonjour?* I knew it thirty minutes ago. Is that a type of onion?'

He shakes his head. 'That's a waste. Just so I'm clear,' he says, 'that means no one kisses you in this spot, here.'

He is standing way too close to me now. He moves a lock of hair out of the way and he kisses the side of my neck, just below my earlobe.

'My licence has been revoked,' I say, after I remind my lungs to move in and out. 'You can't enrol in the CAE for a refresher course. They don't make training wheels my size. It's even possible things have grown over, down there. Anatomically. I don't know how to do it anymore.'

I rest my hand against his shoulder with the honest intention of pushing him away, but all I achieve is the feeling of his skin and bones and muscles through the fabric of his shirt, transmitting up my arm and across my chest and up my neck and into my brain. This is a mistake.

'Tell me to stop any time,' he says, as his lips move down my neck toward my collarbone. 'Go on. Do it.'

'You've been working out, haven't you? I haven't been working out,' I say.

'Go home, Alec. I don't fancy you,' he breathes. 'Say it.'

But instead I say, 'Is there a dimmer in this room? Maybe there are some candles under the sink. Or the dark. The dark is good too.'

'I do not want to make love with you, Alec. Say it.'

I say, 'This is all very sudden. I could have toned up a bit, if I had a bit of notice. Sit-ups, leg-raises, it all seemed a waste of time after I took my vows. I'd have waxed. Some bits at least. Not everything. I'm quite fond of body hair, in moderation. I've got an idea. Maybe I can text you when I'm in front of my diary.'

'What about here?'

He lifts my left arm and rolls up my sleeve, neatly, evenly, and bends his head to kiss the white flesh underneath and brush it with his teeth and his tongue and oh Jesus I can feel every cell of him, every muscle, and every molecule of the air he breathes.

'Alec.'

'We used to be very good at this. What would be the worst that could happen?'

The worst thing that could happen would be that I might never recover. There's been no one for years, yes. But there might be. There could be, possibly, at some stage in the future. I still have time. I still have hope. But if he touches me again, that would be it. I would be unmade. It would be the end of me.

I know all this. And yet, and yet. And yet, when it comes to it, standing here in front of him, I'm the one who does the kissing. Hard. I grab hold of his shirt near the neck and I twist it in my fists and bring him closer, closer, and his mouth is on mine again and I can feel him and he's right there, along the length of me, arms tight around my back. This is a reprieve, of sorts. It's a phone call from the governor when you're already strapped in the chair.

He lifts my feet from the ground. I'm suspended in his arms. I try to lift his shirt over his head, but that means we have to stop kissing.

'Off,' I grunt. Taking off his shirt is all at once the most important thing in the known universe. Empires have been traded for less.

'Uh huh.' He's doing nothing about his own shirt, but I'm back on my unsteady feet and he's pulled my shirt out of my jeans and he's smoothing his hot palms over my back, along the ridge of my spine, across my stomach, down toward the top of my pants.

Then we unbalance and fall back on to the couch behind me and he's lying between my legs and we both stop for an instant to look at each other, me and Alec, and there's something about being horizontal that is like the sound of a starter's gun for both of us. I cannot get enough of him. My legs tighten around the back of his thighs, he brings his shirt up over his head, then does the same with mine. I scratch his back, I want to mark him, I want him to bear evidence of my hands, I can't help it, and he opens his mouth wide against the hollow of my throat. He is supporting himself on those glorious arms and as he slides against me I feel his buckle digging and I reach down to unzip his fly and I inch my hand down his pants where its hot and hard and this makes him moan. This is the sound I've imagined for years, the taste and the feel and the smell of my dreams.

Janice, he mouths against my neck. He slips my bra straps off my shoulders and bends his head.

Then the doorbell rings.

It's a strange sound, like a cat's collar tinkling from the other end of a long tunnel. It is hardly worth worrying about, that cat. It'll go away, surely. Neither of us can hear it.

It rings again.

He stops. He's breathing hard. 'Should we…?'

'No,' I say, and pull him down again.

Then there is a heavy knock on the door, like the heel of an open palm. Then a heavier one again, like a fist. 'Hello?' a voice calls out. 'Janice? Are you there?'

'No,' I yell back, as I lock my legs around his thighs. 'Wrong number.'

'Janice?' That selfish, spoilt, horrible, indefensible voice says, the voice belonging to my mortal enemy. It's a woman, this despicable, persistent person whom I loathe bitterly, passionately, without even having set eyes on her.

Alec opens his mouth to speak, and I clap my hand over it. Now I have my hand over his mouth and that in itself is turning me up another level. He takes one of my fingers between his gorgeous teeth.

'We're asleep,' I call out. 'We're dead.'

'You're not dead,' the voice calls out, after a pause.

'Not yet. We're in quarantine. If you come in here you'll get one of those viruses that make you a zombie. I'll give you my kidney. Both kidneys. I'll throw in a liver. Please, please, I'm begging you. Go away.'

'Help me Janice. I've got no one else to turn to. I've got nowhere else to go.' Then the loathsome voice begins to cry.

'Bugger,' I say.

Alec kisses my forehead. 'We've got all night,' he says, and he leverages himself off me.

But I know we haven't. I know we are out of time.

I watch him stand apart from me now, back to where he belongs. I use my arms to bring myself to sitting. I stand before the dizziness takes hold, and before I shatter into pieces I turn away to put my shirt back on. It's a stupid display of modesty, as though I can still salvage some kind of dignity. When I turn around, Alec is creased and flushed and breathing hard, but dressed. I try to put it all behind me: how close we came, that I was ready to offer up my peaceful existence for this one hour, like an addict. Now the equilibrium I've worked so hard to cultivate is gone and I don't even have a memory of one final time with Alec in exchange.

'This can never happen again,' I say to him, then before he can answer, I open the door. Standing there, alone, is Martha.

'Those discount flights give you nothing,' she says. 'It's like parcel-class. It's a disgrace. And the luggage bunfight at Tullamarine. Mental. An old lady tried to steal my suitcase. Can I have a cup of tea?'

'You were in Noosa.'

'"Were", exactly. I am no longer, as you can plainly see. I found a late flight and now I am here.'

'And you are here why?'

'Why? Your sister arrived, that's why. Just showed up in reception and started World War Three when we came down for a swim. I tried to reason with her. Extend the hand of friendship. She should be thinking about this next phase of her life like a grand adventure.'

'I'm guessing she's wasn't in the mood for a grand adventure,' I say.

'I don't intend to have a stand-up argument in a resort foyer like some kind of fishwife. Talk about unattractive, two women fighting over a man. Demeaning. Henry can sort it out by himself. Besides, if you don't run off now and then, you're never going to be chased.' She winks, then looks from ruffled me, to ruffled Alec, and back again. 'Tea? Someone?'

Alec shrugs and heads toward the kitchen.

'I used to make out on the couch when I was babysitting too, but I was sixteen,' Martha says, when Alec is out of range. 'Who's he?'

'Never mind. What do you want?'

'I'm getting the floor done at my place, seeing as we were supposed to be away. And I'm not springing for a hotel. So I figured, why not here? Caroline's in Noosa. I can spend quality time with the girls.'

'Yeah, nah. I don't think so.'

'Be fair, Janice. It's late. I've been travelling for hours. I'm exhausted. Caroline has crashed my holiday. I don't want to be petty but every action has a reaction.'

'Listen. Maybe things are done differently on your home planet. But here on earth: no fucking way.'

'Did I break any vows to anyone? Why am I considered the bad guy? I'll tell you why: generations of women making excuses for men who don't keep their commitments, that's why. As though we were put on earth to be the emotional handmaidens and they are little boys who can't be expected to take responsibility for themselves.'

Her eyes are dark-rimmed and puffed, like tiny Yorkshire puddings. She's sagging, it's true. Her arms wilt by her sides. There's a stain on her blouse in the shape of a paw print. Economy travel leaves a watermark upon the spirit.

'Caroline'd have a fit. She'd dismember me.'

'I'm very tired Janice,' she says. 'It's one night. I won't be any trouble. She'll never know.'

'She will. The girls will tell her.'

In a sudden flash I remember small me, sitting on Mum's bed swinging my legs and Mum, squatting, with her hands on my knees. *And in Daddy's bathroom*, Mum's saying, *how many toothbrushes are there? Are there any jars in Daddy's bathroom? Do you remember what the jars looked like? Like from a supermarket? Or expensive ones, from David Jones? What does Daddy's flat smell like? Like perfume? And in the kitchen, is there any Tupperware? Any salad bowls?* I'm wearing new red patent shoes on my swinging feet, so glossy they look wet. They're a present from my mother, and they're a reward, and a down payment.

You're a clever girl, Janice. You notice things, Mum's saying. *Tell me everything.*

'The girls are exempt from our conspiracies,' I tell Martha.

'Fine, sure,' she says. 'I get that. I'll be gone before they wake up. I'll be like the wind. They won't even know I'm here.'

There are clattering sounds from the kitchen: mugs are being moved around, the kettle steams and drones. I know what Alec's like when he's determined. He won't be going home tonight and I clearly can't be trusted. If I have sex with him, I will unravel.

'Milk?' he calls out.

'You must be joking,' Martha calls back.

'You've got a bad back,' I say to her.

'No I don't,' she says. 'Who even says "bad back" anymore? How old do you think I am?'

'One night. And only if you take the bed. Say you've got back problems, you can't sleep on the couch. Insist on it. And Caroline can't find out.'

'Whatever,' Martha says, 'But we're going to be a family. All of us. It's only a matter of time.'

The day I stopped taking the pill, Alec and I celebrated with faux-champagne in coffee mugs in our rented bedsit. *Hang the expense*, Alec said. *Who knows? By this time next month, you might be off booze for a while.*

You mean 'we', I said. *We might be off booze for a while.*

We said these things as if we were joking, as if to say no, no, it won't happen that quickly. We looked skyward like we were on the red carpet being asked our chances of taking home the Oscar, but our fear of seeming cocky was inversely proportional to our actual cockiness. We were certain, absolutely positive, that everything would proceed according to plan. It was our destiny, Alec and me, being together. What else is destiny for?

We clinked mugs, and we drank.

Alec always knew he wanted children. Fatherhood, he said, was the most important contribution any man could make. He wanted to be young, able to piggyback and handstand

and remember what it was like to be a child himself before the weight of mortgages and careers and general disillusionment took hold. He talked about 'the firsts', making them sound like the only thing that could fend off the inevitable ennui of ageing. Imagine watching someone ride on a tram for the very first time, he said. The first time someone saw a giraffe or read Seuss. Imagine helping them. The privilege of it. Becoming a father would be a way of starting his own life anew.

He was awed by the female body, almost jealous of the power to hold babies inside ourselves. He wanted to share the feeding, share the waking. Most of all, he wanted to be honest, he said. On maybe our third date, we were nestled around a small table at the Italian place that soon became ours.

When I was six or seven, he said, *I used to wheel our cat around the neighbourhood in my sister's stroller.*

What a chick magnet you must have been.

I don't like to brag, but in grade two Kate Burns was so determined to sit next to me at big lunch that she yanked Gail Nguyen's ponytail and they had to be separated by a teacher. I was engaged five times by my seventh birthday.

You must be set for toasters for the rest of your life.

He filled up my wine glass. *You're a biologist*, he said to me. *You understand that this is what we're born to do.*

Those randy, selfish genes behind the wheel of our gigantic lumbering robot bodies, as Dawkins would say.

Listen, Janice, he said. *I'm not being fair, I know. I don't want you to walk away. I'd be devastated if you did, I'd think I was a dickhead and I'd be right. If you get up from this table right now, I am a dick. What do you think?*

I've seen no evidence yet that you're a dick. I don't have an actual detector, though. I've been fooled before.

Maybe you could tell me this. Is the idea of children a deal-breaker for you?

No, I said, to his soft, earnest eyes.

We didn't talk about it again. We dated some more, we moved in together, we married in the usual fashion and all the while it was marinating there, in the back of my brain. It was a deal we'd made. Finally, on the tram home from dinner one Wednesday night, he asked if I was ready.

I said I was. And maybe I actually was. Or maybe I was carried along by Alec's wave of certainty.

In Iceland, babies sleep in cardboard boxes. In Africa, women carry them against their bodies in fabric slings. We would be hippy parents, raising our child with values and imagination instead of toys made by child labour from carcinogenic plastic. Alec scrounged some sessional tutoring on the Medieval Plague and the Great War and worked the bar at the pub on the corner of Smith Street on weekends. He made good money in tips as night turned to morning and patrons lost the fine-motor skills required to pick up change from the sticky surface of the bar. The chef, a colourblind ex-lawyer ex-bikie who was studying tattooing, made us both standing offers of free ink and wrapped the leftover schnitzels in foil when the kitchen closed on Saturday nights, for us to eat for the rest of the week. I submitted my PhD and, in the relief, almost forgot the great sweeping existential angst of devoting my intellectual life to the tiniest kind of creatures imaginable. I even stopped wondering what that said about my vision and ambition, whether it implied a narrow, reductionist world view, an inability to engage with the sweeping grandeur of life. I'd picked up some hours as a part-time research assistant at a biotech firm on the train line outside Dandenong: nothing exciting, writing SOPs and running electrophoresis, filling in on the HPLC when they were busy, that's all. It would be a struggle, we knew, but we were young and we were strong and we were plenty stupid. We didn't need a car or better clothes or an overseas holiday. Strolling the lanes in Venice? Climbing Kilimanjaro? Vapid externalities. We knew what was important.

For three months, there was something special about the way we made love. Something extra. Sometimes when Alec came, he would look into my eyes and I would look back into his, as though there was a beam of light that ran between us, as though we were a pair of young idiot lovers in some big-haired daytime melodrama. This was the time we would make our baby. Our baby would have Alec's patience and his hands and my heart and my eyes. It would be the luckiest baby in the world, or at least the best loved.

We talked about the things we believed in and wanted to teach it, the type of school we wanted. Alec and his 'firsts': standing up in the tiny waves at Elwood beach, seeing the goats at the children's farm. The museum. The zoo. We settled on Will for a boy, Lucinda for a girl. We had a furious disagreement about the role of godparents. Was it anachronistic in our rational world, or a tangible link to community? This was vitally important, it was emblematic of the world we'd raise our child in. How could he think that way? I cried; Alec paced. Now, of course, for the life of me I can't remember which of us was arguing for what.

In the back of my mind, I never stopped thinking about him. Our baby. There was equal likelihood of a girl of course, but surely after me and Caroline and Mercedes and Paris, our baby would even things out in the marketing-driven pastel cultural construct department.

I couldn't stop staring at babies and toddlers in the street: their impossibly tiny nails, pores around their noses, the way each hair on their head existed not as an individual but as part of a silken wave. The marshmallow palms and satin fingers that lock with such force around adult pinkies. When you stand back and observe them, babies are like small explorers from a distant planet. They watch, they listen. They take it all in. Every single shop I passed sold fleece jumpsuits the colour of warm porridge and dear little fur caps with kitten ears. One Saturday afternoon I woke groggy from a nap on the couch and there was a toddler standing next to me, pulling on my arm to tell me something. I could feel him. Almost see him, almost reach out and pull him close and hold the tight warm package of his new skin. Yet when I woke fully, there was no one and I was alone.

Perhaps our boy would have a face that hid nothing, and behind it, a mind that dreamed of being a father when he grew up. Perhaps we should get a cat, so he could wheel it around in a dolls stroller.

Nothing happened the first month. Or the second, or the third.

Humans are inefficient, I told Alec. I remembered a physiology lecturer saying if humans were domesticated animals, our farmer-masters would have given up on our unpredictable, unreliable, underachieving fecundity. Both sperm and eggs must be close to perfect, for a start. Fallopian tubes unblocked and open for business, embryo genetically first-rate. Eggs are only viable for twenty-four hours. Sperm deteriorates as it gets older. Rabbits breed like rabbits, rats breed like rats, humans breed like incompetent clowns who need perfect vaginal acidity, optimal cervical mucous levels, ideal scrotal temperature, pin-point timing and Serge Gainsbourg on shuffle before they even consider producing so much as one offspring every other season. Alec and I were fit and young and strong. We just needed more time.

Maybe it's me, he said. *Maybe I shoot like a stormtrooper.*

Practice makes perfect, I said.

Three more months. Six. Twelve.

One afternoon in late spring my period was almost an hour late so I dug out the test kit that was counting down the months to its use-by date in my bedside drawer. I peed and I waited, and when those two blue lines appeared, I thought: this is fair. This is right. It hasn't come easily, but that makes it better. Sweeter. No one can say we don't deserve it. We've had plenty of time to change our minds yet we persevered, and now we have triumphed. I looked around me, I remember doing that. This very lounge room here, where I'm sitting, will be part of our baby's first memory. That tree, the white one I can almost touch from the balcony—that will be something he'll gaze at, and when he grows older, trees with that kind of scarred bark will hit him hard with a nostalgia he won't understand. He'll learn to walk on this floor. It will support his first few steps and when he falls, he'll feel the certainty of it underneath his bottom.

When Alec came home, I was lying on the couch holding a pillow to my middle in a state of wonder. All the possibilities of the universe were open in front of me. I said nothing. I showed him the blue-lined stick.

For a moment he seemed afraid to touch me. I thought he was unhappy: his face looked different, like he was not my Alec, but a close relative. He wasn't unhappy, I understand that now. He was remaking himself as a father in that instant.

You wonderful woman, he finally said to me. *You wonderful, wonderful woman.*

Three weeks later I was in my car, waiting at the lights about to turn into the lab carpark, and it flooded out of me.

After that there were doctors and tests and referrals and more doctors and pills and more tests. We ate better and walked more and we drank not at all. People advised us to buy organic, to align our bed north-south, to meditate. We played hypnotherapy discs as we went to sleep and our dreams were filled with the sound of waves and American women whispering. We sat in the office of a highly regarded acupuncturist surrounded by other desperate women with ageing eggs and waning confidence, waiting for shiny silver needles to slide into our dull energy channels.

All these things, I realised later, are a kind of prayer for non-believers.

It's you, overthinking things like always, said Caroline. *Don't think about it.*

As if that was remotely possible.

It's stress, she said. *Get smashed on tequila and root him senseless. Weed, just a little. Go on a holiday.*

In Mission Beach, we stayed at a motel with a pool as blue as ice and lazy ceiling fans on the off-chance she was right. She wasn't.

And when everything else failed, we had science.

Science. The obsession of my working life. Clever people in white coats, people who could make miracles. I read everything in the literature that I could find. Yes, the cost was substantial, but a few years had passed since we were two kids in a bedsit. We had good jobs now. We could sell the car. We could borrow, cut back. Chickpeas, public transport. Prahran market late on a Saturday afternoon when the traders begin to sing *ten dollars a tray only ten dollars*. We'd been broke before. We knew how to do it.

This isn't how we imagined it, said Alec once, as we held hands on the footpath in front of the clinic.

Don't think about the process, I said to him. *Think about the baby.*

It turned out that I was one of those end-justifies-the-means people, when sufficiently self-interested.

All day at work I sat in front of my fume hood and subbed and fed and cared for my bacteria. I adjusted the temperature of their incubators if they looked a little peaky and I improved their culture media by trial and error and hard work. Chocolate and serum and yolk and blood; bubble, bubble, toil and trouble. Grow, darlings, but not too fast. Make your little towns and cities, surround yourself with daughters so that part of you will live forever.

I had exploratory surgery through a small hole near my navel that left me swollen and sore, but the scar after it healed was too small to notice if you didn't know where to look. I took tablets that made me gain six kilos and made me cry and every night Alec injected the fat of my bottom with hormones that we kept in the fridge beside the bags of vegetables for juicing. His artless face showed more pain from wielding the needle than mine did from being punctured. He hesitated, he wiped my skin over and over with the swabs, he rotated the exact spot in a clockwise direction every day so that the injections were evenly spread across my flesh. The hormones were to make me a better, proper, functioning woman, to fix whatever was lacking, to cure me. I was weighed and tested and measured. I was harvested, fertilised and implanted.

Each month passed with an unreasonable optimism that sometimes leached over into certainty. The endless reflection and the obsessive scrutiny at home and at work. Surely I don't pee this much, normally? I feel a little queasy, don't I? Just a little? My, I'm tired today. Strangely tired. Meaningfully tired.

Every month I bled and bled.

At least you don't have to worry about your relationship, said Caroline. She knew Alec would always do the right thing.

We were counselled and we were consoled and we handed over our credit cards. As more of our friends had children in the normal, thoughtless way, we lost touch with them one by one. It wasn't us, I'm still convinced. I watched Alec smile at every birthday and every christening of every baby in our widest circle, saw him visit every mother we knew in any hospital, armed with gifts that cost more than we could afford, yet still the invitations shrank to nothing. The sight of us, I guess, was too difficult for our lucky friends so every night now it was just Alec and me alone at home, sitting in front of the television while it showed something we had no interest in. Current affairs programs, though, filled Alec with fury. A baby in a hot car outside the pokies, the kind of thing that used to make him shake his head and tsk, now made him wild. Once he kicked the hallway wall, though he was an amateur at acts of violence and there was no permanent damage to either plasterboard or foot.

Don't lose faith. It'll happen, Alec said. *It has to.*

Lots of people have IVF, Alec said. *We're both young, we're healthy. There's no reason why it won't work.*

It's just a matter of time, he said.

One morning, I was emptying the centrifuge when Gary called me to the phone that hung on the wall of the corridor. It was the doctor's office. They wanted to see me soon, in the next few days. I made the appointment and then I rang Alec, straight away. We went to all the appointments together, even though all he did was sit beside me while the doctors explained what they would do to my body. We were in this together, he always said.

'Hey,' he said. 'What's up?'

The walls of the corridor were white prefab. The whole place could be sealed or disinfected with pressure hoses. The floor was blue rubber that never cracked or split or made any kind of place for bacteria to hide, and at the other end of the corridor was the emergency shower over a drain. Everything was safe here, everything was contained. In my hand, I held a test tube. I must have taken it out of the centrifuge and brought it with me when I was called to the phone. I can't remember now what bacteria it was. The species doesn't matter. What matters was this: the reason we centrifuge cells is to separate the heavy parts of the cell from the lighter parts. The pellet of cells at the bottom was grey like mid-July, and the supernatant floating above it was a sunny viscous yellow. If I held it very carefully I wouldn't have to spin it again. If I moved too vigorously, though, the compressed cells in the pellet at the bottom would disperse back into the supernatant and I'd have to start again.

'Are you there?' he said.

Then I said, 'I just wondered if you wanted to see a movie tonight. Tightarse Tuesday. Maybe we can even spring for a pizza after. It's been weeks since we've been out.'

'Sure,' he said. 'Listen, I have Heresy and the Inquisition about to start. I'll meet you at the Nova, six-ish?'

'See you,' I said.

I hung up the phone. The test tube was warm and smooth in my steady hand. I'd kept it still enough. The separation was still in place.

I was alone, then, as I sat in front of the doctor a few days later and he told me my latest batch of eggs had died not long after fertilisation. No cell division. No growth. He didn't know what was wrong with these fragile eggs or, for that matter, what had been wrong with any of them since we started down this road so many months ago. He talked about cytoplasmic quality, about more tests on my general health to make sure I didn't have something scary and undiagnosed. (I didn't.)

Why, then? We don't know why. We don't know what the fault was, deep in the very fabric of my cells. We mortals don't know everything, medicine doesn't know everything. All we can do is try. Even science isn't an exact science. Some things about the human body are still a mystery.

One thing he did know: he couldn't in good conscience let us stay on the program. He saw no possibility of success.

'Tell Alec to ring me if he has any questions,' the doctor said. 'Or to ring one of the counsellors. That's what they're here for.'

'I'll tell him,' I said.

'I'm sorry we couldn't manage a better result,' he said.

On the way home I detoured to the beach. I parked near the baths and looked through the windscreen at the waves crashing on the rocks, at those crazy stubborn icebergers beginning their afternoon swim. Some of them must have been in their eighties and they were still churning the water in tight coloured caps and Speedos. Testing themselves, finding out what they were made of. I hoped for an old age with that much determination.

I thought of lots of things, sitting there in the car. Perhaps I should have fought harder. Maybe I should have stood up in that doctor's office and insisted we continue. People have miracle babies every day, or so the tabloids tell me. Alec's baby would have been worth fighting for, except for this: it was my own body who was the enemy, so how was I supposed to fight? Mostly I felt bad for the small boy who once wheeled a cat in a pram. I wondered what love really meant, when you got right down to it.

I'd always imagined us taking up mountaineering in our eighties, or paragliding for the first time on our sixtieth wedding anniversary. Now, safe in the bubble of my car, it seemed that life would turn out very differently from the way I'd imagined it. For a while I kept the radio on, hoping for inspiration, but all I could find was eighties classic rock and ads for mobile phone plans. As the sun set, my phone started vibrating in my bag: Alec, wondering where I was. I didn't answer. I stayed in the carpark for a while longer, looking at the sea.

I would not deprive some child of the perfect father. I would not spend my life as someone's *right thing*. I knew he would be stunned, and he was. I knew he would be willing to make any sacrifice, any compromise but I did not intend my next fifty years to depend on gallantry and pity. I would have to be believable, and I would be.

By the time I pulled into the driveway, I'd made up my mind.

I wake to an inching, crawling sensation on my calf. It's creepy. It's either a spider or a scorpion. I'm not afraid of small creatures so I play possum, hoping it will mistake me for an inanimate object and continue on its way.

It's not fooled. I feel it dance up past my knee. City insects are scared, grovelling things that know their place, like those strange lace-winged beetles that swarm dense clouds in late spring and disappear in minutes. This is a hardier kind of semi-rural bug, I can tell. Its course is determined, not meandering. It pauses before the hill of my thigh to steel itself for the climb, which it tackles with a strategic run-up. When it's on the top of my hip, I crack open one eye.

It's not an insect. It's a tiny plastic car with a face, the kind given away by fast-food restaurants to incite children to badger parents into leaking money. Paris is in her princess pyjamas, sitting cross-legged on her bed beside me. She's holding the car by the doors in a pincer and steering it expertly up and down the hills and valleys of me.

Now I remember. Last night Martha took Caroline's bed reluctantly, in deference to her bad back which, as she explained with unnecessary detail, still gave her grief from the time she caught a seven-year-old who was trying to retrieve a cricket ball off the roof of the art building. *Honestly, burden of care and all that, but I should have let the little treasure fall*, she said. *Young bones heal fast and god looks after innocents.*

When I introduced Martha to Alec, he was charmed and charming, sympathetic because there's nothing worse than back pain, nothing worse, and he would take the couch, he said, all the while smiling his complete disbelief. I tiptoed into Paris's room by the glow of her pink butterfly nightlight. She was sleeping like a starfish, assuming starfish snore like miniature timber workers chainsawing old-growth forests. I manoeuvred her limbs together and rolled her over on her side, and then I crawled in beside her dead weight.

'Steady on, Danica Patrick,' I say to her now. 'Watch the corners.'

She flies the car to my arm where it does a reckless 360 around my elbow before progressing up to my shoulder.

Alec is here. In this house. It's been years since I woke up in the same house as Alec.

The life of the divorced person is hard enough without waking in the vicinity of your ex-spouse. It's like your surgeon, sitting on your post-op bed and saying *now that I've removed your leg, would you like it to stay over occasionally?* The amputation might have been clinical and quick; it might have been a bloody, struggling rip. Regardless, no one wants the limb to visit. A phantom one is already in its place, throbbing away in the vacant air. Ex-spouses should have mandatory containment zones, like nuclear accidents. It's difficult enough to retrain your brain. For months after you separate, it's all: *I must remember to tell Alec about that new wine bar in Gertrude Street*, or *That shirt is nice, I wonder if it's his size?* A noise in the hall is assumed to be him, coming home. Two tickets to a Darren Hanlon gig are bought, an article about the Dismissal is circled in a magazine, rum and raisin ice-cream is brought home—and greater love hath no woman, in my book, than the voluntary purchase of rum and raisin ice-cream. It's a frozen reminder of the first time I was pissed beyond comprehension, aged thirteen on Bundy and Cokes.

Despite that, I bought it. There is rum and raisin ice-cream in my freezer at home right now. It's a reminder, or a eulogy. It's been there for months. I've never opened it.

This strange void between being single and being half a couple. This altered reality.

'Did you sleep OK? I slept amazing. No wonder princesses always look so well-rested. This is a great bed. I want one for my place,' I say to Paris.

The little car careens down my shoulderblade.

'Maybe it's time you said something in actual words. I'm getting worried.'

She shakes her head. Her pyjamas are bubblegum pink and the sheets are piglet pink in complete contrast to the walls, which are a cross between flamingo and watermelon. It's like sleeping inside a body cavity.

'When, do you think?'

She shrugs.

'How do you feel about bribery? You say a complete sentence and I'll take you shopping for the princessiest dress you've ever seen.'

She gives me an unimpressed expression: downward tilt of the chin, raise of the eyebrows and I'm pleased with myself for understanding. I could moonlight as a body-language 'expert' and appear on morning television to comment on politicians innocuous gestures.

'Is Uncle Alec still here?'

She nods.

I roll away from her, onto my side to improve the course for the little race car of materialistic brainwashing. It soon resumes chugging up my curves. I must admit it's nice being touched there, even if it is by an anthropomorphised plastic vehicle.

'Being a grown-up is really, really difficult,' I say.

Paris leans over me from behind. Her upside-down face is smiling and I take that for sympathy.

Through the hair curtain, Mercedes appears in the doorway.

'Remember that time we went to that zoo and you had to go in that dark room to see the platypus and Paris was too small so Daddy lifted her up and then he dropped his ice-cream and a bird came and got the cone?' Mercedes says.

I nod.

'That was fun, wasn't it?'

I tell her it was.

'If you had a baby, we'd be its cousin. Emma from school,

she has a cousin called Travis and he's at our school too.'

I sit up and drag Paris on to my lap. 'No cousins, sorry.'

Mercedes casts her arms wide and spins in the centre of the room, hair flying, feet shuffling in awkward circles. When she stops, she exaggerates weaving and swaying like a small drunk. 'We've been quiet because Miss Roland is still asleep,' she says. 'Uncle Alec is making pancakes. I showed him and Lesley the spare toothbrushes and stuff. We've been flying kites already, in our jammies.'

'Wait. Miss Roland is here, did you say?'

'In Mummy and Daddy's room. We seen her. She went to the loo before.'

Bugger. 'You really can't trust anybody.'

She nods. 'That's what Mum says. Are you getting up?'

'I'm busy. I have a new job as a racetrack.'

Mercedes sits beside the bed, cross-legged. 'But pancakes.'

I reach for her hand and interlace our fingers, then I do the same with my other hand and Paris's, behind me.

'I think I've gone deaf,' I say to Mercedes.

She drops her chin and accentuates her dimples—a tiny talk-show host humouring her celebrity guest—and she peers at my ear. 'Nah.'

'I'm no expert, but I don't think you can see deafness from the outside. Paris still hasn't made a peep.'

'Remember when she used to be a dog?'

Oh yes. For a good six weeks around her fourth birthday, Paris communicated only in woofs and growls and responded only to pats on the head and ruffles under her chin. She went around on all fours, sniffing. For her birthday she wanted one of those kid harnesses and leads that would have seen Caroline publicly shamed by some child welfare advocate.

'I preferred her dog period to this silence business. Although she's eating on the table now, so that's an improvement.'

'Some kids at kindy were really mean to her, when she was a dog. They called her names and said she smelled like poo so she punched them and Andrew's nose started bleeding and Mummy had to go and get her and she wasn't allowed at kindy any more.'

I blink. I can't think what to say to this: I look at Paris, she seems unperturbed. 'I had no idea,' I say.

'So we're not allowed to fight. That's a rule. Not ever. Especially not Paris, because if you do that at school you get expelled and then you have to stay home forever and then you'll never be prime minister.'

'Why do you think Paris is so quiet now?'

Mercedes shrugs. 'Her mouth is having a rest, I guess.'

We both look at Paris. She also shrugs.

'It's not just Paris that I can't hear. Listen.' The three of us still, Mercedes shuts her eyes. 'That's the sound of nothing. No garbage trucks, no messy couples coming home from night-clubs, no urgent 4 am free-range bacon deliveries to cafes by eejits who leave the engine running with "Highway to Hell" on loop under my window. No tap-dance studio in the flat upstairs. No Ned Kelly lookalikes on skateboards with hand-carved wheels from Etsy with Tibetan prayer bells in the hub. No sirens.'

'We don't have those here. We have cicadas.' She cups one

hand around an ear. 'You can catch them in jars if you be quick but they die so it's cruel and we're not allowed.'

Sure enough I hear it now, that country chirrup: a drill bit through soft plastic. It's loud. It must be close, either just outside the window or somewhere in the room. I don't know how I didn't hear it before. I specialise in the lives of things that are smaller than us, I should have noticed.

'That's a love song,' I say. 'She's singing about missing her boyfriend and wanting him to come home. It's very romantic.'

'No it isn't,' Mercedes says. 'It's rubbing its legs together. And it's only the boys that make that noise. And it's not in love. It's calling for a mate. They haven't even met each other and you can't be in love with someone you don't know.'

'How do you know so much?'

'School.'

'Is that how people learn to be grown-ups, do you think?' I ask them both. 'Is there a class? Maybe in the last week of high school? Because that was the week I had that sinus infection.'

'I dunno. Me and Paris are going to stay kids, we've already decided. If you're a grown-up you have to eat cauliflower and broccoli every single day and you have to pretend to like it. Plus, you have to wear boring clothes with no princesses on them. Not even on your jammies. Not even on your slippers. You have to like movies that are super boring. Then when you're a mummy, you get sad a lot and you cry when you think no one's looking.'

'When you put it like that.'

'I can bring some pancakes in here, if you're sick. If you're sick you're allowed to stay in bed. Sometimes grown-ups can't sleep in their own beds, I think. That's why they sleep in other people's beds, even during the day. Because they're really tired.'

I kiss the back of both their hands. 'I'm not tired, and I'm not sick. I just want something I can't have.'

'I know,' she says, 'you can put it on your Santa list.'

'The elves are geniuses,' I tell her, 'but what I want is seriously hard to wrap.'

By the time I shower and dress, Martha is reclining on the couch in Caroline's dressing gown, flicking through a magazine, and Lesley is in Henry's chair with her knees tucked to her chest, bent over her mobile. She's in yesterday's clothes, with stern, black-framed reading glasses on the end of her nose. Alec, floral apron over his jeans, is holding a spatula and making a leaning tower of pancakes on a platter. The girls are staring at the pancakes, hypnotised. The table has been set by Paris. I can tell this because the knives are on the left and the forks are on the right.

'And receding hair in boys comes from the mother's side,' Martha is saying. 'Big thighs and bottoms, that's from the mother's side too. You can blame Caroline if you get them. Eyesight, that's from the father's side.'

Mercedes and Paris nod without averting their eyes from the pancakes.

'Finally,' Martha says, when she sees me. 'I'm starving.'

'I'll be gone before they wake up,' I say to her. 'I'll be like the wind. They won't even know I'm here.'

'Don't be so literal,' she says. She licks one finger to help her turn the pages of her magazine. 'That's the trouble with people who talk too much. No feeling for subtext. In early childhood learning, we call that an overemphasis on the verbal. You, Janice, need to develop a multimodal approach to communication.'

'Who told you I talk too much? Was it Henry?'

'Right,' she says. 'Because you think that's something I need to be told.'

What was I thinking, letting her in last night? Was I insane? Mercedes and Paris deserve to grow up in a house with their father in it. It's a terrible thing, to miss someone when you're small and utterly powerless. While I have breath in my body, they're not going through that.

'Martha has to go, right now,' I say to the girls.

'What do you think of this one?' Martha holds the magazine up to Mercedes and Paris and they both come closer to peer at it.

'It's too skinny,' says Mercedes. 'It'd be better if it puffed out at the bottom more, like Cinderella's. And the sleeves need to be puffier too.'

'Eek,' says Martha. 'No thanks. I've seen photos of my mother from the eighties. She went the full Alexis Carrington on a daily basis. I still have nightmares.'

'How about that one?' says Mercedes, pointing to a page.

'Lord, I don't have the cleavage for that,' says Martha.

'Why is the colour so boring? Don't they come in pink?'

'My mother would have a fit, but I like the way you're thinking.'

I see now that Martha's magazine is *Australian Bride*. The girls sit on the couch one on either side of her, and together they gaze at the pages of wistful, dreamy models with their Caucasian accessory husbands.

'Why are none of the husbands smiling?' Mercedes says.

'Maybe they're selfish handsome jerks who don't know how lucky they are,' says Lesley, without looking up from her phone. 'Maybe the brides should realise they're about to tie themselves to someone who will never appreciate them and they'll spend the rest of their lives looking over their shoulder. Run, glossy brides, run.'

'That's not it,' says Martha. 'They want to get married, men. They're dying for it. It's their only chance to experience real intimacy.'

Lesley snorts.

'They're frowning because they look sexier that way,' says Martha. 'No one wants a grinning idiot husband. Do you think Mr Darcy did stand-up on the side? Tortured is way better. Deep. Brooding. Scars are also very hot. Personally, I've always rather fancied an eyepatch.'

Mercedes nods.

'Girls, say goodbye to Martha. She needs to go,' I say. 'This second.'

'No I don't,' Martha says. 'Due to circumstances beyond my control, my weekend is unexpectedly free and I can't think of anything better than spending it with my two favourite girls.'

'She means us,' Mercedes says.

'Don't look at me like that,' Martha says to me. 'All's fair, etc. I'm not here for a haircut.'

'Two minutes to pancake lift-off.' Alec reappears around the corner of the kitchen. 'I've got the first batch keeping warm in the oven.'

'And you. Kite boy. An apron?' I say. 'Seriously?'

'Don't you like it? The girls like it, don't you girls?'

'We think Uncle Alec looks pretty,' Mercedes says.

'Thank you,' says Alec. 'I feel pretty.'

'Alec,' says Lesley, eyes locked on her screen. 'What's your email password?'

'That's private,' Alec says. 'It's between me, my email provider and a few hundred thousand people who work for a couple of dozen federal agencies with no judicial or regulatory oversight and god only knows what political or social agenda.'

'I mean, what is it? Is it the name of your first pet? Is it your date of birth backwards?' Lesley says.

Martha yawns, and stretches her legs and rests her feet on Caroline's coffee table. 'It won't help you,' she says. 'Men are infinitely variable, the little dears. They don't all think the same.'

'On some things they do,' says Lesley.

'Even if you crack his inbox, then what? You're only letting yourself in for a world of pain.' Martha flicks another page with wild insouciance. 'My advice is don't try to change him. You're not his mother. You need to out-think him. Beat him at his own game.'

'I'm Caroline's friend, you know that, right?' says Lesley.

'That's so last century,' says Martha. 'I'm not the enemy here.'

'Miss Roland's not an enemy, is she?' says Mercedes to me.

'No one's an enemy,' I say, though I could probably take Martha down if it came to that. She's wiry, yes, but a bit fragile across the shoulders and thinner than me. If I had the element of surprise, I could clamp my hand over her mouth and twist her arm behind her back, then frogmarch her up to the road and hail a passing taxi.

Don't overreact, Janice. Be calm. There's no excuse for the use of force.

'Get 'em while they're hot, good friends,' says Alec.

'You're cute,' says Martha. 'Isn't he cute? I should introduce you to my sister. She's a photographer, very arty. I'll text you her number.'

'They're getting back together,' says Lesley, nodding at me.

Martha shrugs. 'Who has a crystal ball? No one. He can keep it until he needs it.'

Anyway, taxis never drive past this far out of the city. I'd have to book one in advance.

'It was just an idea. We're all friends, remember,' she says, when she sees my face, and she pats my shoulder like I'm a German shepherd. 'Good friends.'

Martha sits at one end of the table and I sit at the other, facing each other: in the lists, before a joust. Alec plays mother and passes syrup, jam and butter. Lesley rolls each pancake into a cigar, then eats them with her fingers. Martha cuts hers into lots of triangles all at once, then she dips each piece into a puddle of syrup.

'How you eat with your job, I'll never know,' says Martha. 'I'd be seeing germs everywhere.'

'They are everywhere,' I say.

I want to tell her that we Eukaryotes are a tiny addendum to the story of our planet. That the Mesozoic was not really the age of reptiles and the Cenozoic isn't the age of mammals but every single second of earth has been and always will be the age of bacteria. We are pathetic, compared with them. Of course they're everywhere. They're all over us, for a start: every human alive is a planet for our own specific microbial population, so my bacteria are mostly different from hers, and hers are different from Alec's.

'Germs make you sick,' says Mercedes.

'No, darling,' I say. 'Well yes, in the sense that germs are defined as pathogenic bacteria. But very few bacteria are germs. Some are, but very few. Mostly they make us well.'

I tell her about *Mycobacterium vaccae*, which is one of my favourite bacteria. Not my very favourite, which remains the beautiful and resilient *Helicobacter pylori*: a gorgeous purple under Giemsa stain, lives in stomach acid, which can get as high as pH 1. That's seriously acidic. *Mycobacterium vaccae* is commonly found in soil. It's thought to stimulate an immune response in the prefrontal cortex that increases serotonin in the brain. Increasing serotonin is how a lot of anti-depressants work.

'Is it in my clay? Because nothing makes me happier than making pots,' says Lesley. 'Gardening is good too. You hardly ever meet a sad gardener.'

I tell her it's very possible.

'Germs are germs are germs,' Martha says. 'That's what Dettol's for. What's that, Mercedes?' Martha points her knife at one of the triangles.

Mercedes peers at it. 'Isosceles,' she says. 'And that one's a scalene.'

'Impressive,' says Alec.

'We just did it on Friday,' Mercedes says.

'I also teach introductory French. The earlier they learn a second language, the better. What's this?' Martha taps her fork on the edge of Mercedes' chair.

'La chaise,' says Mercedes. 'That means it's a girl.'

'Of course it is,' says Lesley. 'You rest your weight on it. What sex is a mop? What about a bucket?'

'Can you hear that? That buzzing? What is that?' says Alec.

I tell him it's the male-only cicada orchestra in rehearsal for *Eltham's Got Talent*.

Martha takes her phone from her back pocket. 'I could drown it out, but they don't have bluetooth speakers. This house is like the middle ages.'

'I have a portable CD player at home. I could get it if you want,' says Lesley. 'What's your favourite band?'

Martha looks at Lesley like she's suggested making fire with two sticks. 'Modern music, Nanna. You won't have heard of it.' Then, to me: 'I might have a quick lie down after breakfast. I'm exhausted.'

'Sorry,' I say. 'I have to disinfect the sheets after you slept there last night. Germs.'

She raises one eyebrow at me. 'That's a pity. This afternoon I was planning to teach the girls some of my old cheerleading moves.'

'Seriously? You know how to do that?' says Mercedes.

Excellent. Martha's lofted drive soars effortlessly over my head for a six.

She smiles right at me, the insolent cow. 'I used to work for the Lions when I was putting myself through uni.'

'I want to be a cheerleader,' says Mercedes. 'Miss Roland can stay, can't she? Please?'

'Fine,' I say, 'sure. Caroline can't kill me twice.'

'Why is Mummy going to kill you?' Mercedes says. 'Because we didn't brush our teeth last night?'

'I'm joking,' I say. 'Mummy loves me very much.'

'I know that,' says Mercedes. 'You're her sister. You've got to love your sister, it's a rule. You can't pick your family, Mummy says.'

'So why did you two split up?' Martha says, pointing to me and Alec with her fork.

'Us?' I say.

'The usual, I guess,' he says, looking straight at me. 'Someone let someone down.'

Martha shrugs. 'All our cells change every seven years. Literally and figuratively, we're different people. How can you make promises on behalf of someone you haven't even become yet?'

'That's a complete cop-out,' says Lesley. 'That's an excuse for spineless, pathetic liars.'

'Some things are more complex than they appear on the surface,' I say. 'People are more complex. But that seven-year thing is an urban myth.'

'You're agreeing with her?' says Lesley. 'Her?'

'You have twins, right?' Martha says to Lesley. 'That must

have been shocking. Were you big?'

'I was a whale,' says Lesley, as she polishes off another pancake. 'I was the *Hindenberg*. I was one of those American cruise ships the size of a small city with its own ice-rink and climbing gym and mega-mall. I listed from port to starboard as I walked. I could feel my onboard swimming pool sloshing.'

'That sounds revolting,' says Martha.

'Did you really used to be a cruise ship?' says Mercedes.

'Not really, sweetie,' says Lesley. 'Really I was the moon. Fishermen up and down the coast would run aground on sand bars and lose their crab pots because I altered the movement of the tides.'

'I'm never getting married,' says Mercedes.

After I left Alec, I ate breakfast in a cafe by myself every weekend. By 7 am, I was up and dressed and moving, wearing lipstick and earrings and looking, for all intents and purposes, like a real person. In the first few weeks the cafe was out here, near Caroline's place, but soon I found a favourite around the corner from my new flat. For a whole hour I sat upright in my chair and ate eggs and read a novel and spoke to waitresses in full and complete sentences. I smiled. I told myself that eventually that robotic hour would stretch to two and then six, and before I knew it, probably even before I retired to spend my twilight years in some facility for divorced people, I would manage the whole day upright and alert and looking for all the world like a fully functioning member of society.

That was the plan. Until then, I spent early mornings walking through the laneways near my new home, head down. I ate toast for dinner. I bought new clothes to save the waste of the half-load in the machine but I lacked the pure, sweet suffering of the wronged.

You cannot tell any of this by looking at the outside of me.

Martha presses her serviette to her lips and leaves it on top of her plate. She stands, and leaves her chair out. 'You,' she says to Alec, 'are a treasure,' like he's cured cancer or swum the English Channel, miraculously insulting both competent women and competent men at once. I could make pancakes at twelve.

'I aim to please,' Alec says.

'Some women don't know how lucky they are,' Martha says. 'Henry can't manage to pour juice in a glass without getting it all over the bench. So cute.' Then, to all of us, as she leaves: 'Nighty night. Just go about your normal business, don't mind me. I'll have my earbuds in and besides, I sleep like the dead.'

After we clear the table, I tidy up the lounge room. My phone had fallen down between two cushions on the couch and when I pick it up, I see six missed calls. It isn't cicadas that Alec has been hearing. It's Caroline.

I walk out to the patio and slide the glass doors tight behind me. The early sunshine is fading now and the clouds that started off scattered and wispy are joining in the far horizon. From the sky, dozens of rainbow lorikeets look down on me as they swing and loop but they're not hooning around, they've got somewhere to be. The silver gums along the road are twisted and writhing and the grey-green of their leaves sets off the few leftover golden balls of wattle. Perched on this slope above the valley, it seems as though the world is only a few miles across. Imagine this land when it was wild. Even now, tamed and tidy and Sunday-pruned, it's another planet. The air against my skin is already clammy.

'Where were you?' Caroline says, when she answers. 'I've been calling and calling.'

Where did she think I was? I have two small children in my care. You can't put them in a cupboard while you nip to Shoppingtown for a manicure, apparently.

'Well excuse me for breathing,' she says. 'I just wanted to check that everything's OK.'

Of course everything is OK, I tell her. Why wouldn't things be OK?

'No reason. It's good for you to have a weekend away in a proper house instead of cooped up in your shoebox. Any time you want to babysit, you're always welcome, no trouble. Just give us a ring first.'

Thanks, I tell her. She's generosity itself.

'There's some washing I didn't get to,' she says. 'It's in the basket at the bottom of the stairs. You could pop it in the machine if you're bored. Make sure you spray the collars. And check the girls' uniforms for stains. In the light. You might need to pre-soak. Should take you half an hour, tops.'

I sigh, which she takes as agreement.

'So you're having a relaxing time then.'

Oh, yes. Nothing much happens in the outer suburbs. It's just like a spa retreat. A nudist, adulterous spa retreat populated by guerrilla amateur psychoanalysts. Is it always this boring at her place?

'Excuse me. Once a month there's drinks at the art gallery and the pub has early-bird jazz on Saturdays. Over by nine, in time to drive the babysitter home. Everyone's very friendly, actually.'

They certainly are. I know exactly how friendly it is out here, with its friendly Neighbourhood Crotch program. Caroline is still talking: about the exorbitant last-minute fare and being sandwiched between two armrest hogs (*although the window one was cute, a little hairy but cute, a lot of women love pelt anyhow and I get that, it's masculine, Henry looks like he's been dipped in toffee, window guy was some kind of elevator mechanic, dating him would have a lot of ups and downs eh eh?*), about her private-eye flair in tracking Henry and Martha from his credit-card statement to a gilt and chrome all-suite hotel right on Hastings Street (*the kind of place that Henry, the old Henry, my Henry, would have said was for pretentious dicks before he apparently became one*) and yes, the 'adult discussion' in the lobby that 'might have become a little heated'. The future of her family was at stake and sharp looks from bystanders, while embarrassing, and the eventual intervention of the management, which, yes, might be considered humiliating, were way down her list of concerns. Once the coward Martha had bolted, Caroline followed Henry up to the poncy suite with its views of the overpriced sea to sit him down and talk like mature adults about their family and the girls and the vows they'd made, but he didn't speak at all. He only cried. She hadn't seen Henry cry since Paris was born.

'If only he could communicate better,' she said. 'Men. They're emotionally catatonic.'

'He cried. That's gold-standard, world-class expressiveness.'

'He said he doesn't love me anymore. What do you think he means by that?'

'It's a mystery.'

'They don't listen. He's from Mars, I'm from Venus. If only you could buy a Martian phrasebook. You know why they're like that? The bit that joins the two halves of their brains together is too narrow. All men have it, it's like a birth defect.

Normally it's wider, except for Martha, probably. Her brain bridge is probably man-skinny.'

'Firstly, women don't have a thicker corpus callosum, that's a myth. Secondly, even if we did, it doesn't mean anything in terms of anything. And thirdly, your argument is that because Martha slept with your husband, she's also from Mars?'

'Martha is from Pluto,' she says, snorting. 'All hail Martha, queen of the underworld.'

The sound of the cicadas is louder, until I realise it's coming from the phone. It's like she's in a wind tunnel. 'Look, Caroline. He told you what he wanted yesterday. He went off with her, to Noosa. That's the problem you have to address. Chasing him across state lines won't change that.'

'He was crying,' she said. 'What does that mean in terms of male psychology, do you think?'

'I'm no expert but here's a stab: perhaps he's sad.'

'But why is he sad? Because he planned a romantic trip with the wrong woman? With her, instead of me? Or maybe he felt guilty for stringing her along? Probably. He regretted the whole thing and wished he was back home, that's why he was crying. Remorse, that was it.'

It's like explaining particle physics in a foreign language to a deaf person on the other side of a soundproof door. 'Sure, Caroline. It's your story. Why not.'

'I knew it,' Caroline says. 'Anyway. I spent the night.'

'There? With him?'

'No. Somewhere else, with no one you know. Of course with him. Anyway, nothing happened. Or not much. I even. Well. I thought if I gave him a little, you know, oral encouragement. I know what he likes. What he used to like, back in the day.'

'Jesus.'

'Blowing someone while they sob is not very sexy, actually. It's depressing, to tell you the truth.'

'I'm pretty sure that's assault.'

'Don't be ridiculous. When you're in a long-term relationship, it's normal for one person to start and let the other one catch up. You'd know that, if you were still married. I thought his enthusiasm would, you know, grow. That hotel had a king-size bed, did I mention? With satin sheets. She obviously chose it. No class. One peek under a black light and you'd wrap your privates in clingfilm permanently. Yes, even you, germ girl. But still. Who can resist an appetiser? I thought that if I stayed there in that bed, naked, Henry would come in.'

'Did he? Did he come in?'

'I lay awake all night. He slept on the couch. We've still got a lot to work on, I know that,' Caroline says. 'I left first thing this morning. He needs time to think, a few hours by himself. God, I wish this taxi would hurry. This lane always fills up, I told him that. See? I told you this lane fills up.'

In the distance, I hear a man's voice. 'Lady they shut off one lane for fixing or somethink. What can you do? Nothing, that's what. They do what they want. You vote, you pay tax, you get no say in it.'

'See that sign?' she says. 'It says one hundred. That's how old I'll be when we get there if you don't make an effort. Look. There. A semi could pull into the space in front of that ute.'

'You speed up, you slow down, you zip across, and for what? Wear and tear on the gears and high blood pressure, that's what.'

'Hang on a second, will you darling?' Caroline says to me. Then her voice muffles; she's holding her hand over the bottom of her phone, ineffectively. 'If we were in the right lane from Mickleham Road I'd be home by now,' she says.

'Everybody rushing these days. No time for nothing. It's crazy.'

'My sister is in charge of my children, for god's sake. All of her houseplants commit ritual suicide within days of being brought home. Anything could be happening.'

'My wife, she turned into a real stress-head,' says the man's voice, even more distant now. 'Then, boom. The doctor gives her hormone pills, abracafreakingdabra, now she's a sweetheart like when I married her.'

'It's like I'm in a hearse. Or a nightmare. A hearse in a nightmare,' Caroline says.

'Taxi, did you say?'

'You'll be glad to know I'll be relieving you soon. I'm sure you've got things to do. FarmVille, or make soup and freeze it in single servings, or buy things from the homeshopping network. Pinterest. Whatever.'

'Wait, where are you?'

'In a taxi,' she says. 'I wish you'd listen. I'll be there in twenty.'

I'm trying to reply, but my brain is buzzing with the force of a thousand cicadas.

'I'm going to make a special dinner for Henry tonight

when he gets home,' she says. 'And he will come home, I can feel it. A roast, maybe. Wife-food. We can start again, now that Martha's gone for good.'

'Martha's gone for good?' Through the glass of the sliding door, I can see Lesley painting her toenails, then stretching out her legs and wiggling them. Mercedes and Paris are sitting on the couch, knees to chest, flicking the pages of Martha's bridal magazine and admiring Lesley's glistening toes. I can't see Alec.

'Maybe. Probably. Why else would she have bolted like that? Guilt, I reckon. She knows what she's done is unconscionable. And unprofessional, for that matter. I've a good mind to contact the education department. There's probably some kind of blacklist for women like her. They shouldn't let her anywhere near a classroom.'

'It's a tough job, teaching,' says the distant man's voice. 'Ought to give 'em a medal.'

'What?' says Caroline.

'All credit to them. I couldn't do it, that's a fact. Texting, sexting, getting on the gear. Bud and choof and green. Twerking. Selfies. Kids today, total nightmare.'

'Hang on,' Caroline says to me, then, 'Excuse me, but the minimum standard you expect from a teacher, the very minimum, is not shagging the father of her best student.'

'Humans are only human, 's all I'm saying.'

'What complete nonsense. We put up with that kind of behaviour and then what? Anarchy, that's what. The collapse of the family unit.'

'My wife, I met her in the cab. Door opens, someone gets

in, I pay no attention, she says Northland mate, and can you put the air on, and then I look up and there she is, shining in the rear-vision mirror. One look, nearly run into the back of a tram. I end up waiting for her outside the video store and taking her home again, I tell dispatch I've got a flat.'

'Riveting,' says Caroline.

'Fourteen years come September.'

'You were single, though. And so was Miss Northland, I'm presuming. My husband already has a wife,' Caroline says. 'Obviously.'

'The heart wants what the heart wants,' says the man's voice. 'Plus there's always more to the story.'

'Did I ask for your opinion?'

'Nothing is black and white, lady,' says the man. 'All I'm saying.'

'That's a frightening attitude from someone charged with following the road rules,' Caroline says.

'I don't think you should make any assumptions about Martha,' I say.

'Trust me,' Caroline says. 'That's the last we'll see of her. She's probably at home writing her resume as we speak. She's probably halfway back to Brisbane by now. Land of the husband-stealers.'

'Halfway to Brisbane by now?'

'Not me,' she says. 'Martha. I'm on the Ring Road. Twenty minutes.'

'Twenty-five, maybe thirty,' says the man. 'Karingal Drive this time of day. Need a crystal ball.'

'I was being generous, taking your driving into account,

but I could jog it in twenty-five,' she says. 'It'll be closer to fifteen.'

'Lady, I do this for a living.'

'Yet you seem surprisingly well fed,' says Caroline.

'You're on the Western Ring Road?' I say.

Even on the phone, I can feel Caroline roll her eyes. 'Will you please pay attention?' she says.

Once, on a Friday afternoon before a Saturday access visit with Dad in those early days before he moved away to start his new family, I was lying on my belly, making little piles of my money on my bed. I was a good saver, unlike Caroline, who spent every cent on Siouxsie and the Banshees or Bauhaus or The Cure and was into Mum for twenty-seven years of pocket money advances by the time she turned twelve. In front of me was my life savings, nineteen dollars and seventy-two cents in towers of coins balancing on the taut bedspread. I looked up to see Mum walking past the doorway to my room with the laundry basket on her hip.

'I knew I'd hit the jackpot with this motherhood caper eventually,' she said. 'I've been meaning to ask for a loan. I'm good for it.'

I distrusted paper money. It was insubstantial. You couldn't stack it or jangle it or see which one could roll the farthest. I changed any notes Mum gave me at the milkbar. It was incomprehensible to Mrs Stanopolous that every teenager in a three-block radius would voluntarily sit in her shop in sunny weather and feed their coins into her Space Invaders machine, expecting nothing in return. It couldn't be right.

She gave change at speed, whenever anyone asked for it, as if disposing of evidence.

'You can have fifty cents,' I said to Mum, 'but that's it. I need the rest of it.'

This was a substantial sacrifice. The fifties were my favourite, the only dodecagonal coin in the world.

'For what?'

'I'm going to take Dad out to lunch,' I said. 'Somewhere nice, not just a pie. But it's not enough.'

There are many different kinds of promises, I know this now, not just those we break and those we keep. Big promises, little ones. Those we make to other people and those we make to ourselves. Sometimes sworn in words; sometimes more an understanding, a tacit kind of agreement that never truly bubbles up to the conscious part of our brains. A promise can be a silent vow about the kind of person we wish to become. Sifting through my life now, I see hundreds of promises, so many of them in direct opposition to each other. If I choose to keep one, it's at the cost of another. It becomes a question of priorities. Somebody's heart is going to break. Sometimes you have to choose the lesser evil.

But that's the adult me talking, the divorced me. The child me, sitting on that taut bed, on the clean sheets washed and dried and folded by my mother—what was I thinking? Nothing I owned was really mine. My life and everything in it had been constructed from my parents' money and time and care.

From Caroline's room next door, I could hear the muted roar of her music. Even now, if I shut my eyes, a song flares like an animal whining, quietens and flares again. My childhood was spinning toward its end. My mother's face was tired and blank and dull. I had not yet seen her as a person separate from me.

Now that I am a grown-up, I can line up all my promises in front of me like piles of shiny silver coins. This one is higher than this one, that one glistens and another teeters under its own weight. Some have already collapsed, and litter their debris over my life. From where I sit, it seems I am surrounded.

'It's strange,' my mother said. 'I almost put some blusher on this morning, but when I opened the compact, do you know what? It was all dried out and cracked down the middle. Completely stuffed. It looked like the Nullarbor.'

'It's too old, maybe,' I said. 'You can get more at the chemist's next time you're at the shops.'

'I could certainly do that,' she said. 'Everything is replaceable. I'll just throw out the old and dried up and get something brand new, something shiny. Next time I'm doing the shopping, I'll be sure to drop in.'

She stayed there, leaning in my doorway with the basket on her hip until I wondered if there was something I'd forgotten or something she'd forgotten. I rarely saw her being still. My mother had been athletic in her teens but in those days, exercise and sport belonged to children, not mothers. By then she was broader and softer, even though she was always in motion. Whenever I saw her dashing from the bathroom to her bedroom after her shower, I felt bad for her soft, white middle and her chicken-skin thighs.

'Thanks for the clothes,' I said, because when in doubt, resort to good manners.

'I wonder what your father is doing right now.' She fidgeted with the peeling plastic on the edge of the laundry basket; she picked at it with her nails like she sometimes did with the skin on her knuckles or the edges of her cuticles.

I shrugged.

'Is he doing housework, do you think?'

'Housework?' I said. 'Dad? What do you mean?'

'Maybe he's out somewhere with that woman. Somewhere nice. Maybe they're having an early tea and later they'll see a band. We used to see bands, before we got married. Or maybe they'll cuddle up on the couch with a movie, just the two of them.'

All single mothers are great multitaskers and ours had a particular tone reserved for when she was chopping vegetables or reading something but wanted to maintain a kind of connection with us, so that we didn't ever feel that something else was more important than we were. That was the way she spoke now, without looking at me, as though her attention was elsewhere and these words were plucked from the spare edges of her awareness.

'Every time you eat, you remind me of him,' she said. 'The way you make a well in your mashed potatoes for sauce. That goddamn orange juice. The colour of your hair. The shape of your face. Every single day, I can't escape him.'

I made myself very still.

'A hundred years ago, your great-great-grandmother would have cooked chops and mashed potatoes and peas for tea, just like I do, and her children would have smothered everything in sauce. Cooking meals is like the discovery of time travel. It's a hell of a legacy, generations of women who die with skin that smells of sheep fat.'

She hoisted the laundry basket higher on her hip. 'Follow me.'

I did. I moved quickly. There was something in her voice. All at once, I was severely, adrenally motivated.

She wore a deep blue sundress, I remember still. Following her down the hall, I could see the flat plates of her shoulder blades lifting and falling beneath the straps as she walked. In the kitchen, she rested the basket on the counter next to the sink. She took pairs of my underwear from the basket, and two or three t-shirts, and a denim skirt and some socks. There might have been other things, I don't remember. There were things of Caroline's in the basket as well, and a slip and a pair of checked cotton pedal pushers of hers, but these she left where they were. She dropped my things in the sink. Then she turned to the tall thin cupboard that served as our pantry and she brought out a bottle of tomato sauce, one of those indifferently designed old-style glass ones. She took off the lid. She held the bottle upside-down, suspended over my clothes.

She hovered it there in space for a moment. The sauce was old and had dried to a darker claret-red crust around the neck.

Then she moved her arm hard and sharp and smacked the bottom with the flat of her hand—one, twice, again—before it glugged out in a great crimson splat over my clothes. Her face was calm. She was looking vaguely above the refrigerator, I think, certainly not at me. I could smell the sauce as soon as it hit the fabric and when she turned on the tap and gave my wet clothes a good mix with a wooden spoon, the whole kitchen filled with sweet and rich overcooked tomato.

When the sink was full, she turned off the tap and put the lid back on the bottle, though not much of the sauce remained now. She returned it to the cupboard and left it upended and balanced on its lid, resting between a tupperware container of spaghetti and a bag of no-name brand oats, so that the dregs would slide down the neck and life would be easier for the next person to use it. There was a line of sauce splashed on her inner arm and she licked one finger and rubbed it clean. My clothes had clogged the drain and the sink was full. The tomato water was closer to pink, but the red on the clothes was almost blueish, like someone had opened a vein.

In the days to come, I'd scrub my clothes and soak them in bleach but nothing worked and finally I wrapped them in a plastic bag and hid them in the very bottom of the bin because if she saw them, we might have to talk about it. I didn't want to talk about it. My mother was the one who took us shopping for Father's Day presents and did his ironing. *Girls, keep it down, please. Your father's had a hard day. Girls, pick up your clothes from the bathroom floor. Your father wants to shower.* She taught us how to love him, and she broke into tiny pieces when he left.

In the days to come, I'd make a mental pile of my belongings in an old scarf and tie it to an imaginary stick. I'd hike along pretend railroad tracks until I was adopted by a family of gypsies who saw my inherent, sparkling goodness and could identify with the injustices I'd suffered. I'd never come back. My mother would be in my untouched bedroom shrine, sobbing; kneeling at the altar of my dresser, drowning in her remorseful tears.

Back in the kitchen with my saucy clothes, though, the possibility of life as a gypsy hadn't yet occurred to me. My mother loved us wildly, I know that now. Parents were gruffer with kids back then. It wasn't a popularity contest like it is now. Everyone we knew was raised with a kind of benign indifference. No one thought anything of it.

'When you and your father are having your nice lunch, maybe you could ask him to do your laundry,' my mother said to me, utterly unremorseful. Then she headed for her room, and closed the door.

'We borrowed Lesley some of Mummy's nail polish, from her bathroom,' Mercedes says, when I get back to the lounge. 'She won't mind. She has lots of colours but she never uses them anymore because Binh does her nails now.'

'That's good. Listen, where's Martha's bag?'

'I felt this burning need for more red in my life.' Lesley is sitting in Henry's leather recliner with her sensible tweed skirt hitched up to her knees, her black boots discarded on the floor. She stretches out her legs and wriggles her squat little toes, which glisten like blood. 'See? Like ten tiny fire trucks speeding to a rescue. My rescue.'

'Lovely.'

'Binh used to work at a university before but here she's a nail lady. But that's OK because at least she's here. Being here is better and being a nail lady is a good job. You meet people, you're practically your own boss. Binh lets us sit in the massage chair. It tickles and it makes your voice go funny.'

'Why are you pacing? Stop it,' says Lesley.

'I'm not,' I say. 'Am I?'

She shrugs. 'Fine, pace if you want. It's your ulcer.'

'Ulcers are bacterial. *Helicobacter pylori*. We've known about it since 1982.'

'It's just an expression,' she says. 'I didn't know it would be on the exam.'

Typical. Bacteria get no respect and a groundbreaking, Nobel-winning discovery (Barry Marshall and Robin Warren, for the record: two of my personal heroes) is completely erased.

'The fingers are next,' she says. 'I haven't painted my nails in, oh, ten years? Clay strips it straight off, no point whatsoever.'

'All the brides have pink nails, like shells.' Mercedes holds the magazine open at a photo of one pale hand bearing half a dozen sparkly rings with fat jewels of all colours. The rings are some kind of flamboyant tumour, a diseased but organic extension of the female body. The pink and shiny fingernails, though, are too natural in this context. They seem like they're stuck on. Fake. 'See? Look at hers,' Mercedes says. 'They're like pearls.'

'More fool them.' Lesley beckons Mercedes over and she flicks pages until she finds faces and entire women instead of disembodied parts, and then she speaks directly to the flat brides, her mouth close to their cheekbones and their button ears. 'Red, you idiots. Wear red. Get a tatt. Ditch the sky-blue chair-covers with dinky bows and spend the money on leathers and a motorbike.' She taps one of the airbrushed brides on the head with a fingernail.

'Maybe there's a rule for weddings. Maybe husbands don't like red.'

'If a man doesn't want his wife to be hot, she shouldn't marry him. Never let anyone repress your sexuality, girls.'

'Twelve boys love me. Lachlan, he's my boyfriend but I like Matthew too. He's my second boyfriend. Lachlan and me, we're going to go on dates when we get to be sixteen because that's how old you have to be.'

'But you don't have to worry about that yet,' I say. 'Right now, we've got plenty of other things to worry about. Now, Martha's bag?'

'Anyway, I don't want to get a tattoo. Becca's mum says it hurts. Not as much as babies, but still.'

'A woman's life is full of pain,' Lesley says. 'That's what you've got to look forward to.'

'Lesley's joking,' I say.

'No I'm not.'

'She's kind of joking. Sort of.'

'Don't lie to them,' she says. 'The sooner they learn the truth, the better.'

'Once I fell off the fence when me and Paris were playing tightrope and my arm was really sore and I had to go to the doctor,' says Mercedes.

'I hope you screamed and kicked something,' says Lesley. 'I hope you said a really rude word.'

'Like bum,' says Mercedes. 'Or willy.'

'Nobody likes pain, darling,' I say.

'If men gave birth, there would be a separate section of

the newspaper for birth stories, between sport and real estate,' Lesley says. 'There would be birth judges and live broadcasts and world records in the speed of dilation and the length of your labour in hours would determine the size of your payout from the state.'

'That's silly. If daddies could have babies, they wouldn't be daddies. They'd be mummies.'

'We are braver than them, by miles,' Lesley says. 'Bolder. We are bloody frontline warriors.'

'Boys are soldiers, girls can't be soldiers,' says Mercedes.

'Historically, boys were soldiers, yes,' says Lesley. 'But that's because historically, boys were everything. Historically, boys were also poets. The very idea of a soul was thought up by a man, way back in history. That's why they're the ones who run religions. Men can pretend they're made from higher stuff, but we know from girlhood what we're made from: blood and mucous and weeping flesh.'

'Gross,' says Mercedes.

All the while Lesley's giving her dissertation in women's studies, the clock is ticking and the taxi is coming and I've done nothing, not yet. What can I do? What should I do?

'It's not gross. We've got to own it. We should strap our used menstrual pads to our wrists like Wonder Woman's bracelets,' says Lesley.

Mercedes raises her mercifully naked wrists—'Pew pew pew!'—deflecting imaginary flying bullets as she careens around the lounge room.

'OK, thanks Germaine,' I say, 'but sanitation, that's a pretty good thing too. Let's move on from blood, shall we? I know. Mercedes and Paris have been dying to see your potters wheel.'

The eager apprentice potters manage to hide this wild desire. Mercedes is dodging behind chairs, flinging her wrist back like Spiderman, middle finger folded to her palm, sending bursts of invisible arachnoid mucous roping across the room. Paris is still gripping the bridal magazine, huddling in front of it as though for warmth. Lesley takes a hit from one of Mercedes' invisible spidergirl shots and dies gurgling, sprawling sideways across Henry's leather recliner with arms dangling over the armrest, her wet toes stretched wide in her last throes.

'I'm not surprised,' she says, upside down. 'My wheel's a beauty. One and a half horsepower, four hundred pound centring capacity. Electric, of course, that's important. Kickwheels are for hippies, you sit there all day throwing, you soon figure that out. My left shoulder, I can't tell you.'

'Maybe they could have a try? Girls, would you like to make a pot?'

'They're too young for the wheel. Best to start with a coil. Pushing your fingers through wet mud, it's a sensual experience. Everyone should do it.'

'What does sensual mean?' says Mercedes.

'It means figuring out what feels good for your own body from your own perspective, instead of from someone else's. Being empowered by your own body instead of the effect it has on someone else,' says Lesley. 'It takes some people years to manage.'

'Girls, why don't you go with Lesley back to her place?

She'll let you play in mud. Take the shortcut, across the yard. Run run run, go on, don't look back. Whoever gets there first gets an ice-cream.'

'We're not allowed to get dirty,' says Mercedes. 'We can go downstairs to the playroom and make a book with Hello Kitty stickers if you want. We do that sometimes when Mummy is having her rest.'

'Of course you're allowed to get dirty,' I say. 'Go ahead. Roll in it.'

Lesley groans. 'I know you think you're being a good feminist but you're not. If you're a woman, the only thing dirt means is the labour required to clean it up. Being still and doing nothing, that's a feminist act,' she says. 'A little help.' She waves her arms until Paris abandons the twelve-year-old bride-models and Mercedes stops superheroing and they stand on either side of her, hauling her upright with one arm each while avoiding her sticky toenails.

'Lesley. Work with me here, please,' I say. 'We are fifteen minutes away from a natural disaster of biblical proportions.'

'Work, did you say? Do you know what my middle name is?'

'Is it Grace? That's mine,' says Mercedes.

'No. It's Catherine, after the patron saint of unmarried women and lacemakers. My parents have a lot to answer for. There's nothing like useless busy-work to keep the unemancipated from plotting revolution.'

'You can be as still as you like at your own house,' I say. 'You can be like a frozen paralysed petrified cadaver if you want.'

'Can I just. I have twins. I work from home. I can't let my husband out of my sight for twenty minutes, apparently.'

'Look,' I say. 'I admit Craig sounds hard to love.'

'You'd think that, wouldn't you?' Lesley says. 'That would make everything so much easier.'

I stand behind her and massage her shoulders. They're amazingly muscular, there's almost no give under my fingers. 'He's your husband. You've made a commitment. You've got to communicate. You can't walk away at the first sign of trouble.'

'You should pitch a show for the comedy festival,' says Alec, who has appeared at the top of the stairs. He has a tea towel over his shoulder and the empty compost bin in his hand and despite that I bet he still smells of the eggs and sugar and syrup of the pancakes.

'Thank you for your contribution,' I say.

'Right.' He stalks across the lounge and flings the tea towel in the sink. 'That's it. I need a moment of your time.'

'Not now. As they say in the classics, winter is coming.'

'Yes now. Outside.' He opens the glass doors to the patio and stands there, foot tapping.

'Auntie Janice is in trouble,' says Mercedes.

'No, no,' I say to her. 'Grown-ups sometimes have private discussions, that's all. Nobody's in trouble.'

'If you say so.' She turns to Paris. 'Better put the TV on like Mummy does. Loud.'

Outside, I close the glass doors firmly behind us. Alec is standing in front of Caroline's white roses with his arms crossed.

'I'm a little pressed for time right now,' I say.

'Tough.' He runs his fingers through his hair, then gives his floppy fringe a sharp tug. 'You are the most impossible person that I've ever met, do you know that?'

'Alec. I'm not disputing the validity of what you're saying. I'm nodding. See me nodding? But we don't have to talk about that now. You could have written that down and texted it to me.'

'Look,' he says. 'I've had a job offer.'

'That's great. I'm glad. You've been there too long, you need a new challenge. Or as new as challenges get, in the history department. A new old challenge. Happy to talk about it later, for as long as you like.'

'It's at MIT.'

'RMIT? Do they have a history department now?'

'No. M for Massachusetts. Massachusetts Institute of Technology.'

And even as I hear it, I know that part of my brain will be colonised by Wherever, Massachusetts, from the day of his arrival onwards. It'll be unavailable to me, that part of my brain. I'll know the season in Massachusetts, and the weather, and the news. Someone here in Melbourne will ask me the time and I'll say *Almost six*, and inside I'll think *and two in the morning, in Massachusetts*. The better to picture Alec, and what he's doing, at any given breath. It will be automatic, autonomic. I will have no say in the matter.

'I need a new start,' he says. 'Too many memories here, everywhere I look.'

'Of course you do. Good call. Excellent decision.'

'So it's fine with you if I move away.'

'Of course it's fine with me.' It's perfectly fine that Alec will be moving to the other side of the world, half a planet away.

'So last night was nothing, was it? You felt nothing, I felt nothing. We just forget that ever happened.'

'Genitals have a mind of their own. Lust has nothing to do with anything.'

He shakes his head. 'You can't possibly believe that.'

I don't, of course. I'm not sure what percentage of our intelligence is actually held in our brains but it's pretty small. My arms have their own intelligence, I know this because for all those months and years when I haven't held our baby, the feeling, the lack of him is mostly in my arms—and deep in my tissues and organs, too, where I should have held him, where he should have begun to live, where his heart should have started beating. And the cells of my skin miss Alec, and my lips do, and my legs miss lying next to his legs, and my fingertips miss the feeling of his hair and his stubble and the hollow at the base of his throat. The human gut does lots of thinking, and why shouldn't it? Brilliant, organised bacteria live there, lots of them, going about their day, making neuro-transmitters that change the way we think and feel. A billion heads are better than one. My body understands how I feel much better than my small, stupid noggin.

All at once, I'm very tired. If you forget about sperm whales and elephants and horses and rhinos—the mega-fauna that grossly distort our narcissistic impression of life—and instead compare us to the other 99.99 per cent of beings we share the planet with, we're monsters. Too big for our own good. It's exhausting, dragging this enormous fleshy human carapace around all day. If I was the size of a colony of *Staphylococcus aureas*, Alec could pick me up and put me in his pocket and I would nestle in there and then Caroline could come and go and Henry and Martha could run away together or not and Lesley and Craig could make up or split apart and none of it would matter.

But there's Mercedes and Paris. They would still matter.

'We're divorced,' I say. 'I don't love you anymore. Go to Massachusetts and marry some Massachusettsian.'

'Great idea. I'll pick one out when I get there. There'll be a woman at the airport. Maybe someone waiting at the luggage belt, or maybe I'll propose to the woman who drives the bus to the hotel. You could write me a reference, former wife to future wife.'

'You're a dork, you know that?'

'Everyone is a dork on the inside,' he says. 'Everyone is hoping no one else notices.'

Before we moved in together, we caught a train to Cairns and slept on wide verandahs with views of the sea. Once we climbed a mountain with packs on our backs and slept under the stars and woke to see a morning like there had never been before, not anywhere on earth. Once, on a very hot night, we caught the tram to St Kilda and sat on the damp sand with our feet in the wavelets and took turns telling each other stories of Nordic people and their cold, cold lives and imagining the ice that settled on their skin and hair until the sun came up over the bay.

'Do you ever feel like you've been waiting your whole life

for something to happen?' I say. 'Something special, I mean. Your moment, whatever that means.'

He breathes out in a rush and leans against the side of the house, he tilts his head back and rests his hands on his thighs. 'I think everybody feels like that.'

'What if it never happens? What if we're all here, getting ready, like our entire life is the night before the first day of school, and we're waiting and waiting and the moment we're preparing for—it never actually comes?'

'All that means is that your moment is still ahead of you, Janice.' He reaches out and takes my arm, he holds me by the wrist and rubs his thumb over the blue veins and the tendon strings. 'That's good.'

'Maybe I'm dreaming,' I say. 'Maybe I'm in one of those strange dreams where you know you have to do something important and you run around like a maniac but somehow you can't manage to do the very important thing you've been trying to do. And then you realise you've got no undies on. And your teeth fall out.'

'What are you trying to do, Janice? What's so important?' he says.

Then I hear a toot. At the top of the hill, I see a car. A taxi. It's coming down the drive.

'That was never twenty minutes,' I say.

Caroline is waving from the window. 'Yoo hoo,' she yells. The taxi stops and she flicks some notes over the front seat. The driver observes them, fluttering idly, then he scoops them up and moves fast to peel himself from his beaded seat and bolts toward the opening boot without bothering to close his door. He hands Alec a plastic shopping bag from the boot, quickly, like it's a transplant organ that really should be in the fridge. The bag is full of clothes. There's a bra strap poking out the top.

'You see?' Caroline opens her own door and hoists herself out, standing with her hands on her hips, while the driver closes the boot and rushes back to his seat. 'You don't listen, that's your problem. You ignore my advice. Your GPS is rubbish. The rise of the machines my arse. Attention idiot computers: good luck exterminating humanity if you can't even comprehend a no-right-turn.'

'You got lucky, don't make a federal case,' the driver says.

'You always have to be right,' she says. 'You and your whole bloody gender.'

'Keep this up and you'll go on the list. I mean it. You'll never get a cab to this address again.'

'My sister's had a stressful few days,' I say.

'Don't you apologise for me,' she says. 'Don't you dare.'

'And hello to you too,' I say.

'I don't have to put up with this,' the driver says. 'I've got three taxis now. I'm only driving today because of my useless brother-in-law's lumbago.' He turns to Alec. 'Fancy word for hangover.' He sits back behind the wheel and slams the door, then he winds down the window and yells, again to Alec, 'Better you than me, mate.' Then he swerves as he reverses up the drive and oversteers to the left, his tyres leaving the cement and running over two of the lavender bushes before he corrects back to the driveway. The lavenders are snapped clean in half. They're goners.

'That's wilful damage.' Caroline yells after the reversing taxi, waving her arms. 'You couldn't drive your way out of a paper bag. I should send you a bill, shrub killer.'

'Yikes,' I say. 'That is a shame.'

As soon as the taxi is out of sight, Caroline shrugs. 'Not really,' she says. 'Henry put those in. I've always hated them. Makes the whole house smells like nanna's undie drawer.'

'Oh. Welcome home,' I say, but she floats right past me.

'Darling Alec,' Caroline says, kissing him on both cheeks. 'I'd completely forgotten you were coming around today. I hope it wasn't awkward for you, with Janice here.'

'Not at all,' says Alec.

'Me neither,' I say. 'In case you were about to ask.'

'I wasn't,' she says. 'I've had an epiphany. You were the dumper, and my sympathies are now entirely with the dumpee.'

'Mummy!' yells Mercedes from behind us, and she and Paris burst from the house and fly into Caroline's arms.

'Hello my babies,' Caroline says. 'Paris, put something on your feet. How many times. Your toes will spread and then you won't be able to wear pretty shoes when you grow up. Mercedes, didn't Auntie Janice put your hair up?'

'Nope, and you know what else? We didn't have any vegetables and that's what gives you scurvy and I think one of my teeth is wobbly and that's what happened to Captain Cook,' says Mercedes. 'See?' She bares her teeth at Caroline like an angry chimpanzee.

'There there,' says Caroline, 'Mummy's here now.'

'You'll never guess who else is here, Mummy. She's just

like Goldilocks and you and Daddy are the bears.'

'Lesley. Lesley's here,' I say. 'She and Craig have had some kind of disagreement.'

'Of course they have.' She kneels down beside Mercedes and Paris and gives them both a long cuddle. 'Their marriage is out of the spotlight for five seconds because of me and Henry. Little Miss Earth Mother has relevance deprivation syndrome.'

'But Mummy, Mummy, someone else is here too. Guess.'

'Mercedes, what are our interrupt words?' says Caroline.

'But it is important,' says Mercedes.

'And?'

'And excuse me, Mummy,' Mercedes says.

'That's my good girl,' says Caroline.

'Excuse me, Mummy,' she says again.

'I think it's more than that,' I say. 'Lesley suspects that Craig is very good friends with someone around here. Special friends. She's very interested in discovering the identity of Craig's special friend.'

Caroline freezes, still kneeling, and looks up at me. 'What?'

'We're all good friends,' says Mercedes. 'Auntie Janice said.'

'Mind you, some of us are better friends than others,' says Alec.

'Well,' says Caroline. She stands slowly, moving her handbag to one shoulder and then the other. 'Does Lesley suspect who Craig's special friend might be?'

I shake my head. 'It's a mystery.'

'Though I'm beginning to form a theory,' says Alec.

The patio door slides open. It's Lesley, standing inside the door, balancing on her heels. 'Welcome home, Caroline,' she says. 'That waxing salon up the road. Does it do Brazilians?'

'What kind of a greeting is that? For a start, A, your pubic hair is of no concern to me, and B, do I look like Mrs Google?'

'Um, Alec,' I say. 'Caroline would love a cup of tea after her trip, wouldn't you Caroline? Maybe while I'm making Caroline a cup of tea, you could move the bag that's in her bedroom?'

'Your bag's in Paris's room,' says Mercedes. 'I saw it. It's green.'

'No,' I say. 'The other bag. The new one. It needs to go out.'

'Sure,' he says. 'The bag. No problem.'

'I'll help,' says Lesley.

Alec and Lesley both disappear inside. Caroline turns to follow them.

'Um, just a moment,' I say. 'Wait a sec.'

Caroline rubs the back of her neck with one hand. 'I hardly slept last night. I'm wearing yesterday's clothes. I want to take a shower, and change, and have a cup of tea and a nice lie down on my own bed.'

'Sure, of course. It'll only take a second.'

She sighs. 'What?'

Alec and Lesley are inside now. I watch them through the kitchen windows as they head down the hall toward Caroline's bedroom, and they look efficient and mature. They are resourceful people and they will get Martha down the stairs and out the back and everything will be fine. I only have to keep Caroline occupied for just a little longer. I take her by the arm and steer her away from the girls to the edge of the driveway, and point her away from the house, towards Lesley and Craig's.

'For heaven's sake, what is it? I've been travelling, I need a cup of tea,' she says. Then she stops and says, 'Oh, I am so not in the mood for that.'

Craig is right in front of us, marching through the hedge. His arms are swinging and he's marching like a sergeant-major on parade.

'Where is she?' Craig says. 'This is bloody ridiculous.'

'Hello, Caroline,' says Caroline. 'How are you, Caroline? How was your mercy mission across state lines to rescue Henry? You're an angel, the way you've opened your heart and magnanimously, for the sake of the children and beyond any reasonable expectation, taken him back.'

'You're forgiving him?' he says.

She blinks. 'Do I look like Nelson Mandela?'

She's joking, of course. She'll take Henry back. We had the same childhood. There's no way she'll put her children through that.

'Of course you will,' says Craig, reading my mind. 'How do people sleep on their own? Where do you put your arms? When you're the back spoon, at least the front spoon takes some of your weight. Plus, there's more of a depression in the mattress to make space for your underneath arm. Last night I had an hour, two at the most.'

'I would have thought you could sleep anywhere,' says Caroline. 'You, of all people.'

'I woke up with pins and needles right down to my fingers. I thought I had a stroke in my sleep. This arm's still fuzzy, even now. Colder than the other one. Could be permanent nerve damage. Here's a business idea: mattresses with arm-shaped holes in them so single people can sleep on their side.'

'Just sleep on your back, for heaven's sake,' says Caroline. 'It's not rocket surgery.'

He snorts. 'Tried that. Two till four-thirty, flat as a flounder. You know what I thought? This is exactly how I'm going to look in my coffin, that's what I thought. Staring straight up at the cream satin, smelling the gardenias, listening to the string quartet and the women, sobbing and wailing.'

'Oh, pet,' says Caroline. 'You won't be staring, for a start. The mortician glues your eyes closed.'

'We had a quiet night after you left,' I say. 'Quiet quiet quiet. Nothing happened.'

'Then I started to think: maybe it won't be cream satin, maybe it'll be baby-blue taffeta over black teak. Before I knew it, I'd planned my whole funeral. Music, newspaper notices, video tribute, press release. Message for the skywriter. And the eulogy: will my brother be out on parole by then, or do I need someone with a higher profile? It's not pretty. I mean, the ceremony will be, obviously. The whole idea of being dead, it's a real downer.'

'The ones that open at the top are called caskets,' says Caroline. 'And you probably won't have one of those. Polyester stapled onto chipboard, probably. Couple of verses of Psalm 23 and straight into the fire.'

'It'll be a stroke, odds on,' says Craig. 'And quick, hopefully. Otherwise you got months, years ahead of you. Nappies, bedsores. Blink once for yes, twice for no. Stroke is what gets all us Coxes in the end.'

'Your surname is Cox?' I say.

He nods. 'Why?'

'No reason.'

'My future in the hands of minimum-wage carers who spend all shift playing Candy Crush and hitting on my grieving almost-widow.'

'Aunt Janice slept with Paris in her bed,' says Mercedes. 'Guess why. Guess who was in Mummy's bed?'

'Where's Lesley?' Craig says. 'She needs to come home now.'

'You'll never guess who,' says Mercedes, 'not in a million years.'

'Lesley's inside,' I say, 'but she's right in the middle of something. Give her a second.'

'Sleeping by yourself is like being eight years old,' he says. 'Alone and cold, listening to your parents fighting in the next room. My asthma, god, it used to play up. If I go get Mum while they're fighting, will I cop it? If I don't, will I run out of air and cark it?'

He scratches his face; slowly at first, then faster and faster until I grab his arm.

'Lesley's inside. Just give her a minute.'

But he's already walking toward the house. 'Lesley,' he

sings out. 'Come home, darling, I'm begging you. It'll never happen again. I mean it this time.'

'Craig, wait,' I call after him. 'Don't go in there.'

'Well? What did you want?' Caroline catches hold of my wrist.

Nothing, I tell her, and I shake free and rush after Craig with Caroline on my heels and the girls trailing behind her. Craig's inside the house now, he's in the lounge, he's nearly in the hall. It's dark down that long hall because all the bedroom doors are closed. It's a long, dark, gloomy hall of despair. Craig stops dead, halfway along.

'Well, well, well,' he says. 'This is cosy.'

I hear Lesley's voice before I see her. 'What are you doing here?' she says to Craig.

'I came to get you, in a spontaneous romantic gesture,' Craig says. 'I didn't realise I'd be interrupting something.'

'You're not, mate,' says Alec.

'Auntie Janice slept with Paris, did she,' says Craig 'I wonder why. I wonder who was sleeping in Caroline's bed.'

'If no one's going to make me a tea after my taxi ride from hell, I'm making my own,' says Caroline. She starts rustling things in the kitchen.

'Look who I found coming out of your bedroom, Caroline.' Craig is shepherding Alec and Lesley down the hall to the lounge, a collie with his straggling sheep. 'Standing in the dark, arms around each other. Whispering secrets.' He crosses his arms. 'You two seem very comfortable together. Very, very at ease.'

'Look, Craig,' says Alec.

'I'm not a dill, you know. No one's ever accused me of being a dill,' says Craig.

'You should cultivate a wider circle of acquaintances,' calls Caroline, from the kitchen bench. 'Tea? Anyone?'

'Seriously,' Lesley says. 'You want to have this conversation with me? You?'

'Lesley was helping me fix something,' says Alec. 'Something unresolved that really should be seen to. That's all.'

Craig squints at him. 'Really?'

'Scout's honour, mate,' says Alec.

'Course, mate, of course, I didn't really think,' says Craig. 'Ha ha. Can't you take a joke? I don't for a minute believe that my Lesley'd get up to anything.'

Lesley stops dead in the hall, at the entrance to the lounge. 'Not for a minute, heh?'

Oh Lord. There's a mad look in her eye, halfway between a matador twirling her red cloak and a bungee jumper on the parapet. I have a sick feeling.

'Of course, sweetheart.' Craig chuckles. 'The very thought.'

Lesley plants her legs akimbo and her hands on her hips and tosses her hair. 'Think again. I confess. Me and Alec,' she says, 'we've been at it for months. You haven't even noticed.'

'What?' says Craig.

'You heard. Me. Alec. At it like teenagers.'

'You're joking, right?' says Craig.

'Is it so hard to believe that someone wants to make passionate love to me? Is that what you're saying?'

'No. Yes,' says Craig. 'You?'

'I felt bad about it at first,' she says. 'For the first, oh, four minutes. Then I felt really, really good. I mean, sensational.'

Craig begins to giggle in an unhinged way, like someone has tightened the screws in his temples, which are connected to the sinews on his neck, which are standing out like wire under the skin. 'How long, can you tell me that? You and him. How long have you been doing it?'

'Forget the tea. Bloody mary, anyone?' Caroline opens the fridge and as she swings the doors, I see Mercedes' and Paris's artwork of crayon suns and flowers suspended by magnets, iconographs for happy families.

'I'll have a double,' I say.

'I tried to tell you,' Lesley says. 'I just couldn't find the right words.'

'How about these words: I'm literally cutting off your metaphorical manhood with some random historian. That would have made things very clear,' says Craig.

'Did you use all the celery?' says Caroline, with her head in the fridge.

'No,' I say.

'Years and years, we've been at it,' says Lesley. 'I was driven to it, married to you.'

'Ah, just one minute,' says Alec.

'Sugar?' Lesley rests her index finger across Alec's lips. 'I'll handle this.'

'Sugar?' says Craig. 'You call me "Sugar".'

'Let's see,' says Lesley. 'We first met here, at Caroline and Henry's. At a barbecue. Henry's birthday, was it? Or a New Year's Eve? We couldn't help ourselves. We erupted, like embers left over from a campfire that everyone thought was out but wasn't really out and when you kneel down and blow on them, maybe drop some dry leaves or some tissues on the little glowing bits, they burst into wild, uncontrollable flames that only had eyes for each other. Right then and there, in the bathroom. One foot on the soap dispenser and the other on the towel rack.'

'Well it's not here,' says Caroline. 'I had half a bunch. Organic, from the farmer's market.'

'Why would I take your celery?' I say. 'You've been gone for less than a day. No one could go through half a bunch of celery in a day. Celery is not chocolate.'

'It's logistically impossible,' says Craig. 'There's not enough hours in the day.'

'How would you know?' says Lesley. 'You never come down to my studio. There's plenty of space, right there among the clay. And it's right near the Cronins' back fence, for convenient access. Plus, I drive around a lot: suppliers, galleries. Lots of time built into the schedule for detours. If my GPS could talk.'

'My life is a lie,' says Craig. 'The love of my life. My queen. My every breath.'

'Well it didn't grow wings, did it? It didn't wake up this morning and feel neglected, lying in the crisper, and just wander off of its own accord. It wasn't affronted by lying next to the conventionally farmed broccoli. We haven't, presumably, been burgled by a gang of starving biodynamic rabbits.' She plonks the tomato juice down on the bench statement-style, then she wrenches the freezer door open and retrieves the vodka, icy and glistening. 'Always getting into things that don't belong to you, aren't you, cactus legs?'

'I am rubber, you are glue,' I say.

'My makeup, my clothes. I know what happened to my black lipstick, don't think I don't,' says Caroline. 'For the last time, keep out of my stuff.'

'First, Petty Hetty, the statute of limitations on your black lipstick has well and truly expired, and second…Hold it,' I say. 'Mercedes, Paris.'

There is no answer.

I look around. For a while I can't see them, then I notice a small foot poking out from the back of the couch.

'Come on,' I say. 'We need to talk about grown-up stuff.'

'Wait,' Mercedes says. 'There's something I have to tell you first.'

'What?' says Caroline.

'It's very important,' says Mercedes.

'Then what is it?'

'Just a minute.'

'You're stalling,' Caroline says. 'Downstairs. Now, please. Both of you.'

'Up, down, up, down. You people are driving me crazy,' says Mercedes.

'I beg your pardon. What did you say to Mummy?' says Caroline.

'We're not allowed to climb in the bathroom so why is Lesley allowed?' Mercedes says. 'We're not even allowed to reach the bath stuff on the top shelf because that belongs to Mummy and Daddy says climbing is too dangerous.'

'That's a good question,' Caroline says. 'I'll answer it later, when you come back upstairs for ice-cream.'

'Plus, how are we ever supposed to learn how to be a grown-up if we have to go downstairs every time things get interesting? Plus, when's Daddy coming home?'

'It's because we trust you to amuse yourselves down there,' says Caroline. 'If you were just babies, you'd need someone looking after you.'

'It's not fair,' Mercedes says. 'It'll be forever until I get to do adultery.'

We all stop and look at her.

'You know,' says Mercedes. 'Adult stuff. It'll be years.'

'Never fear,' says Caroline. 'You'll be a grown-up before you know it. Now, downstairs please.'

Paris crosses her arms and Mercedes stamps her foot and points her finger right around the room, pausing at each of us in turn, staring us dead in the eyes. It's creepy, like she's a kid in a Stephen King novel. Any minute now furniture will be flying everywhere and drawers will be opening and closing.

'We'll go,' she says. 'But you all just wait. When you're all old and you're all in wheelchairs and you haven't even got proper teeth and I'm the boss of everyone, just you wait.'

She's right, of course. She'll be the one choosing Caroline's nursing home and probably mine as well, seeing as she'll be my closest living relative who's still compos mentis by then. Caroline and Henry and me, we'll be sitting by the windows in our publicly listed nursing home (*Shrivelled Lakes: mostly adequate care for the inadequately superannuated*), looking out at the sun on the concrete outside, struggling to remember what it felt like on our skin, and scratching ourselves for entertainment. Watching for Mercedes' car, hour after hour, day after day, praying that she'll bring her kids for a visit and smuggle a bag of mini salted-caramel scrolls and a bottle of average whisky past the nurse's aide, asleep at the front desk.

When all this is over, I'll make it up to her. In the meantime, she takes Paris's hand and they head off down the stairs, slamming the door behind them. We all stop until they're gone from our sight: a frozen tableau in a strange drama-school exercise.

'Oh Alec,' says Caroline, reanimating when they're out of sight. 'I'm very surprised.'

'Form an orderly queue,' says Alec.

'Lesley, on the other hand,' Caroline goes on. 'I saw that coming a mile off.'

Craig buries his face in his hands.

'Multiple times a day, seven days a week, every position you can think of. Upside down, right-side up, bent over, bent under, clothes on, clothes off,' she says. 'I can't get enough. Once I sucked him off as we were going through the McDonald's drive through. And then I had a Quarter Pounder and a large chips.'

'Oh Lesley,' says Craig. 'All those trans fats.'

'That sounds terribly unhygienic,' says Caroline. 'I hope you waved your card at the electronic whatsit and didn't hand the poor girl cash.' There's a clink of ice cubes. She half-fills five glasses with tomato juice and tops them up with vodka. She shakes the little bottle of tabasco with a jaunty flourish.

'You nearly caught us, once.' Lesley pokes Craig in the

chest with her index finger. 'I had to hide him in the shower behind my wet naked body. Once I dressed up in a nurses uniform—white stockings, suspenders—and strapped him to the bed frame. Your bed frame. I tied him down by his wrists using your belt from your jeans. I rode him like a rented mule.'

'My belt?' says Craig. 'This one? The one that's holding my pants up right now? I have to sit down.'

'So do I,' says Alec. He sits heavily in Henry's chair.

'Give it to me now. Smash me against every wall of the house.' Lesley swings her leg over Alec's lap and sits astride him, crotch to crotch, and grabs his lapels in her fists. Her tweed skirt is stretched over her thighs, inching up her legs. It doesn't look so sensible now. The fabric is thinning and worn near the side zip, so tight it could give at any minute. She plants both hands on the back of the chair, on either side of his head.

'Lesley,' says Alec, 'I'm very flattered.'

'I want you inside me,' she says to him.

'I'm going to punch your lights out,' says Craig.

'No you are not,' says Lesley. 'You're not touching a hair on his beautiful head.'

'You call that beautiful?' says Craig. 'Seriously.'

'Feel these arms,' Lesley says, squeezing Alec. 'Go on. These biceps are gorgeous, and the top bits, near the shoulders. What are they called? And the chest. It's lovely.'

'I've got those,' Craig says, flexing everything at once. 'I've got the exact same bits, but better. Look, see? Besides, his body might be OK but he's got a face like a walnut.'

Alec's mouth is open and his head is turning first to Lesley, then to Craig, and that means I can look at him now, as much as I want. And I do look. At Alec, sitting there with his walnut face and Lesley on his lap with her hands on him, and the non-scary but still ostensibly threatening threats of Craig directed at him. His own hands are in constant motion: now almost touching Lesley's thighs, now flat on the seat of the chair, and he is bewildered and beatific and so pretty, prettier than a hundred roses or a thousand stars, and it strikes me there is no one like him and there never will be. Not now, not if I live to be a hundred.

'Right, let's everyone calm down,' I say.

'Our grandmother went quite barking toward the end, you know.' Caroline stirs the bloody marys with an index finger, then sucks it clean. 'Kept humming "Jesus Wants Me for a Sunbeam" and never left home without a potato in her pocket.'

'I'd forgotten all about that,' I say. 'The potato business.'

'She kept her favourite one in a bowl near the door, so she could slip it in her pocket on the way out, when she picked up her keys and handbag, remember? It came in handy, she said. She pressed walk signs and lift buttons with it, if she was in the city. Mostly I think she just liked the feel of it.'

'There's something soothing about a spud, if you get a nice one,' says Lesley, from her perch astride Alec, fingers entwined in the front of his shirt. 'It's firm without being hard. The shape of it, like a nice stone, the kind me and Clinton used to skip across Eildon as kids. A good potato has got a bit of heft.'

'But why a potato, do you think?' says Caroline. 'Why not an onion?'

'All those little flakes of papery skin everywhere,' Lesley says. 'You'd be forever turning your pockets inside out. Drive me mad.'

'I don't think she did it for the way they felt,' I say. 'Anxiety, we'd call it now. Nanna liked to be prepared in case a famine hit while she was on her way to the TAB to put on her quinella.'

'They give me hives,' says Lesley. 'The peeling, not the eating. Could eat them for breakfast, lunch and dinner. Those little Swedish pancakes, the ones with the sour cream. What are they called?'

'Potatoes, potatoes, who cares about potatoes?' says Craig. 'I've been played like a cheap accordion. I've been a prawn.'

'You mean a pawn,' says Lesley. 'Though you have also been a prawn.'

'Oh for heaven's sake,' Caroline hands the celery-free bloody marys around and we grasp them like lifebuoys. 'She's making it up. She's a fantasist, anyone can see that. Her and her dead people's clothes.'

'I only allow natural fibres near my skin. Feel the material, go on. They don't make them like that anymore. They're vintage.' Lesley picks up Alec's hand and rubs it up and down her blouse.

'They're creepy, that's what they are. I bet your drycleaners have a sweep, guessing which bodily fluids are responsible for which stain. They're an olfactory wonderland, your clothes. You can see the worn patch at the front where the paramedic was banging on some poor old girl's chest.' Caroline layers one hand on top of the other to perform CPR on the kitchen bench.

'A fantasist, am I?' says Lesley. She takes a huge swig of her bloody mary, slams it on the coffee table, then takes hold of Alec's collar and she holds him steady and she kisses him. Full on, on the lips. She's still at first, she's determined but somehow tentative and we all just stand there and stare. They're kissing and the room melts around me, Dali-style, walls and chairs and windows dripping like watches.

'Well,' says Caroline. 'That escalated quickly.'

'I need to sit down,' I say.

Lesley breaks it off with a final smooch and looks at Alec with a smile that could melt the poles. She's a twelve-year-old who's caught Santa delivering a Malvern Star with pink handlebar ribbons on Christmas morning. She gives him a quick peck on the forehead. Her glasses are fogged up and crooked across the bridge of her nose. Alec, on the other hand, looks vaguely concussed, as though someone has smacked him across the head with a tuna.

'Right,' I say, in a voice that sounds close enough to mine. 'Enough. You've made your point.'

'What?' Lesley says, to Craig's gaping stare. 'It's called sex appeal. Look it up.'

'Get off him,' I hear myself say. 'Right now.'

'What's it to you?' Lesley says to me. 'You had your chance, you blew it.'

'You,' says Craig, to Lesley. 'You. You. I've never seen you kiss someone else before.' He runs his hands through his hair. 'That was incredibly hot.'

'It's taken you this long to realise?' Lesley tosses her head like she's in a shampoo commercial, then she dismounts Alec and wiggles her skirt down. 'You really are a prawn.'

Alec drains his bloody mary in one gigantic swallow and holds the glass up to his eye to check if any drops remain, then he jiggles it to decide if he could squeeze more out of the ice cubes if he poured them into his fist. I take the empty glass from his hand and replace it with mine, which he also drains.

'Hit me,' he says, handing me back the glass. I start for the kitchen to make him another.

'I don't think he was referring to the drink.' Lesley winks at Alec. 'Plenty more where that came from, lover.'

All at once, we hear a noise from the front door. It's wide open. 'What are you all doing here? Where's Martha? And what the bloody hell happened to my lavender?'

Standing in the doorway, with an overnight bag at his feet, is Henry.

Right about now, I'd like to go hiking somewhere far, far away. Somewhere inaccessible by road. Maybe I'd camp. I'd be the kind of person who knows how: competent, good in a crisis, someone who could save marriages instead of watching them crumble around her. How do you reserve a campsite, actually? How do you find them, book them, pay the deposit? Identify which patch of ground is yours so two people don't attempt to camp in the same spot and get tent rage and stab each other to death with tent pegs. I'd have to buy a tent first, I suppose. A single-woman tent. The camping-store woman could teach me to put it up and I could practise in my bedroom. Can you put up a tent in a bedroom? Maybe I need a real tent and also a practice tent without pegs, with velcro instead to make it easier on the carpet. I could buy water from the supermarket, and tins of tuna, and live in my new tent, in the wild, and I would never again, for the remaining years of my life, have even the smallest thought about any part of the entire continent of North America that wide ocean away. I'd purify water from a stream. I'd buy chocolate and Russian novels: not a lot of jokes but heaps of alcoholism and existential angst, which would come in handy. I'd miss my bacteria, of course. Maybe I could culture roo poo or something. The first definitive study of the microflora in marsupial excreta. Maybe I'd become famous, the Rebecca Lancefield of poo. Maybe there'd be a town nearby and I could drive in every Sunday and have a coffee and a salted-caramel scroll. Yes. Coffee once a week, sure. That's doable. People manage that, people who live in places where they don't drink much coffee or where they still think that instant coffee really is coffee instead of whatever it actually is. The coffee would have to be takeaway because I'm not showering or washing my clothes at the campsite so I'd smell, probably. A bit. I'd be brushing my teeth, though; think Thoreau, not Ted Kaczynski. Maybe I could ring and order the coffee and a salted-caramel scroll and charge it to my credit card and have them leave it outside the cafe door. I could get a job as the town eccentric. *Here comes crazy Janice Brankovic*, everyone would mutter out of the corner of their mouth. *They say she was a normal, functioning member of society once, before her family drove her loony. Just put the coffee and the scroll down and get back in the car. Keep your extremities within the vehicle at all times.*

'Earth to Janice,' says Caroline. Her face is about six inches straight in front of mine, and she's frowning. 'Honestly, my whole life, she's been like this. It's a miracle she successfully found her way down our mother's birth canal. Vague as.'

'But how do I recharge my phone, to order the scroll? A

solar phone charger? Is there such a thing?' I say.

'Scroll?' says Henry. 'Who's she calling, Papyrus R Us?'

'We think we're the ones researching bacteria but what if it's the other way around? What if they're looking up at us? They're probably laughing their slime layer off at our big stupid bodies, our ridiculous clothes. If we had a half-decent peptidoglycan cell wall we wouldn't need clothes at all.'

'She's having a turn,' says Lesley.

'We think we're top of some anthropocentric evolutionary tree of our own invention. We can't even bud off identical daughter cells using simple asexual plasmid replication. We're pathetic.'

'Did she say "asexual reproduction?"' says Lesley.

'Where's the fun in that?' says Craig.

'We think we're so smart,' I say to them. 'We're not.'

'That's becoming increasingly clear,' says Henry.

'We should be more like bacteria. Co-operative, non-competitive, just happy doing our thing.'

'Janice, are you okay?' Alec says. 'Squeeze my hand if you can hear me.'

'Alec. Darling Alec,' I say.

'Throw water in her face. Slap her. Here, let me, it's no trouble.' Lesley raises her hand and lets fly.

'What?' Alec deftly catches Lesley's arm before I can even flinch. 'What did you call me?'

'You're all still here.' I blink. 'Terrific.'

'I live here,' Henry says, and when everyone turns to look at him, 'or I did, until recently. My name is still on the mortgage anyway.'

I'm slumped in the recliner, surrounded by a sea of faces staring at me. Henry is crumpled and tired, his shirt is untucked and he hasn't shaved. There's a weariness about him: he looks like a fugitive from justice who's joined the French Foreign Legion and ended up lost in the desert, leagues from home with an empty canteen, wearing a pillbox hat with a skirt at the neck, at the mercy of some sadistic French officer.

'Why must you always be the centre of attention? It's not all about you, Janice,' says Caroline.

'Oui, mon capitaine,' I say.

The recliner is like something you'd imagine at a retirement home. It's squishy and incredibly comfortable, like a marshmallow chair. I inch my way to the edge and struggle to vertical.

'Potatoes in her pockets—any day now,' Caroline says. 'Wake up, Janice. Henry said hello to you.'

'Thanks for staying with the girls Janice, but this isn't a social call. Where is Martha, Caroline? What have you done with her?' he says.

'Trouble in paradise, Romeo?' Caroline whips a tea towel over her shoulder. 'Woken up to herself, has she? Don't blame me if your bit of fluff has done a runner.'

'Fluff? She's got her masters in early childhood education,' says Henry.

'Maybe she's the right person for you after all,' says Caroline.

'Who wants another drink?' says Alec. 'I do. A big one.'

'Look, she messaged me last night that she was coming

here,' says Henry. 'She was on her way. She was upset, after that big scene of yours at the hotel. Vulnerable. I've been calling and calling. Her phone is off.'

'You think I'm hiding her?' says Caroline. 'Perhaps you'd like to search your children's rooms, or under my bed? Janice has been here the whole time. She is utterly loyal, so believe me when I tell you: that woman isn't here.'

'Is that true, Janice?' says Henry. 'You've been here the whole time?'

'And I feel a bit stir-crazy,' says me, the defender of Caroline's interests. 'I know, let's go over to Craig and Lesley's. You've still got that pool table, right? We could relax, play some pool, have a few laughs, everyone would calm down.'

'Regulation size, World Eightball Federation rules. Two penalty visits for potting the cue ball, for potting an opponent's ball or for failing to make initial contact with one of your sequence of balls. All IOUs settled at the end of the night,' says Craig.

'Or are you accusing me of something more nefarious? Maybe I've chopped her up and put her in the freezer. Maybe she's fertilising your lavender as we speak.' Caroline executes a few karate chops in Henry's direction and follows up with one rubbish kick that almost unbalances her into the pantry. Henry doesn't move.

'Marriage has ups and downs. You can work this out,' I say.

'Cash only. No credit facilities,' says Craig.

'No offence mate, but are you here for a reason?' Henry says to Craig.

'Ask him, your former brother-in-law,' says Craig. 'I'm here to claim what's mine.'

'Leave Alec out of this. I can make up my own mind, thanks very much,' says Lesley. 'It's not just sex with us. Not just incredibly fulfilling, athletic sex, not just the exhilaration of bracing myself against the headboard while he goes down on me and I shudder with orgasm after orgasm and then later, after he makes me dinner and does the dishes, watching *The Notebook*. Together.'

Caroline stares at her. 'I don't know you anymore,' she says.

'Baby.' Craig drops to his knees and takes hold of the edge of Lesley's skirt. 'Take a look at him. Surely you can see he's not to be trusted.'

'Him' being Alec, and I admit he doesn't look very trustworthy right now. From his facial expression, an alien foetus might be about to erupt from his chest.

'Do you need a glass of water?' I say to him.

'Fucking hell,' says Henry. 'I thought I had problems.'

'Alec respects me,' Lesley says, freeing her skirt from Craig's fingers.

'This is all one big misunderstanding,' Alec manages, as I ease him to the couch.

'Maybe Martha's had an accident,' says Henry. 'Maybe her car's run off the road. She's unconscious, trapped, lying in a ditch somewhere.'

'Unlikely,' says Caroline. 'Unless my luck's done a complete one-eighty.'

'Martha's probably with another lover.' Craig looks at Lesley with puppy eyes. 'She's probably got her skirt pulled up to her hips right now. She's got one foot on a soap dish, moaning, knickers around her ankles, hard up against the wall with some prune-faced stranger.'

'Surely you two can put your differences behind you, for the sake of the girls? Caroline? Henry? I know you can,' I say.

'Don't pay any attention to him.' Lesley sits beside Alec and cups his chin in her hand. 'He's jealous. I love your face.'

'He's talking about my face?' says Alec. 'Me? Is he saying I have wrinkles?'

Henry shakes his head. 'You don't know her. None of you know her.'

'All your devotion, all your adoration. Your years of faith-fulness, by and large, all of it tossed in the bin. Your feelings, ground underneath her pointy black patent leather thigh-high stiletto boots,' says Craig. 'All the years of marriage counsel-ling you put up with, all that pointless talking about your feelings, blah blah blah.'

'Moisturiser with a built-in SPF30,' says Caroline. 'Two minutes in the morning, after your shower.'

'Will that help?' says Alec.

'Of course not,' says Caroline cheerfully. 'But you'll feel less futile in general.'

'Martha doesn't have thigh-high stiletto boots,' Henry says. 'She's not the type.'

'Wake up, mate. All women are the type,' says Craig.

'And maybe an eye cream, for your bags,' says Caroline.

'Bags?' says Alec. 'What bags?'

'The heavy ones are no good,' says Caroline. 'That's a rookie mistake. You think heavier means richer means more moisture but all it does is weigh down your eyelids and stretch the skin and make them even droopier and believe me, that's the last thing you need. I'd keep Botox up my sleeve for now. Do you exfoliate?'

'Exfoliate what?' says Alec. 'Wait. Botox?'

'Don't look so surprised. Lots of men use Botox,' says Caroline.

'You certainly don't look surprised,' says Lesley to Caroline. 'Ever.'

'They reckon *we* think with our genitals? They're the ones who think with their genitals. They just have higher standards than us,' says Craig.

'They don't sound very practical,' says Lesley. 'If they're thigh-high, how do you walk in them? How does your knee bend? Do they have, like, a gusset at the back? You wouldn't want to run for the train. Unless the whole point is knee support, like a brace. In which case, sure.'

'There's no way she's with another man,' says Henry. 'Not Martha. We have something very special.'

'I haven't been able to walk in heels since I was twenty-two. I have huge bunions. I mean huge. See?' Lesley rests one hand on Alec's shoulder and balances her heel up on the recliner.

I don't know how I missed them earlier when she was showing off her toenails, but she certainly does have bunions. Huge is an understatement. It's as if the head of a conjoined twin is growing out of her foot.

'You can hardly notice them,' I say.

'Thigh-high boots are practically orthopaedic, now that

you mention it,' says Craig. 'I could get you a pair. Online overnight delivery, wrapped in discreet brown paper, completely unidentifiable. No one will know. The neighbours'll think they're sex toys. You're a nine, right? I could get a few other things, if we're paying for delivery anyway. Might as well. You're not allergic to latex, right?'

'Do they come in a sneaker?' says Lesley, then, to me, 'I also need serious arch support.'

'Martha's not like that at all,' says Henry. 'She's vulnerable. Uncomplicated. She needs me.'

'You know who else is vulnerable, uncomplicated and needs you?' I say to Henry. 'Your daughters. Why don't you go downstairs and say hello to them? They've missed you. Caroline, why don't you go downstairs with Henry? Spend some quality bonding time with your children. Together, as a family.'

'Not if he grovels on his hands and knees,' says Caroline.

'Not going to happen,' says Henry.

'Henry, if you and Caroline go downstairs for a little while, I bet Martha will show up any minute. Then you can seriously discuss your priorities, your responsibilities,' I say.

'She'd better not show up,' says Caroline. 'Not if she knows what's good for her.'

'You're under the thumb, mate. Martha's got the whip hand,' says Craig, 'and by that I mean: she has a leather whip in the palm of her hand, ready to flay you. Leaving you, Henry, on the bottom. Bound, naked, defenceless, under her power. Begging for release.'

'I was expecting something more exciting than this,' says

Lesley. 'I don't want to be ordinary any longer. I want to shock people. I want hardcore.'

'I hear you,' says Craig. 'I can change. I'm open to anything. Give me a chance.'

'It's still too pale. It's bloodless. If I'm going to take the trouble to spice it up after all these years of dead-boring vanilla, I want more,' Lesley sits on the recliner and swings her feet up to the horizontal, wriggling her toes. She reaches towards the bottle of nail polish. 'I want full-on crimson. The colour of sex and death. I need another coat.'

'Allow me,' says Craig.

The bottle is on the coffee table; Lesley points to it with her extended foot and Craig snatches it up and shakes it back and forth, back and forth, vigorously, rhythmically, repetitively, in his right hand, with a practised kind of action. Then he drops to his knees in front of her and cradles her foot as though it's a sacred object, laying the flat of her sole on the meat of his thigh. He could be fitting her for a glass slipper.

'I've never seen your toes look like that before.' He bends his head low to inspect them, and he sweeps the tops of her feet with the back of his fingers. 'That colour. So hard. So shiny. They're magnificent, like tiny red nubs of ecstasy.' He looks up at her and swallows, then he unscrews the handle and wipes the excess polish from the brush on the inside neck of the bottle.

'Just watch it,' Lesley says. 'Go outside the lines and you'll wish you'd never been born.'

'Yes, ma'am,' says Craig. He sticks his tongue between his teeth and begins slow, controlled strokes. When he finishes the big toe, he purses his lips and blows on the nail.

'Is that mine?' Caroline comes closer to peer at the bottle of polish. 'I turn my back for five minutes. First the celery. I have a house full of kleptomaniacs.'

'Controlling, much?' Lesley pulls the handle on the side of the recliner so the mechanism shifts back. She stretches, interlocks her fingers behind her neck and rests her other foot on Craig's shoulder. 'Look where that's got you.'

Caroline does her best to laugh. 'You must be joking. I'm not controlling. Tell her Janice.'

'Maybe a bit,' I say.

'None of you know me at all,' Caroline says. 'I'm easy-going. Relaxed, actually. Or I would be, if everyone else would just get in line.'

'I'm calling the hospitals,' says Henry. 'Where's my phone? Caroline?'

'Because I am the keeper of all your possessions,' she says.

Henry searches his pockets for his phone, then unzips his overnight bag and rifles through it, throwing clothes every-where and all at once I see it, plain in the desperation in his face. Henry is in love. The microscopic twitch of his eye, the teeth pressed to the inside of his lip, the concentration, the sharp overblown despair. I've know Henry's face for years and it's changed, the result of the use of particular muscles and the disuse of others. Months of a new kind of smile and saying someone's name out loud, over and over, when no one else can hear. The very architecture of his features has changed. His hands are searching for the phone, driven by something more than logic and there's a shadow beside him as though his whole body knows that Martha's not where she belongs, which is next to him.

'You're a different man,' I say.

'If anything's happened to her.' He upends his bag and shakes it above his head. Boxer shorts, a roll-on deodorant and a packet of mints fall to the floor.

His actual brain has changed. When he thinks of her, a vesicle opens somewhere deep in his amygdala, then another, then another. A neurotransmitter, one among many in a holding pattern in the synaptic cleft, rubs itself suggestively against the mouth of a receptor and wham! With only the barest whisper of foreplay, it dives deep inside. This is the origin of everything, this carnal penetration on a molecular level. Hormones surge. Blood flow changes direction, unaccustomed capillaries swell and throb. This kind of cellular transformation is rare. It happens only a handful of times during the course of even the most fortunate of lives. It is a rollercoaster ride for adults, like being high without the drugs. Right now, Henry is in agony. He's defenceless.

'It's microscopic,' I say. 'Everything about love is bacterial.'

Glances are bacteria, and twitches and itches and the way your eyebrow rises and your nostrils flair and the words you use when you speak only to your beloved, they are like bacteria too. Love colonises your whole body. The symptoms of love are caused by your autonomic nervous system doing its finest work, responding to the infection. Love is not something you think about, not something you can reason yourself into or out of. Do you breathe with your conscious mind? Do you decide to send enzymes from your liver, or knowingly control the heart valves as they open and close? Then why would anyone assume that reason can manage something as important as love?

'What the hell is she talking about now?' says Caroline.

'Don't worry about Martha,' I say to Henry. 'She's fine. There's something I have to tell you.'

'What?' he says.

'Wait,' Caroline says. 'Can you hear that?'

Caroline's bedroom door opens, then slams shut. The noise is strangely loud and sharp. We turn our heads in the direction of the hall, we freeze and we wait. Time expands just like Einstein said it would. There are footsteps, a rustling sound. For an instant, a shadow creeps along the hallway wall, then Martha appears like a model down a catwalk. Her earbuds are hanging loose around her neck and her phone is in her hand. Her hair is tousled, her feet are bare. She's wearing Caroline's quilted mauve dressing gown, holding it closed with one hand between her breasts; she's thinner than Caroline so it's slipped off one shoulder to reveal a silken raspberry bra strap and below that on her upper arm, a blue and green tattoo of a swallow. It seems like there's a light behind her, only there isn't. If she stood in a clam shell and let the dressing gown drop, she'd look like *The Birth of Venus*.

'You're here,' says Henry. 'You're safe. I've been so worried.'

'She's here,' says Caroline. 'Janice, she's here. What is she doing here?'

'Trying to have a nap, but you people don't make it easy.' Martha has that warm, sleepy aura that young people have, and she looks much younger than the rest of us and she is. In our defence, though, we all look older than we did on Friday afternoon. She yawns. 'I'm dead. Any chance you could keep it down?'

Alec buries his face in his hands. Henry grins, Cheshiresque, and as I watch, he exhales and his shoulders drop and the tension seems to scatter from the tips of his fingers. Caroline has turned into one of those laughing clowns from sideshow alley: blank eyes, wide lips, head turning from side to side while she waits for someone to pop a ping-pong ball in her mouth. Lesley sits forward in the recliner like she's about to reach for popcorn and as she does, Craig turns so abruptly that the brush slips. He paints a wide red streak of polish over the top of Lesley's foot.

'Oops.' He looks up at Lesley. 'I've been a very naughty boy.'

Caroline's face turns puce. As I watch, the skin at her temples becomes first grainy then scaly, then horns begin to form. Her eyebrows thicken and stand on end, her fingers arch and hook themselves into green claws like the Wicked Witch of the West, except without the reasonable excuse of some foreign teenage runaway flying a house without a licence and landing it on her sister's head and then stealing the shoes from her still-warm corpse and flaunting them all over town with her attack dog and gang of genetically-modified ruffian mutants.

'Okay,' I say. 'Caroline. Caro. I can explain.'

Storm clouds gather above the tops of the curtains and around the architraves, obscuring the downlights. Wind begins to swirl: little eddies in the corners first, then faster and faster squalls that rustle magazines from the table and in no time at all will be picking up cushions and eventually, furniture.

'You let her stay here? Her? Here? In my house, where my children were sleeping? In my bed, where my children were conceived? Explain that. Go on,' says Caroline.

'Actually this is a new bed. We bought it last year, remember? The Salvos took the conception one,' says Henry.

'You can shut up,' says Caroline. 'I'll get to you next.'

'Janice has been such a dear. I've been very comfortable, despite the state of your pillows,' says Martha.

'Why don't you just stab me?' says Caroline. 'Why don't you cut out my heart and drain my blood all over the floor and dance in it with my husband and your new best friend, his mistress?'

'Caroline,' I say. 'We can talk about this.'

'Allergens,' says Martha. 'Ducks have all kind of mites. At home, I sleep on memory foam. Honestly, you won't go back. Tell you what, I'll send you one. It's no trouble.'

'My sister. My own flesh and blood. Et tu, Judas?' says Caroline.

'If you like it, keep it,' says Martha. 'If you don't, well, we can always use a spare pillow, can't we Henry? For when the girls stay over.'

'You're blaming the wrong person,' says Alec. 'This isn't Janice's fault.'

'Everything is Janice's fault,' Caroline says. 'Me and Mum and Dad were doing fine until she came along. She's the one who ruined everything.'

'Alec's right, don't blame Janice,' says Martha. 'Blame him as well. They were so sweet, going for it like teenagers on the couch.'

'Wait, I thought Alec and Lesley were together?' says Henry. 'Wait, my couch?'

'Listen to the voice of experience on this, Janice,' Martha says. 'Ex sex. It's not smart.'

'What?' says Henry. 'Which ex did you have sex with? It was that footballer, wasn't it?'

'I was only a toddler. I wanted a puppy,' says Caroline. 'You know what I got instead? Six pounds four ounces of parent-stealing interloper.'

Craig walks over to Alec, pointing the bottle of nail polish at him. 'You better not be about to break my wife's heart, mate.'

'Alec,' says Lesley. 'I'm as open-minded as the next person, but this can't continue. You have to choose. Consider this an ultimatum: me or Janice.'

'Nothing has happened between us,' says Alec to Lesley. 'It's an imaginary relationship.'

'Is that how you rationalise your slutty behaviour?' says Lesley.

'Exactly, mate,' says Craig. 'Lesley deserves so much better. I'm starting to think it's time to take this outside.'

'You'd do that for me?' Lesley says to Craig. She's gazing straight up at him, as though she's never seen him before.

'Of course,' says Craig, looking straight back. 'I'd do anything for you.'

'I got completely shafted,' Caroline says. 'I had the room next to Mummy and Daddy, but no, that's the baby's room now and you, Caro, are banished to the sewing room at the other end of the house. The baby gets your daisy wallpaper. Your cot? Gone. Your rocking horse? Ownership transferred. Say goodbye to everything you own, Caroline.'

'You don't know how lucky you were, at the other end of the house. You didn't have to listen to everything they said to each other,' I say.

'I've flushed your head before, I can do it again.' She takes a step closer. She makes her hands into fists, her biceps tighten and firm.

The human nostril has evolved to point downwards, which works brilliantly with falling rain, but not so well when you're upended in a toilet bowl. I should have left a video to say goodbye to the girls and explain everything to Alec. *Fellow Australians, if you are seeing me now, it means I have been murdered.*

'You'll end up in the Hague,' I say to Caroline. 'Water-boarding is illegal under international law.'

'What rubbish,' she says. 'If it was illegal, democratic governments wouldn't be allowed to do it.' She takes another step toward me.

I turn, so that Alec's face is the last thing I see before I'm flushed to death. Martha is oblivious, yawning into the back of her hand with her dressing gown half adrift, and Henry bolts in front of her and stands with his arms wide like he's a less-attractive Kevin Costner to her Whitney. Alec also steps forward between me and Caroline, but in a more graceful (yet manly) way than Henry. Caroline opens her mouth and we all brace ourselves.

The back door slides opens. Two small heads peek around the corner, one above the other.

'Excuse me,' says Mercedes.

Everybody stops, like clockwork dolls that need winding.

Beyond the sticky silence, somewhere in the distance a dog is barking. It's probably something authentic, I think. A kelpie or one of those grey cattle dogs with a black eyepatch—some proper suburban animal seemingly unrelated to the bat-eared miniature French bulldog with the diamante collar or the whippet with the collection of skivvies who live in apartments near mine, both of which barely look like dogs at all and are walked by uniformed people wearing headphones. Dogs in the suburbs probably don't have staff.

'Oh,' says Caroline, after a moment. 'Hello darlings.'

'I know we weren't supposed to come upstairs but is Daddy here?'

'Yes, Mercedes, I'm here,' says Henry.

'Why are you all standing like that?' Mercedes says. She squats down a bit, with her legs wide and her arms out, in an unflattering yet accurate impression of all of us. 'Are you playing Simon Says?'

'That's exactly what we were doing,' says Henry. 'But now you're here, we'll stop. Won't we, everyone? Oh I missed my gorgeous girls so much.'

Mercedes and Paris run to him, the way you do when Daddy's been away and you haven't known if you'll see him again, ever, and then out of nowhere he reappears, alive and well and remembering you. Henry puts out his arms; the girls wrap themselves around one leg each. Then Paris raises her head and sniffs. Soon Mercedes also looks around. There's an air pressure differential here, the type noticed by children and animals and devices that measure imminent earthquakes.

215

'Miss,' says Mercedes. 'Are you wearing Mummy's dressing gown?'

Martha hitches it over her shoulder. 'Your Mummy lent it to me. Isn't she kind?'

'Yes,' says Caroline. 'I lent it to her. Mercedes and Paris are good sharers too, aren't you?'

'Are you fighting? Mummy? Is everyone fighting?' says Mercedes.

Paris folds her arms and glares at all of us. She looks as though flames are about to erupt from her nostrils.

We look at Caroline. Caroline looks at us, and she makes a face like she just swallowed a medium-sized rock, but she says, 'Fighting? Of course not, darling. Of course not.'

It's like being part of some strange cult, except no one is a movie star. We are sitting in the lounge room like mature humans, and Caroline is walking between us, pouring tea for her husband and his mistress and her next-door neighbour and her husband who is also Caroline's lover, and her sister, who is me, who is without a lover of any description, and her ex-husband, who is soon to be moving to Massachusetts and marrying the first woman he sees and is not actually the lover of the next-door neighbour. The girls have lemonade.

We sip our tea and look at our feet.

'So I was boarding the plane last night.' Martha is reclining on the couch, still in the dressing gown, as though she's at home. 'When this woman in a tracksuit walks past me with one of those blue plastic bags, you know, the lurid, toxic-looking ones that you pick up at the last minute when you've bought too much junk, and it's clearly too big. Miles bigger than the chrome metal size tester thingie, and she's got a handbag as well, and a plastic duty-free bag filled with gin and this massive Toblerone, and do you know what?'

'While taking her assigned seat, she accidentally sat on the lap of someone else's husband?' says Caroline.

Mercedes laughs. 'That's silly, Mummy,' she says.

'It certainly is,' says Caroline. 'What a silly, silly mummy I've been for all these years.'

'No,' says Martha. 'The flight attendant just zaps her boarding pass and lets her straight on.'

'We're basically serfs,' says Craig, from his perch on the arm of Lesley's chair. 'When you step inside an airport, you cease to have any rights whatsoever. Legally it's a return to the feudal system. It's like the Manga Carta never happened.'

The Manga Carta is, presumably, a document drafted in 1215 by the Archbishop of Canterbury in the form of a Japanese comic book.

'This is very good of you, Caroline,' says Henry.

'Shut up,' says Caroline. 'Shut up and drink your tea.'

'Everyone is so self-absorbed these days.' Lesley is sitting with her feet splayed out in front, tissues wound between her toes to separate them. 'Inconsiderate. I blame millennials, mobile phones and lazy parenting. I hope you said something.'

Martha goes on. 'Excuse me, I said to the stewardess. Did you see the size of that bag? You could fit a whole other person in there.'

'Was it someone else's husband?' says Caroline. 'Folded up very small?'

'They keep you under total control so you can't wander around and catch them loading the planes with the stuff that makes the chemtrails,' says Craig.

'What are you, twelve?' says Caroline to him.

'Only if the scale's between one and ten,' says Craig.

'And do you know what the stewardess said?' says Martha 'She says, "We're not checking size today." And yet,' she leans forward for the punchline, 'when I checked in, they weighed my hand luggage.'

'Bastards,' said Craig.

'That's discrimination,' says Lesley.

'I know, right?' says Martha. 'Have you ever heard anything so patently unfair? I probably weigh less than half of the average person on that plane but do I get any credit for that? I should be able to claim excess baggage fees against the cost of my gym membership.'

'Tim Tam?' says Caroline. 'Brie? I have a chocolate cheese-cake in the freezer. It'd only take three minutes on high.'

Martha shakes her head. 'You're such a wonderful homemaker, Caroline. I'll never be as good as you, even when I get to be your age.'

'Business idea,' says Craig. 'A bespoke fat suit for skinny air travellers. Hidden pockets so you can carry all your stuff on your person without paying excess baggage.'

'That's brilliant,' says Lesley.

Craig shakes his head. 'You inspire me. You're the wind beneath my wings.'

'Oh, and thanks for the loan of the dressing gown,' Martha says to Caroline.

'Keep it,' says Caroline. 'Seriously. I don't want it back.'

'It's a little big,' says Martha. 'And such an interesting design. Did the girls choose it?'

While Martha is talking, Alec rests his hand on top of mine. On top of mine. I keep my hand there, I don't jerk it away. There's a mole and a dusting of freckles on the back of his wrist that I'd forgotten about—they could be the shape of some faraway constellation. How could I have forgotten them? How many other things have I forgotten? If I drew lines between the freckles with a ballpoint pen, they'd make something important like the Emu or the Rainbow Serpent, something that would have inspired our first people to tell stories about gallant heroes and impossible quests. Then he leans closer and his lips almost brush my ear.

'It's a good thing for you the girls came upstairs when they did,' he says. 'I thought I'd have to tackle Caroline.'

'Very lucky,' I manage to say, and I can feel the warmth of his breath against my ear and my heart skips through my chest. He moves his hand away and I look down at my hand where he touched it. Unbelievably, it looks the same as it did a moment ago.

'It wasn't luck,' Mercedes says.

We were speaking quietly, but not quietly enough.

'What's that, darling?' says Caroline.

'We heard Daddy come home.'

'Did you, darling? From all the way downstairs?'

Mercedes nods. 'We waited and waited because we were trying to be good but we were busting to see him so then we came upstairs.'

'You heard him, from all the way down there?' says Lesley.

Mercedes nods. Then she says, 'We can hear lots, when we're downstairs. We can hear it when Mummy has her rest in the afternoon sometimes and Craig comes over from next door.'

All at once, the air temperature drops around fifty degrees. My extremities feel it first: my nose turns red, and then blue. My fingertips and toes start to go numb.

'What was that, Mercedes?' says Henry.

'Of course you don't hear anything all the way down there Mercedes, what an idea. More tea?' Caroline says. 'Who takes milk again? Martha?'

'Caroline, did you say there was cheesecake?' I say.

'Oh yes,' she says. 'I nearly forgot. Cheesecake.'

'I love cheesecake,' I say. 'I like the set kind better than the baked kind, and I know that's controversial, but I'm a rebel, I can't help it, me and condensed milk have a special relationship. It's the lemon juice that sets it, the set kind, although I've never managed it at home, I mean I've tried but cheesecake soup is what I end up with. Which is delicious, by the way. Soupy, but delicious. What kind is it, the one you have in the freezer?'

'It's chocolate Bavarian,' says Caroline. 'Is that set or baked? I have no idea. Ha ha. Mercedes darling, run and get it out of the freezer for Mummy.'

'Stay right where you are, Mercedes,' says Henry.

'But we do hear him,' says Mercedes.

'Oh Mercedes sweetie, you don't have to say every little thing that's on your mind,' says Caroline.

'When you were her age, you used to go up to strangers in the street and tell them the colour of your underpants,' I say.

'I beg your pardon?' says Lesley. 'What exactly do you hear when you're downstairs, darling? When Craig comes over.'

Mercedes and Paris are not being manoeuvred out of the way, not now. Now, Mercedes sits a little taller and looks a little more awake. Eight pairs of eyes are watching her, waiting for what she has to say.

'First we heared him running across the yard, because he kind of groans when he comes through the hedge and then he hides behind the trees. Then we see his legs climbing over the balcony and it's a funny kind of scrambling noise, like the time we had that possum in the ceiling and Daddy had to climb the ladder and put the cage up there. Paris always thinks he's going to fall down on Mummy's roses and squash them but he never does. We can't hear what him and Mummy say, because they're whispering,' Mercedes says. 'Can I have some cheesecake too? And Paris.'

'Whispering,' says Henry. 'They're whispering?'

'When does this happen? Craig visiting your mummy? Is your daddy home?' says Lesley.

Mercedes shrugs. 'In the afternoon. I don't know when, exactly. We go downstairs to play. Daddy's at work, mostly. Most days we're at school but we have school holidays and we have Saturday and Sunday too and we play downstairs when Mummy has naps, especially when Daddy's away. Poor Craig.' She pats his arm. 'You must be really sleepy.'

'Craig. What.' says Henry. 'He, what?'

'If he has to come over to our house to sleep, that must mean he can't sleep in his own bed,' says Mercedes, patiently. 'He must be really tired.'

'Really tired,' says Craig, and he sags in his seat as if he's been deboned. 'Really, really tired. You don't know how tired.'

'You are a piece of work,' says Lesley to Craig. 'When we get home, you just wait.'

'I think I need a safe word,' says Craig.

'Listen, Lesley,' says Caroline.

'Wombat?' says Craig. 'Pineapple?'

'And you?' says Lesley. 'I expected it from him. But you, Caroline? I thought you were my friend.'

'I can explain,' says Caroline.

'Go on then,' says Lesley. 'Explain. I can't wait to hear it.'

'Bieber?' says Craig.

'All this time,' says Henry. 'While I've been feeling so guilty, worrying about you, about letting you down.'

'You're still guilty,' says Caroline. 'This doesn't make you less guilty at all.'

'Are you in trouble, Mummy?' says Mercedes.

'No, no darling,' says Caroline. 'This is just grown-up stuff.'

'And Craig?' says Henry. 'We're *mates*. We share a ride-on mower.'

'I'd say you share a bit more than that,' says Martha.

'We can hear lots, when we're in the playroom. We even heared Miss Roland in Mummy and Daddy's ensuite this morning, but only because she was being sick so loud and we had the side window open when we were getting the kites out. Do you feel better now, Miss?' Mercedes drains her lemonade through her straw in a long, slow gurgle.

We all turn to look at Martha. She takes a sip of her tea. 'Much better, thanks,' she says.

'What?' says Caroline. 'Being sick, did you say? This morning?'

'You know, in the tummy.' Mercedes drops her voice to a theatrical whisper. 'Spewing. It was yucky.'

'What?' says Caroline. 'She was what?'

'It must have been something I ate,' says Martha. 'No need to make a fuss.'

'We all ate the same last night,' I say. 'Pizza. The rest of us are fine.'

'A virus, probably. Twenty-four-hour stomach flu. I'm around kids all day. Little germ factories,' says Martha.

'Is it the kind of stomach flu that only strikes in the morning, Martha?' says Caroline. 'Is that what's going on here?'

'Don't be ridiculous,' says Henry. 'Stop trying to change the subject. Let's get back to the point, which is Caroline and Craig and their afternoon naps.'

Martha keeps her gaze down and sips her tea, and when she replaces the cup on the saucer, it clinks and trembles. Then she digs her hands deep in the pockets of the dressing gown and pulls it closer around her. Her skin looks translucent, like the china cup. I feel even colder.

'Henry,' I say. 'Look at her.'

'I know what she looks like, Janice, thank you very much.

You've all got vivid imaginations. It's nothing like that. Tell them, Martha.'

There is a very loud pause.

And then it's all over Henry's face, the expectations of how his middle age would unfurl. How much money he imagined he'd have, how he thought he'd spend his free time, the places he's always wanted to see. Perhaps he dreamed of a cycling holiday around France or a handicap under thirty. As I watch, Henry's best imaginings float before him in that tiny space between an inhalation and an exhalation. How tenuous our plans are. How heavily we rest on something so gossamer-thin.

Martha folds up the sleeves of the dressing gown with focus, like a tailor making adjustments. She compares the length of the left against the right, she creases the fabric with her deft fingertips. 'Most people over-plan things,' she says as she folds. 'It's important to keep some kind of spontaneity in life. Room for serendipity, detours, the path less travelled. Et cetera.'

'What are you saying?' says Henry.

'I know some might consider the timing isn't exactly perfect,' she says. 'I'm well aware of that.'

All at once, my heart begins to race and there's a pain in my chest. A splinter of something needle-sharp is threading its way through my muscles and my organs. I feel my arms hang heavy at my side and it's a good thing the teacup is on the coffee table, on the saucer, and not in my hand. The surface of the tea is smooth and calm but I can't bring myself to drink it even though my throat is squeezing tight.

'Oh,' says Henry. 'Oh. Oh. OH.'

'I wanted to tell you in private,' says Martha. 'It should have been a special moment, for just the two of us. I didn't plan on a public reveal.'

'This is great,' says Caroline. 'Just terrific. Well done, Henry.'

'I was planning to wrap the stick like a present,' says Martha, 'and give it to you on the anniversary of our first date. I was going to video you opening it.'

'The stick? The one you peed on?' says Craig.

'First date?' says Caroline. 'You are both morons.'

'You are all morons,' says Lesley.

'Like a present,' says Henry, and his eyes glaze and his mouth drops open.

'I get that. For posterity,' Craig says.

Martha blinks. 'For YouTube.'

'Congratulations,' I say, and I smile, exactly as I always do, exactly as I've practised. 'How wonderful.'

'It's very exciting,' says Martha. 'You'll be thrilled, once you get your head around it.'

'I. We. But,' says Henry. 'How.'

'Yes, how?' I say.

'*How*?' says Lesley. 'Seriously?'

'Do you have any idea what braces cost?' says Caroline.

'I do,' says Craig. 'Years of self-esteem.'

'What's happening?' says Mercedes.

'I've already got their names down for high school. They are going to a state school over your dead body,' says Caroline.

'Having the first one under thirty is ideal,' says Martha.

'After you turn thirty, your fertility drops like a stone. All these women who fart around and leave it too late and then have to rely on medical science then it's I can't have a baby, wah wah poor me. How middle class.'

'Maybe we should go,' says Alec. 'Maybe Janice and me and Mercedes and Paris should walk up the shops for an ice-cream.'

Yes. Take me out of this room and take me away from here, to somewhere else, back to when I am Mercedes' age and I could tell myself that the strange behaviour of adults was none of my business and I had my own problems: school and homework and boys and whether I would marry Michael Hutchence or Bernard Fanning (not much of a contest: Bernard, obviously) and my skin was like Mercedes', soft and unmarked and unscarred, and I'd never broken anyone's heart on purpose, least of all my own. Take me away, please. I have absolutely no reason to stay. Take me, please.

'No,' I say.

'Yes,' says Caroline. 'Get up, Janice. I'm talking to you. Are you deaf? Ice-cream would be excellent. Girls, are you ready?'

'I said no,' I said. 'No one is going anywhere. We are sorting this out right now. All of us.'

'I hardly think you are in any position to dictate the movements of my children,' says Caroline.

'I agree with Caroline,' says Martha. 'Little ears are flapping.'

'Your thoughts, also, are utterly and completely irrelevant,' says Caroline to Martha.

'Finally we're communicating,' says Martha.

'Let me communicate this, as clearly as I possibly can. I do not care what you think,' says Caroline to Martha, then, 'Mercedes, Paris: wouldn't you like to go downstairs to the playroom? I know I would.'

Grown-ups think that kids know nothing when really they know plenty, they just don't understand it. Kids only see the beginnings of arguments: the raising of voices, the tension escalating, the black looks and snarls of anger and bitterness unfurling. They never see the truces, the cease-fires, the signing of accords, because they've been tucked away by then on account of their delicate sensibilities. Kids grow up without any idea of how to resolve things. They're left hanging, sometimes for years.

'No.' Mercedes folds her arms. 'We're not going.'

Paris also glares and folds and frowns.

'We're supposed to be mature,' I say. 'Responsible. We're all staying here together and we're going to fix it.'

'We're staying,' says Mercedes.

'They're staying,' I say.

'Fine,' says Caroline. 'Then everyone else is going home. All of you. Shoo.'

'You have no moral authority to tell me what to do. Besides, I'm not going anywhere with him,' says Lesley, nodding at Craig.

'And I'm not going anywhere without her,' says Craig.

'Henry and I do need some time alone, so we'll head off,' says Martha.

'I can't leave the girls right now,' says Henry. 'And I need to think.'

'No rush, though,' says Martha.

'I'm not leaving the girls either,' I say.

'It'd be like walking out at three-quarter time to beat the traffic,' says Alec. 'I wouldn't dream of it.'

'You're all idiots,' says Caroline. 'Stay. See if I care. But we're not talking about anything. Not a thing. Any of us.'

'Nothing? You want us to sit here and say nothing?' Craig says.

'Nothing of consequence, I mean. You can go ahead and be normal,' says Caroline.

*

So we sit. We don't talk; it's like a gynaecologist's waiting room. I know what my sister looks like, of course. I know what my nieces look like. But I don't think I've ever just sat and looked at their faces before, at every facet and plane and dip. I look at the faces of my sister and my nieces and think about the blood that runs between us: the Serbian blood of the Brankovics, the Irish blood of my mother's side. I think about the women who've come before us, that long line of great-great-great-grandmothers who birthed at least one baby and are responsible for us being here.

I think of Anne Mullany, the first in our line in this country, a fifteen-year-old famine orphan from Golden, Tipperary, shipped to Australia in 1845 with four thousand other destitute girls from the workhouses to supply the growing colony with the feminine touch. I think of Anne, sardined below deck on that long sea voyage, stricken on a damp straw mattress on a tiny bunk and all around her the dark sea and the creaking ship bowing and praying and lifting as if it was about to fly. Perhaps she was seasick for weeks on the Southern Ocean, perhaps a girl on a bed inches away died of typhus or scarlet fever and was wrapped in sailcloth and consigned to the deep. Frightened, alone in the world, guilty of no crime yet parcelled out to the other side of the planet with no practical hope of ever returning home. No money and very little understanding of where she was headed.

Which turned out to be into the arms of one Patrick Carney, illiterate with a ruddy complexion, red hair and two scars on his forehead (semicircular, left side of forepart of head). Patrick was the entrepreneurial type: back when he was a twelve-year-old errand boy in Inchageelah, County Cork, all four feet ten and three-quarter inches of him took it upon themselves to tie a kerchief around his face and attempt to hold up a stagecoach. Seven years transportation, with hard labour.

Anne had six children to Patrick and then, after she buried him, six to her next husband. She was one up on Patrick in the reading department (their marriage certificate is signed in her own hand, next to his X) but odds are she was half-scurvified when she landed here, with teeth missing and pock-marked skin. Twelve children is an outstanding effort. We owe everything to her and her splendid reproductive organs.

We know quite a bit about Mum's family, courtesy of Great-Aunt Marjorie, the family's obsessed amateur genealogist since retiring from thirty years behind the counter at Centrelink with an inadequate pension, too much time on her hands and a deep disdain for the living.

After a few champagnes at every wedding and a few whiskies at every funeral, she tells us of her new discoveries and lines us up to compare chins and earlobes. I can see it in her face as she tries to position me. She knows it and I know it.

'Dead end,' I say. 'Blind alley.'

'What?' says Caroline. 'Where?'

'Nothing,' I say. 'Nowhere.'

'Do you have any pets?' says Craig.

Mercedes looks at Martha. 'Not yet.'

'How's school?' says Craig.

'Still good,' says Mercedes.

'What grade are you in?' says Craig.

She holds up three fingers.

'When I was your age, I had this teacher. Miss Heffernan. Lovely woman. Lovely. I adored her. It's a miracle I learned anything.'

'Was that the beginning of your…preoccupation?' says Martha.

'What preoccupation?' says Craig.

'I have Miss Roland,' says Mercedes.

'It's okay to call me Martha now, sweetie,' she says.

'This is why I drink,' says Caroline.

'Paris has Mr Brown and we have Mr Brown too but only for sport which is Fridays,' says Mercedes.

'Steve's a sweetie,' says Martha. 'I'm sure as he gets more experience, he'll start to be a tad more organised.'

'Is he married, Mr Brown? How old do you suppose he is?' says Caroline.

'You've got enough on your plate,' says Henry.

'Have either of you noticed that Paris is a little bit quiet?' I say. 'As in, mute?'

'We allow our children to express themselves in any way they like,' says Caroline, 'within reason.'

'Children don't have to conform to your expectations. They're individuals. It's not all about you, Janice,' says Martha.

'Exactly,' says Caroline.

Paris's silence has an ease about it. Imagine me or Caroline keeping our mouths shut for five minutes: our lips would be pinched tight against the strain of it. When Paris was a baby, she couldn't bear anything touching her feet. Shoes, socks, booties—she would kick them off or peel them down with the toes of her other foot or even lift them to her mouth like a yogi to gum them loose. Mercedes was calmer. She barely cried. She watched everything as though she'd be commissioned to write a report about it later, sitting in her highchair like a miniature tennis umpire frowning down upon us. It was unnerving.

When Caroline was pregnant with Mercedes, she could smell onions cooking three houses away and made Henry go around and tell the neighbours to shut their windows or else have something less whiffy for their dinner. The smell of bread made her gag; also green apples, broccoli, lettuce, grass. She loathed even the sight of anything green except olives (*stuffed with almonds, I said, not pimentos. Do you not know the difference between an almond and a pimento? Honestly. What is wrong with you people? One is cream and the other is red. One is a nut and the other is...Henry, what is a pimento, actually? Other than revolting*). She wanted pickled walnuts, pickled onions, boiled eggs, potato chips (packet), candy Easter eggs (in October!) She sucked ice cubes faster than their freezer could make them so Henry resorted to buying bags from the servo. He was happy to do it. Pregnancy, he knew, is a special, magical time.

'I was a bridesmaid six times before I got married to Craig,' says Lesley.

'Lucky woman,' says Caroline. 'Always the bridesmaid, never the bride. It means you're more likely to be safe.'

'It means you had lots of friends,' says Alec.

'No, I know exactly why they asked me. It was because I was the plain one,' says Lesley.

'What? That can't be right,' says Craig.

'It's true. The bride thought she'd look more beautiful in comparison if I stood beside her.'

'Some girls at my school are very mean too,' says Mercedes.

'I always said yes, even though I knew why they asked me. I always had this strange idea that one time—not every time, I didn't expect to be overrun—but I thought maybe once I might hit it off with one of the groomsmen. I never did, though. Not once.'

'It's a strange environment, weddings,' I say. 'Everyone's stressed.'

'It wasn't that. The groomsmen were only interested in ridiculing the groom and getting as drunk as physically possible,' says Lesley.

'They were idiots,' says Craig. 'I should know.'

Mercedes looks like Henry when she turns in profile: the chin with its tiny cleft, the fine nose with the delicate bridge. I'm a Brankovic: I have our father's cheeks, like apples; eyebrows with a mind of their own. Paris's face is all Caroline and Caroline is all our mother, Irish-famine broad and flat and round as a spud, though I'd never say it out loud on pain of death. Mum and Caroline and Paris are part of a straight line of women that stretches back to Anne Mullany in the past and forward into the future, to the children of Mercedes and Paris, whatever they will look like, and their children, and theirs.

Alec says something to fill the air: some sporting team is doing sports in a more sporting fashion than another sporting team, thus delighting people who have assigned their loyalties to a group of professional sporting people they've never met who play some form of sport they've never played and devastating people who have randomly or familially been assigned to some other team that sits in historical opposition. Craig says something about sport building character, and Lesley says something about cross-cultural and inter-socioeconomic ties. Craig says that children should play sport to learn co-operation, and as soon as he says 'children', everyone looks down at their tea.

'I know. Let's watch *Frozen* again,' says Mercedes.

'You can go downstairs whenever you like,' says Caroline. 'And take your sister with you.'

'Never mind,' says Mercedes. 'It's fine.'

'You're quiet, Paris,' says Henry.

'You're observant, Henry,' I say.

Paris and Mercedes both laugh.

Henry can't stop looking at Martha, who is a wonder, a living, breathing person factory. There is not one minute of the day when she is not constructing. Right now she's flat out engineering toe bones or sculpting the cartilage waves of an ear; I can imagine a long line of ant-like workers climbing up scaffolding within her midsection, each toting part of an elbow crease or the base of a hair follicle. One whole division of teeny artisans is responsible solely for eyelashes. No wonder she's knackered. I wonder if she's hungry, and if so, what she wants to eat. I wonder how it feels to have life growing inside you and what kind of child is forming there. Martha has to continue to work and talk and live, though she's intellectually aware of her cells dividing and her plasma rising and all that pain ahead of her, of a life to be spent in thrall to something she cannot control. I wonder if she's frightened.

Alec is an only child. If he dies without children of his own, not one skerrick of him or of his parents Andy and Nola—sociable people, who grew competition orchids and played canasta and mixed cocktails in silver shakers on Saturday nights and died when their car was rear-ended across a level-crossing with the train in sight when Alec was nineteen—will survive. For years he was risking everything, all because he met a woman at a party who liked to look down microscopes and he allowed things to take their natural course. Alec had never known his parents as an adult. He'd been cheated of that new kind of relationship, of meeting them face-on when they were all the same size. His only memories of Andy and Nola are a boy's, looking up at them, bigger and older and wiser. If he never has children, he's marooned without a generation behind him or one in front. He was dancing with the black hole of eternity, being married to me.

'Are you getting a tattoo, Daddy? On account of Miss having one.'

'Well, you never know,' Henry says. 'Maybe. Possibly.'

'Of course not,' says Caroline. 'Daddy's too old for a tattoo. His skin is very old and baggy and wrinkly and he'd just look silly, like a pathetic old man trying desperately to recapture his lost youth. Wouldn't that be dreadful, if people thought that? Besides, Martha's tattoo is a special kind, just for ladies. It's called a stamp.'

'It's here, actually.' Martha drops the shoulder of her dressing gown to show off the swallow.

'It's pretty,' says Mercedes. 'I like the bluey-green wings. I'm going to get one just like it when I grow up.'

'Over my dead body,' says Caroline.

'Grit your teeth and smile, that's my advice. Artistic tendencies can arise in even the most prosaic family. You can't control it,' says Martha.

'Does that mean I can get one?' says Mercedes.

'No,' says Henry.

'No,' says Caroline.

'How about pierced ears?' says Mercedes.

'No,' says Henry.

'Not yet,' says Caroline.

'See how much better it is, having the three of us? When there's only two parents, if one says yes and the other says no, it's a stalemate. Now that I'm here: bingo. Deciding vote,' says Martha.

'Does that means I can?' says Mercedes.

'I agree with your mother: not yet. When you get to high school,' says Martha.

'That's ages away,' says Mercedes. 'Please, Mummy,'

'Well, I understand the appeal of holding a high-pressure spring-loaded gun very close to someone's head and pulling the trigger and thus propelling a sharpened stud through

236

their flesh with great force,' Caroline says. 'Just let me think on that for a moment.' She closes her eyes and smiles.

Bacteria divide right down the middle and then—*congratulations!*—there are two of them. No jealousy, no remorse, no responsibility, no fights about where to spend Christmas or the age that child bacteria can pierce their ears.

My lovely, sensible, predictable bacteria. I could walk out Caroline's front door and get in my car and drive to my lab right now. I know what each one likes to grow on, and at what temperature, and how long it takes for them to lose their vitality. If I look after them properly and keep them from being contaminated, the daughter colony-forming units are identical to the parents.

If I was in the lab right now, I'd line my colonies up in their plastic dishes and admire them like art. Bacteria are beautiful when they are young. The different agars are creamy or reddish or ochre and the colonies themselves are silver or yellow or iridescent orange glossy globules of life. When they get old, they turn darker, murky khakis and muddy greys, and they start to die and decompose and they smell like the worst thing imaginable. But at that point, don't we all.

'I'm hungry,' says Mercedes.

It's past lunch; we hadn't noticed. Caroline makes toasted sandwiches for everyone. We all offer to help but it's only Alec she allows in the kitchen. From the dining room I see him slicing tomatoes in his methodical way, then halving the slices again to cover the bread more evenly. He shaves cheese while

Caroline butters bread. There's a wordless harmony in the way they work together. He's not unpractised at this kind of cooperation. He hasn't spent the last two years alone in the kitchen, of that I'm sure.

'Nothing for me,' says Martha.

'Make an effort,' says Caroline. 'You'll feel better, take my word for it.'

'What about a walk around the yard?' says Henry to me, when we've eaten. 'Just you and the girls. Or maybe Alec can take them.'

'No,' I say.

'I'd love another tea,' says Martha.

Then all at once, Craig stands. 'A little shush. I've thought about it. I am ready to testify.'

'Not in front of my children,' says Caroline.

'I can't keep it in anymore,' he says. 'I will not be suppressed. I'm like one of those twelve-step people. I'm literally erupting.'

'Fantastic. Here we go.' Caroline folds her arms.

Craig tucks his t-shirt into his jeans and clears his throat. 'Could I stand on something? Is there a stool? At Toast-masters, we have a portable lectern.'

'No,' says Caroline. 'No lectern, no stool.'

'At least I should rest my hand on something that has symbolic moral authority. So I can swear to tell the truth,' says Craig.

'There's not a holy book in the world big enough to squeeze the truth out of that man,' says Lesley.

'I thought you were literally erupting? Get on with it,' says Caroline.

Craig shrugs. He stands with his legs apart and his hands clasped behind his back, a boy scout on parade. He bounces up and down on his toes. 'Okay. Well. My name is Craig and I am very fond of women.'

Lesley drains her teacup. 'Where's my handbag?' she says, and she releases the handle of the recliner so that it jerks upright and all but bounces her to her feet. 'I need numbers for a taxi and a real estate agent. Also, if you left-swipe someone by accident, can you get them back?'

'Okay, all right,' says Craig. He takes a deep breath. 'For years I have engaged in a systematic scheme of deceit and betrayal with women who aren't a patch on you, Lesley.'

'I'm right here,' says Caroline.

'Sorry, but that's how I feel,' says Craig. 'No offence.'

Caroline smiles at him. 'None taken, moron.'

'That's not a nice word,' says Mercedes.

'You're right, darling,' said Caroline. 'Naughty Mummy. I meant to say cretin.'

'I think he's afraid of death,' says Martha, leaning forward with her elbows on her knees, frowning at Craig like he's a specimen.

'Yet he courts it, all the same,' says Henry.

'Mate,' says Craig.

'Neighbour,' says Henry.

'Death is scary, right Mummy?' says Mercedes to Caroline. 'You're supposed to be afraid of it.'

'Hang on,' says Craig. 'I played volleyball at high school. I'm not afraid of anything.'

'*Please*,' Martha says, as she counts off on her fingers. 'You're a textbook case: fear of death, fear of maturity, fear of fear, fear of intimacy, uterus envy. Pick one or all of them.'

'Uterus envy? You're making that up,' says Craig.

'It's the awareness that men are mere bystanders in the business of creation which is, frankly, the only important activity in the whole world, and that one day sperm will be made in a laboratory and their very existence will be redundant. Then,' says Lesley, 'pow.'

'Pow?' says Henry.

'Pow. Y-chromosome extinction,' says Martha.

'Extinct? Us?' says Craig.

'Y-chromosomes themselves are outnumbered three to one, because we have two Xs and you have one X and one pathetic lonely little Y. Ys are more fragile, they're mostly junk. They're crumbling away,' says Martha.

'You can't compete, genetically. You're outgunned. I think that's sad,' says Lesley.

'Extinction,' says Craig. 'As in, annihilation?'

'That's an inaccurate understanding of the science. You're talking about a theoretical timeframe of millions of years,' I say.

'Nerd,' says Caroline.

'Ceasing to be. Dispersing into the great cosmic void, returning to nothingness,' says Craig.

'It sounds relaxing, when you say it like that,' says Lesley.

'Relaxing? The last thing it is is relaxing. Extinction is stressful. Caroline, it's very stuffy in here. And hot. Hot and stuffy. There's not enough oxygen,' says Craig. 'Can somebody open a window?'

'When you ask the little boys in my class what they want to be when they grow up, none of them say "a man",' says Martha. 'They all want to be boys for ever, but boys who have a magnet in their chest that prevents anything touching their heart. And that also powers their flying iron suit, so they can live in their penthouse with their car collection and play video games with their friends.'

'And the problem with that is?' says Henry.

'Tell me Craig: when you were growing up, did you feel your father didn't understand you? Did you feel that he was disappointed in you, on some level?' says Martha.

'Every man alive feels that,' says Henry.

'FYI, I'm not feeling very well,' says Craig. 'I think I'm having an existential crisis. I'm pretty sure.'

'Perfect. You and your existential crisis can hang out with Henry and his mid-life crisis. You can double date. Go to exploding movies and eat pulled-pork sliders and then you can both fall asleep on the couch by nine-thirty with your feet on the coffee table and change your sheets once a month and keep food uncovered in the fridge,' says Caroline.

'Don't be ridiculous. I'm not having a mid-life crisis. That's for middle-aged people,' says Henry.

'You're right,' says Caroline. 'You're way past the middle. There's no way you'll see eighty-four, not with your cholesterol.'

'Remember when you and Henry hadn't been dating very long and he gave you that mixtape?' I say to Caroline. 'I remember. He was so romantic, Henry. The first song was "Romeo and Juliet" by Dire Straits. You must have played that tape a hundred times.'

'Relevance?' says Caroline.

'Mark Knopfler. Now there was a man who understood romance,' I say.

'No one worries about cholesterol anymore. That's a nineties thing,' says Henry.

'Don't worry, babe.' Martha pats him on the knee. 'After being vegan for a few months at my place, you'll be good as new.'

'You don't still have that cassette, do you? If we could play that, I bet all the old feelings would come flooding back,' I say.

'Vegan? You're not vegan,' says Henry.

'Not when I'm out, no. I mostly eat raw at home, though. Home vegan, street carnivore. I love to cook. Though I suppose it's not really cooking, is it, if there's no heat involved? I love to prepare food. I'm a mad juicer. It's the enzymes.'

'I've taken you out for steaks,' says Henry. 'Big, fat, expensive steaks.'

'While I've been here eating mac and cheese with the girls, you and Missy here have been going out for big fat steaks,' says Caroline.

'Out, sure,' says Martha. 'Maybe once or twice a month, on special occasions. Not at home. I've been a para-vegan for years. I mean, look at me. Seriously, do you think I look like this by eating whatever I want?'

'Nothing's been decided, actually. About where Henry's living. A counsellor, that's what they need. And maybe a small dose of pharmaceutical-grade ecstasy,' I say.

'When I go to the juice bar, I tell the girl behind the counter my name is Frank,' Craig says. 'Every time. I can't help myself. She seriously thinks my name is Frank. In the coffee place next to Bakers Delight, I'm Franco. "Franco!" they say, when I walk in. "Come stai?" What do you think that means?'

'How are you?' says Lesley.

'You're a habitual liar?' says Caroline, simultaneously.

'I wish I was called Mary or Kate, because they're proper princesses with crowns and everything and they live in castles,' says Mercedes.

'You're very lucky with your names, both you and Paris. Mummy put a lot of thought into them. How would you like to be poor Auntie Janice?' says Caroline. 'Besides, not everyone can carry off a royal name. You have to develop a certain presence.'

'I remember my grandma telling me she loved Princess Caroline when she was a little girl. Is she still alive?' says Martha.

'Frank's a nice name,' says Mercedes. 'Maybe you just like it better than Craig.'

'What's wrong with Craig?' he says.

'Nothing, that's the point. You want to become another person, to transform, to be reborn,' says Martha. 'How was your relationship with your mother?'

'Here we go,' says Caroline. 'Blame the mother.'

'Look, a question. What do you have for breakfast at home? As an example,' says Henry.

'Don't worry,' says Martha. 'I mix it up. If Monday is quinoa porridge, then Tuesday is kale smoothie. You won't be bored.'

'Hear that, Henry? Tuesday is kale smoothie. You won't be bored,' says Caroline.

'I have one of those super blenders. I know it's a bit bogan to buy things from the TV but it changed my life,' says Martha. 'I also have a slicer dicer. Carrots, beetroot, celery, one minute, I'm not kidding.'

'My mum,' says Craig, 'every day she wrapped up my lunch like it was a present. Wrapping paper and blue ribbons and everything. She stuck a little card on the front she made herself that said how much she loved me. I had to unwrap my lunch before I ate it.'

'That's a bit creepy, mate,' says Alec.

'I got beaten up. A lot. Sometimes even by the boys,' says Craig.

'How do you feel about, say, bacon? As a random example,' says Henry.

'You might as well pump a syringe full of Spacfilla straight into your arteries.' Martha pats his shoulder. 'I want us to have a long and happy life together. Discipline, that's the key. We've got a job ahead of us. People are going to think you're the grandfather as it is.'

'You haven't seen a doctor, though, have you Martha? Those plastic pee sticks, they're rubbish, you can't trust them,' I say.

'Dad used to wear a suit all the time,' says Craig. 'I don't think he had any other clothes. He had these pinstriped pyjamas with a collar and a tie. It was a special bed-tie. Mum wouldn't let him actually sleep in it. She said he'd strangle himself overnight and one of these mornings she'd wake up next to his cold dead corpse so he kept it on the bedside table. That way he could take it off last thing at night and put it on again first thing in the morning.'

'That's seriously not normal,' says Alec.

'Every time I made a friend at school, Dad insisted on

meeting the parents. They'd ask him to sit down and they'd offer him a wine and he'd ask if they fully understood the financial repercussions of either of them suddenly dropping dead.'

'Sorry?'

'Sleeping with the fishes, metabolically challenged, red-shirted, taking a dirt nap. He knew the exact likelihood of stroke, car accident, cancer, falling off a ladder, any age, either sex, off the top of his head,' says Craig. 'Chances of being taken by a shark? Anyone?'

'Ten thousand to one?' says Martha.

'Heaps higher than that,' says Henry.

'Not likely,' Martha says. 'Every day someone gets a bite taken out of them in Western Australia and hardly anyone lives there.'

'Eleven point five million to one,' says Craig. 'You've got a better chance of being killed by the ladder.'

'See, girls? Climbing things can be very dangerous,' says Henry.

'Dad also knew how much school fees cost when you extrapolated them over the life of a child and adjusted for inflation. He could recite funeral expenses off the top of his head, including hearse hire, which people tend to forget about. He could calculate anyone's precise insurance needs at any time and he kept spare forms in the glove box, ready for signing. Always prepared, was my father.'

'How very. Organised,' I say.

'Most people are underinsured. It's a sad indictment on the selfishness of modern society. I blame the internet,' Craig says.

'It was like a community service, what your father was doing,' I say.

'None of the other kids at school were allowed to play with me,' says Craig.

'I think you're afraid of sex,' says Martha.

'Sex?' Mercedes presses her hands over Paris's ears. 'She's too little to hear about that.'

Paris removes them and glares at Mercedes.

'Yes. Far too little, miss masters of childhood education,' says Caroline.

'Sorry. He's afraid of gardening, I mean,' says Martha. 'His father was obsessed with the odds of people dying and his mother was obsessed with waking up next to his dead father. His father's necktie was an ever-present, potent symbol of dying while asleep, a noose already knotted, waiting beside the bed for easy post-coital contemplation. In a Freudian or Lacanian, even a Steinian context it represents his own garden hose.'

'Who, me? Are you joking? Are you talking about my hose? I'm not afraid of gardening. That's the last thing I'm afraid of,' says Craig.

'It does sound unlikely, considering how much gardening he actually does,' says Lesley.

'Think about it,' Martha says. 'That's why he's so focused on crop rotation. He has a constant need to plant seed in order to genetically cushion the unconscious fear of his own impending death, yet deep down he's afraid he can't meet the expectations of the other horticulturists, physically or emotionally. Maybe he's a good gardener, maybe he isn't, but either way he's afraid of failure so he keeps moving on, to till new furrows. Other gardeners aren't used to having someone approach them with so much admiration and naturally they feel flattered, but they don't know him very well and aren't comfortable verbalising their dissatisfaction at his poor cultivation techniques,' Martha says.

'Sounds logical,' says Lesley.

'Sounds ridiculous,' says Craig. 'I've got the greenest thumb you've ever seen. I could propagate in the firsts for Geelong.'

'Freud said there are no accidents,' Martha says. 'This is why the girls heard you: you made all that noise because you wanted to be caught.'

'What absolute rubbish,' says Craig.

'Deep down, you want to get what's coming to you. You know what you deserve and your unconscious is determined to get it. You long to be punished,' says Martha.

'Well,' says Craig. 'There may be some truth in that part.'

'Sometimes when you've finished planting,' says Lesley. 'I go back to the garden and tidy things up a bit, when you're in the shower. By myself. Make sure everything's bedded in to my satisfaction, I mean.'

'What?' says Craig.

'With my trowel. The battery-powered one,' says Lesley.

'I don't believe you,' says Craig. 'You always said I was a violinist. Didn't you always say that?'

'I don't think many people are interested in three-minute concertos. Even Andre Rieu needs to take it easy and not rush things,' says Lesley.

'Rush things?' Craig sits heavily in the recliner, as though his legs have given out on him. 'You think I rush things?'

'Only sometimes, when you're not paying attention, you can be, well, goal-focused. Perfunctory,' says Lesley. 'A bit slapdash.'

'Perfunctory? Slapdash? Caroline, help me out here.' Craig's hands flap as he talks, as though he's dog-paddling in a pool without water.

She shrugs. 'Adequate. Extra points for enthusiasm, which god knows I hadn't seen in a while. Mostly I grow annuals at home.'

'That's not true,' says Henry.

'It is so true,' says Martha. 'You told me so yourself. It'd been years, you said.'

'Oh yes, that's right,' says Henry.

'There are two sides to every story. Give and take, that's the ticket,' I say.

'Why didn't you say something?' says Craig.

'I know how important it is to you. I didn't want to make you sad,' says Lesley.

As they're all talking, I'm watching their mouths open and close and I'm hearing their words, but it's all just noise. They're a troop of monkeys jumping from tree to tree and screeching metaphors at each other. It seems strange for a city girl but right now I'd give anything for the sound of the forest after heavy rain, that bubbling frog symphony, the way the colour of everything seems fresher and brighter—or even the desert, vast and pale and quiet as stone.

'Do something,' I say to Alec.

'What would you have me do? They have to sort it out themselves. People aren't like your bacteria. You can't control everyone and everything,' he says to me.

I can try.

'Yo, guys? That's enough,' I say to them.

Nothing. I clap my hands. I try again, louder this time.

'Really, shut up. All of you, shut up.'

'They're not listening,' says Mercedes. 'You're not the boss of them.'

They keep talking. Now Craig is saying something about his gardening implements: the dimensions of his rake, and his raking technique. Martha is droning something about carrot sticks, Caroline is screeching, Lesley is squealing, Henry is groaning, Alec is trying to speak to the girls about music but they refuse to be distracted; even Mercedes has stopped paying attention to me and now she and Paris are staring, rapt, eyes agog, leaning on their elbows. I can't listen to any of it for one more second.

'Mercedes,' I say. 'Can I borrow you a moment? Hello? Mercedes?'

'In a minute. This is a good bit,' she says.

'Now, please.'

I stand, I walk to the kitchen and she follows, dragging the toes of her shoes across the carpet of the lounge room, then across the tiles of the kitchen floor. When I'm around the corner and out of their sight, I climb up on the kitchen stool until I can slide open the very top cupboard. All family homes have a cupboard like this, high near the ceiling, to store the things that weigh down a marriage: the stainless steel cocktail sets and the rainbow of anodised tumblers and the plastic popsicle moulds and the ceramic statues of milkmaids and the handblown vases that look like bongs and the gravy boats in the shape of bulldogs and the pasta makers and ice-cream churns, the results of collections from workmates and sporting teams and spontaneous purchases in op shops and gifts from distant great-aunts. The things that are unused from the day they're cooed over and packed away to their eventual unpacking by the Salvos, fifty years later, after the division of the estate. I reach my hand in and pull out the first thing I touch. It's a prescut glass cake stand with a flat plate where the cake sits resting on top of a fluted leg. It's etched with stars. It's hideous, and it's heavy.

'Does Mummy like this?' I say.

'What is it? A stage for Barbies to dance on? A place for tiny helicopters to land?' she says.

'It's an anchor,' I say. 'You can be minding your own business, scuba diving in deep water, admiring the quiet and the coral and the beautiful fishes and then some ship above you drops this and squashes you flat. Does Caroline use it for anything?'

She shakes her head and does a little twirl. 'Nope.'

I ask her to step out of the way and when she's back in the lounge, I walk to the edge of the kitchen. The cake stand is cold and hard. I can see all their faces, looking at each other, talking nonsense about gardening. All at once I hate everything about this house: the way the throw cushions sit on the couch just so, the ridiculous bottle filled with essential oil of fruit and flowers and stabbed with ludicrous reeds. It's like a secret handshake, the way people arrange their lives. It tells the world everything about them. People allow themselves to be defined by their stuff so they don't have to think about who they are anymore. Family houses, meant for families.

I shut my eyes and picture my mother's face as I drop the cake stand on the faux-farmhouse tiles.

A million shards of prescut explode over the floor, then there's a hard crack like a slap and a sharp ring like a crystal bell being hit with a hammer and all at once, everything is quiet and beautiful. The floor glitters as though it's tinsel, as though it's ice reflecting in a fire.

They all stop. They turn and stare, they gape, they gasp. Mercedes covers her ears with her hands. Only Paris sits still, cool and quiet. She has the beginning of a smile on her face.

'Now that I have your complete attention,' I say. 'I'm sick of the lot of you. You are all selfish, stupid idiots.'

'What the hell do you think you're doing?' says Caroline. 'That big glass thingie was a wedding present from everyone in Henry's office. They took up a collection.'

'I don't care if they carved it with their teeth,' I say.

'She's expressing herself in the only way she knows how,' says Martha. 'We hear you Janice. We validate you. Do you feel better now?'

'I couldn't care less how she feels. That belonged to me, whatever it was,' says Caroline.

'Actually, if you and Henry split up, you'll have to divide everything,' says Alec.

'What?' says Craig.

'Half,' says Alec. 'Roughly. Depending on contribution and capacity.'

'Contribution?' says Craig. 'That's a financial tsunami. You're joking, right? You must be joking. Not half. Can you get insurance for that?'

'Half, Craig. He's right. Half. If it was a gift from Henry's friends in the first place, it would probably have gone to Henry in the settlement,' says Lesley.

'What has got into you Janice? How dare you commit such senseless vandalism with someone else's property?' says Martha.

'Half? Figuratively half. Not literally half. Not the house,' says Craig.

'I'm not angry, Janice. I'm just very disappointed,' says Martha.

I turn my back on their red faces and climb back up on the stool. In the same top cupboard, I find the matching jug tucked in the opposite corner. It's also good and solid: at least a kilo, with its fat base and ugly curved handle.

'One more word from any of you and the jug gets it.' I toss it in the air as though I have vaguely competent hand-eye co-ordination. It does a sideways 360 and, miraculously, I catch it by the handle on its way down.

'You wouldn't dare,' says Caroline.

I hook my pinky around the handle, I'm barely holding on as I swing it to and fro. 'Go on. One way to find out.'

'You're scaring the girls. I won't have it,' says Caroline.

'Mercedes, are you and Paris scared?' I say.

'It's like a million diamonds have fallen from heaven all over the floor. Smash something else, smash something else,' Mercedes says. She's bouncing up and down where she sits.

'Don't you two move,' Henry says to them. 'There're bits of glass everywhere. The floor is officially lava, until Auntie Janice sweeps up her mess.'

'I'm not bluffing,' I tell them. 'You are all clearly the kind of idiots who care more about inanimate objects than you do about people and there's a whole cupboard full of crap here. I could smash things all night.'

'I hardly think…' begins Craig.

'Shut it,' says Martha, and at the exact same time, Caroline also barks, 'Shut it.' Both of their mouths contract tight and they squint as though they're blasting invisible laser beams at my head. Their expressions are close to identical, which is both unnerving and illuminating, but no one makes another sound.

'Right. From now on, you will only speak if I ask you a direct question. Is that clear?' I say.

Not a peep.

'Is. That. *Clear*?' I say, louder, and then they reply with variations of *yes, Janice*.

I hop up on the kitchen bench so I'm sitting higher than them and the cupboard is behind me, within easy reach if I stand up. The jug is balanced on my lap. 'Right. Lesley, you're first. With everything you know now about his past behaviour and his past promises, do you still want to be married to Craig? Yes or no.'

'He's a pinhead,' she says. 'He's an immature, hopeless, illogical idiot.'

'Duh. But unrelated to my question.'

'I'm right here,' says Craig.

'But he's my idiot. He's my whole life, really. Yes, I'll keep him.'

'Seriously?' he says. 'You will?'

'Are you deaf?' she says. 'Do you not understand English?'

'Oh I do. I certainly do. That's the most romantic thing anyone's ever said to me. I'll make it up to you,' says Craig.

'Oh you certainly will,' says Lesley. 'I have a lot of adventures in credit. Years' worth.'

'What?' says Craig.

'You heard. You will be staying home, by yourself, looking after the twins and doing the housework, and I will be going out. Anywhere I want, with whomever I choose. No questions will be asked about my whereabouts or activities unless I decide to tell you about them, which I may do, if you manage to be good. I think, oh, six years ought to cover it,' she says. 'And if you violate that arrangement, that's it. Over. This is a one-time-only, non-negotiable offer.'

Craig swallows, loudly. 'And what will happen to me?'

'You, Craig.' Lesley cracks her knuckles, one by one. 'You will experience a range of sensations that you've never felt before. I intend to keep you entirely focused on the power of one woman, i.e. me. If you behave yourself, you'll be 'thoroughly satisfied, believe me.'

'Oh, I believe you,' he says. 'Just one more question: how would you feel about, occasionally getting in, um, another pair of hands? To help with the gardening, I mean. A bit of variety.'

'Well I can see the appeal, especially as your extra-curricular activities outside the house will be severely restricted,' Lesley says.

'That's just what I was thinking,' says Craig.

'And everything will be under my complete supervision and express direction,' she says.

Craig nods as though his head is hinged at the back of his neck. 'Completely.'

'I'm not totally opposed. We shouldn't allow ourselves to become narrow-minded and provincial. I did some experimenting myself, at uni,' she says.

'You did?'

'Sure. It was a different time then. We were all crazy for gardening,' says Lesley. 'Gardening, gardening, gardening, night and day, that's all we did. Also, weed. Ing. Weeding and gardening, on a diet of Cheezels and two-minute noodles. Those were the days. It's a miracle we graduated. So I'll say a qualified yes.'

'That's wonderful,' says Craig.

'Though of course, it all depends on the bloke,' says Lesley.

'I didn't mean,' says Craig.

'What?' says Lesley, opening and closing her hands into fists. 'You didn't mean what?'

'Nothing,' he says. 'Not a thing. It's all good.'

'You see?' I say to Caroline and Henry. 'Look at how happy they are. Like delusional scary kinky newlyweds, and they had a lot more than one affair to work through. One measly, meaningless, irrelevant little affair that means nothing in the scheme of things.'

'I'm right here,' says Martha.

'She can have him,' says Caroline. 'I'm so over the whole drama. I'll walk him down the aisle and give him away at their wedding.'

I can see our mother in the way Caroline sweeps her fringe out of her eyes and tucks it behind her ear. I blame Henry, and I blame myself and I blame our father and our mother and Martha and this whole stupid life we've constructed. Caroline is sitting on her couch as though her world is not on the edge of a precipice. Blood is continuing to pump through her veins, her lungs are still moving in and out. I'm furious at her earrings, which match her bracelet and are designed to show off her eyes, and equally angry at her stupid teapot and her ridiculous matching cups. Get up, I want to scream at her. Stand, kick, swing your arms, smash something. It's slipping through your fingers and you're just sitting there.

'You can't mean that,' I say to her. 'Little girls need their father.'

'They'll still have him, Janice. I promise,' says Henry.

'Look, Janice,' Martha says. 'Everyone is missing someone. Every single person you see walking down the street, everyone you meet, everyone you talk to, every last one of us has a great gaping hole in our hearts made by loving someone who isn't around. It's the human condition. You want to spare Mercedes and Paris that? You'd have to lock them in a cupboard for the rest of their lives.'

'Let it go, Janice. You don't have to be a scientific genius to feel which way the wind's blowing,' Caroline says.

'No. You can't think that, I don't believe it. Not after all these years you've spent together. Only yesterday I saw you chase after him,' I say. 'To Noosa.'

Caroline rests her hands on her lap, palms up, and pushes down on her wrists to straighten her arms. I can see the backs of all her rings: wedding, engagement, eternity, significant birthdays, flush up against each other like terrace houses. From this angle the jewels are invisible and they're just modest gold bands, thin and plain.

'Maybe you're right.' Her eyes are shining pools. 'But soon I will. I'm just a little ahead of myself.'

'Will we still have Christmas with Daddy?' says Mercedes. 'Mummy?'

Caroline rolls her eyes to the ceiling. 'Apparently, for my sins,' she says, after a while. 'Apparently we will.'

'And can we really have a kitten?' says Mercedes.

'Don't push it,' says Caroline.

This is maddening. If only we were better at loving each other. If only we didn't have such tiny, useless hearts.

'No.' I look down at my naked hand, holding the jug. 'No no no no no. Nope. You are not divorcing. I will not permit it. You have children. You are blessed. God, you are the most selfish, painful people in the known universe. You're pathetic, both of you. How can you not know you have to make sacrifices for the people you love?'

I never shout but I'm shouting now, at all the missing fathers and at all the missing children, everywhere across the world and everywhere in this room.

'Excuse me,' says Henry. 'I hardly think.'

'Don't you dare lecture us,' says Caroline. 'After all, you left Alec.'

'But that's why I left Alec, you lucky, lucky idiots—because I can't. I can't and he could, provided he found somebody else, so of course I left him. I kicked him to the kerb. It was the only way.'

'The only way to what?' says Martha. 'What on earth are you talking about?'

'Children,' I say. 'Babies. I can't.'

It takes me a moment to realise what I've said. And in that moment, everything stops. The air stops moving, and the clocks. All of our breathing. Everything I've kept inside is loose now, free and loose. I've opened my mouth and out it's tumbled. After all this time. I didn't realise what a hard little weight it was, sitting solid beneath my breastbone. Heavy and hard. Without it, my chest feels open. I'm lighter.

'What?' says Caroline. 'You what?'

From high on this bench, I feel like I'm soaring now that I'm free of it, as though everything is water, thicker and cooler and gentle on my skin.

'It was the only way,' I tell them. 'The only way was to let him go.'

'I don't understand,' says Alec.

'I can't.' I'm holding one hand against my middle; the

empty, barren centre of me. 'Something's broken and they don't know what it is. That's why. That was always why.'

'Janice,' Caroline says. 'For better or worse, that's what it means. Alec would have adjusted.'

Of course he would have. He would have been brave and stoic and never, ever bitter, not even when we fought. It was my flaw, my lack, but we would have both been forced to bear it. It would always have been between us.

'It wasn't just for him,' and as soon as I say it, I know it's true. 'I was selfish, in a way. It was just as much for me. Otherwise I'd have to see him look at other people's kids, every day. I couldn't have done it. I couldn't have watched him go through life that way, and known that I was the cause of it.'

I feel as if I'm floating now. I'm attached to the world by a thin cable. I'm an astronaut suspended in the far blue, I'm buoyant, I'm resting. There are no requirements upon me. I did my best: there is nothing more I can do. I look at Alec. He's looking at the floor.

We all wait.

'You lied to me,' he finally says, and his voice when it comes is cold and hard.

'Yes. Yes I did.'

'You just took it upon yourself, did you?' he says.

'I did what I thought was best for both of us.'

'It wasn't your decision to make.' Alec runs his hand through his hair.

'Of course it was,' I say. 'Because you never would have made it. You couldn't have made it.'

'All this time,' he says. 'You let me think.'

I nod. I suck a ragged breath into my lungs.

Then Paris says to me, 'You're not the boss of him. You're not the boss of any of us.'

We all stop, we turn our heads. She seems smaller now that she's spoken, and paler, and her voice is high-pitched but not the least bit reedy after its holiday. There is no evidence of rust, no wobbling.

'I told you. Resting,' says Mercedes.

'You're right,' I say to Paris. 'I've been very bossy, haven't I?'

She nods.

'Yes, she has been very bossy,' says Alec. 'Do you know what you've done, Janice? We're divorced now. It's done. It can't be undone.'

'Yes,' I say.

'Now, because of your decision, we are two single people, with no commitments and no expectations of how our lives will pan out. No resentments, no disappointments. If either of us ever gets married again, we'll be making a conscious decision with our eyes wide open. Clean slate.'

'I know,' I say.

'If you ever get married again,' he says, 'your future husband will know exactly what kind of woman you are.'

'I guess he would,' I say. 'My future husband. If there is one.'

'Any man who proposes to you now would have to be an idiot,' Alec says. 'An absolute dill. Someone who was so stupid, he didn't realise that finding the perfect person to love, and having them love you back, is enough of a miracle for one lifetime.'

'I can be pretty stupid too,' I say. 'Being in love with an idiot doesn't worry me.'

He stands and paces to the front door, then back again. He presses his hands along the wall, along the back of the chair, as though he needs the feel of something solid beneath his cells. 'I've been single for twenty-three months next Friday,' he says at last. 'Do you see any babies? No? That's because there aren't any. No pregnancies, no babies, not even close.'

'You've still got time, mate. So I'm told,' says Henry.

Alec ignores him. 'It turned out that I didn't actually want children in general. I wanted a particular person's children. Janice's children. Someone else's isn't the same thing at all.'

'Is that right?' I say, over the sound of the blood in my ears.

'It's a small but important distinction,' he says, still. Quieter now.

I can't speak. I am literally speechless. 'I'm literally speech-less,' I say.

'The next time a man proposes to you,' Alec says, 'he'll take all that into account. There'll be no divorce, next time. Next time will be for keeps. If you say yes, of course.'

'But you won't get married again, surely Janice,' says Henry. 'Once bitten, right?'

'What is it you want, Janice?' says Caroline.

What I want is to have sex with Alec. A wave of mad lust sweeps over me and yes, it has something to do with my chaste existence, and something to do with the closeness of him, sitting just there on the other side of the room, but mostly it has to do with this new life of Martha's being proof of our animal nature. Soon Martha's baby will be born and it'll grow up and have babies of its own, then they'll have babies and by then, we'll all be dead and who had sex with whom will matter not a jot. I'd prefer not to be lying on my deathbed thinking about Alec and the opportunity I lost when my body was young(ish) and healthy. I'd much rather take him by the hand right now and lead him back to the bedroom, or even the hallway floor, that would do, I'm not fussed. I'd push him down flat and I'd straddle him and feel his hot, hard skin, and I'd taste him.

Bodies are glorious things, every single one of them. Sex is a pulsing, beating proof of life.

'I'd like to kiss you,' I say.

'Me?' says Craig.

Alec looks up. 'I think she means me,' he says.

There is a lifetime in the way he looks at me, and I look right back at him, and I look and I look. All at once I am breathless; spineless; a liquid, molten thing.

'Please, be appropriate,' says Martha. 'The girls.'

'If you're going to say things like that, I might as well not even be here,' says Caroline.

'You want me to disagree with you? Is that what you want? How would that progress our relationship?' says Martha.

'We. Do not have. A relationship,' says Caroline.

Martha smiles, and tilts her head back to rest her chin on her hand. 'Bless, you're so naive. Take your time.'

'Kissing is not allowed,' says Mercedes. 'You're not married anymore.'

'Do you want to kiss me, Alec?' I say.

'Wait, wait. No one is kissing anyone. I forbid it,' says Caroline.

Alec shrugs. He speaks slowly, as though he doesn't want this moment to end, and one side of his mouth curls to a half-smile. 'It wouldn't be the worst thing that's happened this weekend.'

'You always were a sweet talker,' I say.

'You always were sweet,' he says.

There's been some kind of rupture in the space-time continuum. It's been years since the weekend began, possibly decades. I'm young again and my life is in front of me and everything is right with the world. When you're young, you don't realise you're beautiful but when you look back at the photos and see that you were, you're stunned, and also furious with yourself because you were so gorgeous and you wasted it.

Right now, Alec and I are young again. There is no one else here. It's any Sunday afternoon and every single one, and we're in the pub, laughing, and we're just kids again and there is just me and Alec.

I want to see what Alec looks like in ten years, when he needs reading glasses and can't remember where he's left them and buys cheap pairs from the two-dollar shop and leaves them littered all over the flat. I want to see him in twenty years, when his hair turns silver and in thirty, when he complains about his joints and the cold and he wakes early and books restaurant tables for six-thirty and chews antacids after a curry. I want to see us finding joy in small things: a lambswool blanket against our feet, a perfect cup of tea with lemon, the feel of tiny dried chickpeas through our fingers when we cook.

I set the jug down on the bench. Alec stands and comes toward me, sliding his feet across the tiles, wading through the shards. He takes hold of my waist and helps me jump down off the bench. Glass crunches under my shoes. My feet are solid on the ground and yet his hands stay there, touching me, around my ribs. He's looking at me like I'm brand new, like he's never seen me before today.

'Hello,' I say. 'I'm Janice.'

'Hello, Janice,' he says. 'It's good to meet you.' And then, 'Caroline, will you excuse us? Janice and I are very tired. We need a nap, urgently. Right now.'

He picks me up and, from his arms, I take one last look at them all, sitting in the lounge room. I nod at them; they all nod back. I wave; the girls wave back. As Alec carries me up the hall to Caroline's room, the last voice I hear behind me is Lesley's.

'I'm suddenly inspired to do a spot of gardening,' she says to Craig. 'And as soon as we get home, first thing, I'm ordering a pizza.'

We are not the same people we once were. When the door to the bedroom closes, we stand still for a long time, just looking. His hands tremble as he undoes the buttons of my blouse.

'Let me,' I say. I pull his t-shirt over his head. I undo the button on his jeans and unzip the fly. His skin is hot, hotter than mine. Then I take off my skirt and blouse, my bra and knickers.

We stand in front of each other, and we see each other.

Things happen slowly. When he buries his open mouth against my neck, I can hear him moan my name. When he holds me by the waist, when he traces the bones of my hips, he's gentle as though I'm made of glass and every so often he stops and holds me at an arm's distance and stares. He tastes warm and salty. His unshaven chin grazes my nipples. His fingers are in my mouth. He leads me to the bed and pulls me to the edge, then he spread my legs and kneels before me and it's almost more than I can bear. I roll my head from side to side, I reach for the pillow behind me. I plead and pray and then he sits on the edge of the bed and I sit astride him. He holds me below the ribs as I slide down upon him, and his face, his face looks up at me. He pulls me down by the shoulders, again and again, sharp and hard. I wrap my legs around him. When he's inside me, he grinds and stops, grinds and stops, until I fear I'll lose my mind. He's giving and he's gentle, but he's claiming me. He shudders as he comes and grips me to his body. It is everything I remember and it is more. Right now, this second, not even air can come between us.

A long time after that, we lie on the floor gasping like stranded fish, and despite the shift the earth has undergone, Caroline's bedroom looks much the same except for the photos next to the overturned bedside table and one painting that's come off its hook and slid down the wall and the pot plant that's spilling its soil onto the carpet and the bedside lamp that's lost its shade. We're lying on the pillows, on the floor. I don't know where Caroline is sleeping and I don't much care. I have cared, I will care again, I know—and soon. But right now I am tingly and dizzy, drained of blood, weak of limb, swollen of heart. I've pulled a muscle in my shoulder. I can feel a patchwork of hickies blooming on my neck.

We lie on our backs, side by side, staring at the ceiling, breathing like synchronised nuisance callers. The room is barely recognisable with him in it. I can't see my knickers from here, but my bra is hanging on a handle of the dresser.

'I think I fractured something,' he says.

Officially, it's Monday morning. The weekend is over and

in a few short hours, I'll drive towards my bacteria, which are waiting in their Petri dishes exactly as I left them on Friday afternoon when the world was another kind of place altogether.

There's a long scratch on the side of Alec's throat. He leans up on one elbow.

'Listen,' he says. 'It won't be easy. There's a lot we'll have to sort out.' He sweeps my hair away from my face and tucks it behind my ear; he traces the side of my throat with his knuckles. 'Is it too late for us, Janice?'

I don't know what our life together will look like. I can't feel the shape of it. Is it possible to be a family of only two people? Can we *make* a family, if we gather people we love around us? Perhaps we can. Perhaps that's what every family is.

We humans are not so different from bacteria when you get right down to it. Beneath the world of our body, that enormous sprawling planet, there is the world of the cell and beneath that, there is the world of the organelle, and beneath that, the atom. Inside the atom are subatomic particles, the protons and neutrons and electrons and quarks. And at the heart of that, once you delve even further, we are simply energy and its humming. We are thirty-five trillion cells and over a hundred trillion bacteria working together in perfect harmony. We contain multitudes, all of us. That makes us bona fide miracles.

'It's a new day,' I say. 'I have a feeling that anything's possible.'

Acknowledgments

I think it was Mark Twain who said: *It takes a village to raise a novel.* As usual, I've been the recipient of much kindness from talented, busy people who somehow found time to read, comment, research and help me in various ways. Caitlin Burns, Steven Amsterdam, J. M. Green, Kate Richards, Karen O'Brien, Kylie Stephenson, Megan Fisher, Danielle Scorer and Stephanie Kent were wonderful readers. Caroline and Henry's house is a compilation of two stunning semi-rural homes: Jane and Lyndon Dean's, and Lee and Scott Falvey's. One night over dinner, Max Joubert said to me, 'Not my circus, not my monkeys'. I can't remember the context, but it went immediately on my list of favourite sayings and was perfect for this book. Lee Falvey knows more about the weird behaviour of small children than I would wish on anyone, and Bella

Falvey, Will Falvey and Lily McDonald have much clearer memories of being seven than I do. Margaret Klaassen is the queen of family history and Di Cronin walked Myron the Wonderwhippet when I couldn't tear myself from my desk. Two of my RMIT fiction classes suffered through extracts of another novel I wrote before this one: their generosity was unexpected and appreciated and I thank them all, especially Krysia Birman.

At Text Publishing, Michael Heyward, Mandy Brett, Jane Novak, Kirsty Wilson and Anne Beilby were their usual brilliant selves, and Imogen Stubbs is a jacket genius. I'm very grateful.

For a short while in my twenties, I worked as a stock culture collection librarian for a biotechnology company. Possibly this kind of work doesn't even exist anymore: possibly my descriptions of dishes of beautiful bacteria are nostalgia for a time when science meant everything to me. Regardless, any errors are my own.

Finally, many years ago, A. S. Patric was so aghast to hear I'd never read *Anna Karenina* that he bought me a copy on the spot. He was right; it was transformative. Alec is named after him, in gratitude.